This Treacherous Journey

The Mountain Series

Book 6

Misty M. Beller

This book is a work of fiction and any resemblance to persons, living or dead, or places, events or locales is purely coincidental. The characters are the product of the author's imagination and used fictitiously.

ISBN-10: 1979954550
ISBN-13: 978-1979954556

Dedication

To you, Dear Reader.

You inspire me in ways that continue to amaze me.

Thank you for letting God use you as His blessings to others.

I have gone astray like a lost sheep;

seek thy servant; for I do not forget thy commandments.

Psalm 119:176 (KJV)

Prologue ~ Part 1

AUGUST, 1851
ROCKY MOUNTAINS, MONTANA TERRITORY

Simeon Grant glanced at his wife as another moan slipped from her lips.

Nora clutched her swollen belly, bent over from the pain. She'd turned in the saddle so she almost rode sideways. It must've hurt too much to straddle the horse.

Should he stop and set-up camp here? Or press on until they reached shelter? Surely it couldn't be much farther to the smoke he'd seen curling up through a break in the trees. *Lord, let it be a home, and let there be a woman there who can help us.*

His wife straightened in the saddle and offered him a weak smile. "That pain is gone."

He tried to offer an encouraging smile. Nora was always so strong, always taking on the burdens for those around her. If only he could take this burden from her now. He had to get help soon— for both her and the wee one inside.

He glanced around, a scent touching his nostrils. Wood smoke. *Thank you, Lord.* "I think we're not far now." He glanced at his wife. "Do you think you can make it a few minutes longer?"

She gave a weak nod, which turned to a grimace as she pressed her eyes shut and curled into another pain in her midsection.

How had he let this happen? He'd brought the love of his life into this mountain wilderness to chase *his* dream. She'd never once dashed his enthusiasm, just willingly sold off their meager home, loaded what possessions they now carried on the pack horses, and headed out to settle the wild Montana territory.

Never had he imagined Nora might be with child so soon after their marriage. Never had he thought the journey would take so long. And now the remote, unsettled freedom of these mountains that had drawn him was the very thing that jeopardized his wife's life.

But even with the length of their journey, wasn't it still too soon for Nora's time? They'd only be married eight months. Not that he doubted her faithfulness. No, the thought struck a deeper fear in him. Would coming early put the baby at risk? And Nora, too? If only he knew how to stop this.

He would give everything he had to find a doctor right now.

Ellen Scott paused at the porch steps, one hand on the rail and the other balancing a pail of milk. Listening.

She could have sworn she'd heard the nicker of a horse. Not one of their animals, she was sure of it. Quinn would be out in the hayfield for a few more hours yet, which meant it was her job to protect the homestead.

After rushing up the stairs, she pulled the latch-string and pushed through the cabin door. She grabbed the rifle hanging beside the threshold, swung the milk bucket onto the table, and strode to the window in the sitting area. Once again, she sent up a prayer of thanks that Quinn had had the foresight to bring the window glass with them when they'd settled here.

After checking the cartridge in the rifle, she peered through the window again. All she could do now was watch and wait.

She hadn't always been this suspicious. Had almost been as social as the next person back in Virginia. There were times she missed the regular human interaction they'd given up when they'd settled the homestead in these beautiful mountains. But here they didn't have neighbors for miles. The Indians they'd taken to trading with were friendly, mostly from the Apsaalooke bands. However, for every pleasant Indian, there were five more that would rather chase them off. She had no choice but to be cautious.

A horse appeared through the trees. Three more trailed it. Two figures sat atop the front animals. A man, tall and broad on the lead horse, then someone hunched low on the paint mare. Supplies loaded down the horses behind.

The wide, round brim of the fellow's hat bespoke a white man. Which was a good sign but didn't always mean safety.

But it was the pale blue material worn by the other figure that made Ellen's heart leap.

A woman? Glory be. She hadn't seen a female yet this year.

She stepped outside, lowering the rifle so it hung easily from her right hand, yet still at the ready should she need to aim and fire. These people would know her man wasn't around from the sheer fact she would greet them instead of Quinn.

If there was a woman along, surely they meant no harm.

As the couple approached, the posture of the lady ducked lower, cradling something in front of her. She sat sideways in the saddle too, sort of like the women back east rode sidesaddle—but different.

The man led his group right up to the porch and removed his hat. "My wife needs help. Can she come inside?"

Well, that was sure getting to the point. Ellen took a closer look at the woman's face, saw the way it pinched from pain, her damp hair clinging to her face. Then Ellen's eyes trailed down to what the woman cradled. Her very rounded stomach. *Dear, Lord.*

It was the woman's time. *Help me, Father.*

"Bring her inside." Ellen spun on her heel and headed back through the open doorway. She dumped a bucket of clean water in the pot on the stove, stoked the fire, and then strode toward her bedroom. It would be nice to put the woman in the spare room, but it still didn't have a bed.

They'd planned to put a crib in there when the time came, but God hadn't seen fit to bless them with children yet. Not for three years now, but she hadn't stopped praying every day for the gift. So that meant this strange woman would give birth in the large bed Quinn had built for the two of them.

By the time Ellen had a spot on the bed prepared, the man was half-guiding, half-carrying his wife into the room.

"Lay her here."

After the woman eased down, Ellen helped position pillows behind her back to prop her some. "How far along are you, honey?"

The woman looked to be between labor pains, exhausted and white as new snow. "I think somewhere between seven and eight months." She gritted her teeth as another pain hit.

Ellen glanced at the overlarge bulge under the blue flannel. She had to be further along than that. Without asking, Ellen pressed her hands against it, feeling the strength of the contraction. Tight as a drum skin.

"Well, dearie, this baby's comin' whether you're ready or not."

Simeon paced the small bed chamber.

Nora's screams tore his insides apart. How much longer could this go on? How much more could she endure?

"Bring another cool cloth." Mrs. Scott barked at him from her position beside the bed.

Simeon spun on his heel to face her, then as her request sank in, he turned back to the basin to obey. After wringing out the towel, he approached the bed and knelt by Nora's head where he would be out of the midwife's way.

Nora's eyes found his, exhaustion clouding their depths as her lids drooped to half-mast.

With the cloth, he stroked away the beads of sweat marring her face. So beautiful. Yet her skin was so pale it looked almost translucent, and her lips blazed a bright red. Was she feverish?

He pressed his palm to her forehead, but at the touch, her face contorted.

"Another one. Raise up and push, dearie."

Nora's eyes squeezed tight as she curled her chin into her chest. Red flooded her face from her efforts. Or maybe from the pain. He didn't know, but if he could have taken it all on himself, he would have already done it.

Her hand fumbled with the covers, and he slipped his

big fingers around hers. She clutched with more strength than he would have thought possible from her little body. Then another piercing half-moan, half-cry escaped her.

"Here. He's almost come." The midwife's voice raised a notch in her excitement. "Just one more push."

But Nora sank against the pillow. "I can't."

"We'll wait for another pain," the woman said. "Rest a minute."

Simeon wanted so badly to peek. To catch a glimpse of their precious new life. But he couldn't quite bring himself to look. Instead, he stroked Nora's hair and rubbed his thumb across the top of her hand. "You're doing splendid, love. It's almost over."

She didn't crack an eyelid, just kept sucking in deep breaths. But a corner of her mouth lifted just a fraction.

Then another pain hit.

As she curled into herself, the midwife kept up a steady stream of instructions.

"You've got to push harder this time, honey. He has to come out."

Was the child a boy, then? He didn't have time to stop and think before Nora loosed another awful scream.

Then a different cry filled the room. A baby.

Mrs. Scott held up a tiny person, and Simeon couldn't take his eyes from the writhing little body.

"It's a boy." She placed the child on a blanket, then wrapped him up tight. She started to hand him to Nora, but then a frown touched the older woman's face.

Simeon's gaze slipped to his wife. Nora was still

curled up in that ball, as if she hadn't already delivered the baby. Her face was mottled red and white.

Mrs. Scott shoved the swaddled baby toward him instead. "Hold the lad."

Simeon almost dropped the bundle, but scrambled to gather the child and the blankets to himself. Only the little face peeked out at him from the covers. A tiny face, not even as big as his palm. A hint of white residue covered the features, but didn't diminish the awe that surged through Simeon's chest.

The babe's face pinched as he let out another lusty cry.

A different scream filled the air at the same time. Nora.

Simeon glanced at his wife. She still curled in around herself. In pain. No…agony. If he didn't have the child in his arms, he would have dropped to his knees by her side again. Surely there was something they could do to relieve her pain. His gaze slid to the midwife, back to her original post and working hard at something.

Fear sluiced through him. The pains should be gone now. Right? "What's wrong?"

"Looks like another one's coming." The midwife spoke in a clipped tone, obviously intent on her work.

The words struck like a blow, and he swayed a bit from the impact. Another baby? His gaze found Nora again. She rested against the covers now, in between pains.

Clutching the baby carefully to his chest, he lowered himself to his knees beside the bed. "We have a son, love.

He's beautiful. And another on the way."

One of her eyelids cracked open, and Simeon tried to hold the babe so she could see him.

But another pain took her then, and he pulled back to give her space. He shuffled the baby into his left arm so he could hold Nora's hand again with his right. If it helped in the least, he could do that for her.

The pains kept coming. Over and over.

The baby took up crying too, especially as Nora's screams echoed through the bed chamber. Simeon paced with the child, snuggling it close and bouncing it gently—anything to soothe.

Yet nothing he did seemed to help. Every muscle in his body was drawn tighter than a violin string. What was taking so long?

A noise from the other room caught his attention for a moment. Then a male voice called, "Hello?"

"Quinn. Bring me the extra quilts from the trunk." Mrs. Scott barked the words, and if he wasn't mistaken, there was a note of panic in her tone. Did that mean something was going wrong? Surely not. She seemed so competent. And she'd helped deliver this beautiful baby boy already.

A man appeared in the doorway, middle-aged, maybe a few years older than Mrs. Scott. He paused to take in the scene, then stepped forward and laid a load of blankets on the bed. "What else can I do?"

The man's surprise at finding strangers in his bedroom seemed to have passed rather quickly.

"More warm water. Not too hot. Then bring a cup of goat's milk and a spoon."

Nora was in the midst of another pain, and Simeon stepped back to her side. The labors seemed so close together now, barely giving her time to catch her breath in between. Her face didn't turn as red now when she pushed, more like a flushed pink. It couldn't mean the pain had lessened, because her screams surely hadn't. Was she losing strength?

Lord, please help her. Fill her. Strengthen her. He sent up the request for the thousandth time. God would intervene. Nora was His child. He had to.

When Mr. Scott—he assumed that's who Quinn was—came back into the room, his wife barked another order.

"Drip a few drops of milk into the babe's mouth."

Simeon supposed that instruction was meant for him. There was one straight-back chair in the room, and he settled into it as Mr. Scott brought the supplies over. The man nodded a quick greeting to him, then held the cup while Simeon took the spoon.

It wasn't hard to get the babe's mouth open, because he let out another lusty cry. The four drops of milk seemed to stop him short though, and he scrunched his lips together as he worked to swallow the liquid.

"The next one's coming."

Mrs. Scott's announcement forced all thought from Simeon's mind as his pulse gathered speed. He leaned forward to get a better look at Nora. Exhaustion flooded every part of her body.

"Push, darlin'. You've got to push harder or the babe will never come." Exasperation touched Mrs. Scott's voice.

When Nora sank back against the pillow, Mrs. Scott looked over at her husband, standing in front of Simeon. "Quinn, take the baby. I need the husband here to help her."

Simeon handed over his precious bundle, and his legs barely supported him as he rose to his feet.

But when he knelt beside Nora, true fear slipped into his chest. She looked one shade darker than death. *Lord, you have to help her. Please.*

They worked together. Simeon wrapped an arm around her shoulders and helped her curl into the pushes.

After what had to be a quarter hour of agonizing effort, Mrs. Scott finally glanced up at him. A weary smile touched her face. "It's a girl."

Lightness filled Simeon's vision, and he had to blink to bring the woman's face back into focus. A boy *and* a girl?

He pressed a kiss to Nora's damp forehead. "You did it, love. A boy and a girl."

Nora murmured something he couldn't understand as she sank into the pillow.

He took the second bundle from Mrs. Scott and stared down into another tiny face. A smile started in his chest and spread up to his mouth. So beautiful. Just like her mother.

"She looks like you, Nora."

He glanced up at his wife, but what he saw poured dread into his chest.

She was perfectly still, eyes shut. "Nora?"

Her lips moved then, the slightest parting to allow air through. But it only lessened his fear a fraction.

"Nora?" He touched her hand. Cooler than it should be.

He looked to Mrs. Scott, but the woman was focused intently on whatever she was doing at Nora's feet. "What's wrong?" The panic in his voice was nothing compared to what clawed in his chest.

"She's losing blood."

Sheer terror iced through him. "Nora." He turned back to his wife, stroked a hand across her forehead and down her temple, smoothing back the hair from her face. Her lifeless expression never changed

"Nora, you can't leave me. Please." He leaned closer, watching for any response. Nothing, except the faint parting of her lips. At least she was still breathing.

"Nora, please." Tears blurred his vision, slipping down his face. "God, help her." His voice cracked on the words as every part of his heart poured into them. "You can't take her."

His love. Nora. She couldn't leave him.

Nora's lips parted a little more this time, like she wanted to speak. He leaned even closer, not daring to breathe.

"My…love." She whispered the words with the

faintest breath.

Those same words flooded his own heart, too.

Something in his chest cracked until he could barely draw breath through the tears. "I love you, too."

And there, with the baby in his arms, he leaned over his wife…and wept.

Simeon woke in darkness, his knees pressed into a hard wood floor and a pain crimping his neck. He was slumped over the side of a bed, his right arm draped over his wife. He glanced at her face, and a wave of grief pressed down on him.

He touched her cheek. Surely it had all been a terrible dream. She was only sleeping. But the skin there was eerily cold. He cradled his hand around that precious cheek, the one he'd stroked so many times during their short marriage.

How could she possibly be gone? How could God snuff out her beautiful life at such a young age? Only nineteen at her birthday last month. Yet there'd never been a woman so loving and strong and full of life. Never anyone like Nora. No wonder God wanted her for heaven.

As the tears came again, he laid his head against her cold hand and gave in to them.

Prologue ~ Part 2

"Look at how she smiles like an angel in her sleep." Ellen whispered the words to her husband as they sat across from each other by the hearth in the main room. Just like most evenings—her in the rocker and Quinn in his overstuffed chair. The only difference was, tonight each of them held a baby. *A baby*.

How many times had she craved and prayed for a little one, often to the point of tears? And now—for a few special days, at least—God had blessed her desires by sending these two precious bundles. Not that they were hers, but their father had been almost inconsolable most of the day, so she'd taken on their care and loved every moment.

She stared into the little girl's angelic face for another moment. The babies were just over a day old now and eating well from the pap feeder she'd rigged. She glanced over at Quinn, holding the boy child. Rarely had she seen such a soft expression on her strong husband's face. He looked just like a papa.

Quinn looked up to meet her gaze, and the gentle

expression didn't leave his eyes. "What do you think he's going to do now?"

The question stole the light feeling, pressed a weight against her chest. It was a conundrum she'd been afraid to face.

She had no idea where the couple had been headed. They'd had enough supplies on their pack horses to set up simple housekeeping, so it looked like they'd been immigrating somewhere. Although why in heaven's name they would travel out here with the woman so close to her time, she couldn't say. But she certainly wouldn't ask the poor husband. He would likely bear enough guilt as it was.

She let out a sigh. "I don't know. I guess we need to lay her to rest tomorrow. That might help him come to terms with things."

"Has he even come out of the room today?"

"Once for the outhouse, but not more than that. He's not touched any food either. Just a sip of water. I took the babes in to see him after lunch, but he just stared at them like he didn't know who they were." Another long breath eked out as she pondered the man's reaction. "He's in shock, for certain. Deep grievin'."

Quinn dipped into silence, but his eyes took on that faraway, thoughtful look. "Ellen. I been thinkin'."

"Yes?"

"What about if we offer to take the children? For permanent. You know, make them our own."

Ellen sucked in a breath. She'd had that fantasy more than once in the last day, but always chocked it away as a dream that could never come true. After all, what man in his right mind would give up both his children? But hearing the same thought spoken out loud… By her husband. Could it be possible?

"I'd like that more than anything." Her words came out breathy, a little too hopeful. At five-and-thirty, she wasn't exactly past the childbirth years, but she'd not been a young thing when she and Quinn married, and it seemed like they'd been praying for children so long.

"I'll see if I can find the right time to ask him." Quinn nodded, as if the matter were settled.

Lord, if it be Your will, grant us favor with Mr. Grant. Please. And for the first time all day, hope bloomed in her spirit.

Simeon stood beside the simple mound of dirt, his mind playing through memory after memory of Nora. The pretty pink of her cheeks when he first asked to court her. That first pulse-racing kiss. The sparkle in her eyes when he'd brought up the idea of moving a thousand miles away to the mountain wilderness. Her parents had been horrified, but she'd enthusiastically reassured them. They'd said goodbye as if it were the last time they'd ever see their daughter.

And they'd been right.

Another tear slid down his cheek, and he let it fall unhindered. He was tired of the tears. But they wouldn't stop, and he didn't have the strength to force them back. There was no one here he had to stand strong for. No one whose opinion he cared about. No one, now that Nora was gone.

A male throat cleared behind Simeon, pulling him from his fog. He didn't turn to face Quinn. Didn't know what to say to the man. His mind seemed shrouded in a haze so thick he couldn't see his hand in front of him. Couldn't see his next step.

"She must've been a fine woman."

A mirthless chuckle almost escaped Simeon, but he clamped his jaw against it. "She was." But she was so much more than that.

"I can't imagine losin' my Ellen. Our prayers are with you, son."

Simeon pressed his eyes shut. He wasn't ready to face God yet. Nor a conversation about the Almighty.

The man spoke again. "Your wee ones are doin' good. Ellen's always fancied babies, and she's lovin' the time with these two."

The children. He'd almost forgotten about them as memories of Nora engulfed him. He swallowed down some of the cotton in his mouth, but his voice still came out in a rasp. "I'm sorry she's had to take charge of their care. I'll see if I can help some."

But he didn't know the first thing about babies. What if he did the wrong thing and hurt them? They were so incredibly tiny.

Quinn cleared his throat again. "Ellen doesn't mind at

all. In fact, that's what I was hopin' to talk with you about."

Simeon didn't turn to face the man, but something in his chest prickled.

"I don't know what your plans are. From the load you was carryin', it looks like you might aim to homestead. That'll be hard enough without any added responsibility, but takin' care of two babies on your own, well…I can't even imagine."

That prickling feeling expanded, crawled down to his gut.

"Me and Ellen have been prayin' for young'uns for a while now. We just wanted to offer it up as an option that we'd like to take in the children. For permanent. If you think it'd be the right thing."

Simeon's shoulders stiffened. Give up his children?

"Just think about it. No need to decide anythin' right now."

He nodded, his eyes trailing back down to the clods of dirt piled in front of him. How could he give up the offspring that he and Nora had produced? The final evidence of a love that had been deep and enduring. Would Nora want that? Or would she want him to keep the family together? He would do whatever it took to care for the babies, even while he built the cabin and worked to start their new life. The life he'd planned with Nora…

But was it even possible to do those things with not one, but two, newborn babes in tow? What if he neglected some important step with the children and put them at risk? He'd never live with himself if he made another mistake that killed a person he loved.

Simeon's temples throbbed, and he squeezed his eyes against the pain. He couldn't decide now. Not yet.

Ellen nestled the little girl child against her shoulder and looked across the front room at Simeon Grant. The man sat in the ladder-back chair, elbows on his knees, head in his hands, shoulders drooping so much they almost closed in around him. She'd never seen a man so buried in grief. Not even her own pa when Mama, his wife of seventeen years, passed away.

Her spirit ached for Simeon. So young to watch his life turn upside down. The man couldn't be much more than one- or two-and-twenty. If only there were a way to pull him from the depths of his misery.

The babe snuggled under Ellen's chin burrowed deeper, curling her tiny knees so she rounded into a fragile ball. Maybe time with his daughter was the thing Simeon needed.

Cautiously, she approached, stopping a few feet in front of him. "Would ye like to hold the babe? It's time she gets to know her papa." The words stuck like tree sap in Ellen's mouth.

Quinn said the man had seemed shocked at the idea of leaving his children with them, although he hadn't said no outright.

Still, she'd been trying to give up the idea. After all, what she really wanted was whatever was best for the children, right? And staying with a caring father would surely be a good thing. This man had already proved his capacity to love deeply.

Simeon looked up at her with bleary, red-rimmed eyes. Even in the dim light of the cabin, the depth of despair washing through them brought the sting of tears to her own eyes.

Without a word, he cradled his arms to receive the babe.

Ellen carefully placed the precious bundle in the crook of his elbow. "She needs a name, I think." Maybe that task could help distract him as well.

He stared down into the sweet face framed by the white crocheted blanket she'd been saving for their own child—should God ever see fit.

"Nora." The word rasped so much, Ellen barely deciphered it as more than a clearing of his throat.

But as understanding dawned, her chest constricted even more. His wife's name. "It's lovely." Her own words came out hoarse, too.

She thumbed away a tear and turned back to the kitchen to allow the two of them time alone.

Simeon stared at the tiny features tucked into the crook of

his arm. She looked so much like his Nora. The fair eyebrows and long blond eyelashes, the rounded cheeks that would probably spread into dimples when she smiled.

The sweet innocence of this face only made the ache in his heart pierce deeper. This child depended on him. And the other as well.

Reuben was the name Nora had chosen if their babe was a boy. Or Deborah for a girl. But this face that looked so much like her mother—no other name could suit but Nora. She would grow strong and beautiful just like the amazing woman who'd given her life.

But could Simeon handle that? Could he provide for the needs of two babies? He didn't even know what those needs were. They still had at least five days' ride to the land he'd purchased. Was it safe for such fragile bodies to ride horseback? If a deer jumped from the woods and spooked the horses, that could spell disaster for this sweet babe. How could he, a rough farmer's son from South Carolina, raise two children on his own? Without a mother.

He swallowed down the lump clogging his throat. The Scotts seemed like good people. They'd taken him and Nora in without question. Without asking why he'd brought a woman so near her time out into this mountain wilderness.

Ellen Scott had worked tirelessly to help bring his children into the world, and she'd done her best for Nora, too. He had no doubt. She'd cared for the babes without complaint. And this little bundle in his arms seemed content with that care.

He'd been a bit surprised there weren't more sounds

of infant cries filling the cabin. He'd always been given to believe babies cried a lot, just to announce their needs. Or maybe these two did, and their tears hadn't reached through the fog that still clouded his mind.

No, he wasn't a fit father for these children. He couldn't be what they needed. As much as he wanted to try—for Nora—it wasn't fair to these precious babes.

As a single tear dripped onto little Nora's blanket, he pressed his eyes shut against another shot of pain.

"If you'll send us word of your location," Mr. Scott said, "we can let you know how things are going."

Simeon pulled the cinch strap tight on his saddle, then lowered the stirrup. There was nothing left to do except mount up and ride away. And say goodbye.

Slowly, he turned to face the Scotts. "Thank you. That would be good." But did he really want to receive constant reminders of the children he was abandoning? No, not abandoning. He was giving them new life. They would be so much better off with the Scotts than on his struggling new homestead. A place with no shelter or provisions. A place he hadn't even seen before. He'd only created images in his mind from the descriptions he'd been given.

And yes, he did desperately want to know how the children fared. He wanted to know when they took their first steps, spoke their first words, rode their first horses.

He reached for Quinn's outstretched hand and clenched it. So many things he wanted to say, but the lump in his throat barely held his emotions in check.

"We appreciate everything." Quinn's words were deep, filled with meaning.

Simeon met his eye and nodded.

"If you ever want to come see them…" The man's words trailed off, as if he weren't sure if he should have offered or not.

But Simeon shook his head. "No. They're yours to raise. Yours and God's. I don't want them ever thinking they were abandoned. They should only know love."

He let his gaze drop to the babe in Quinn's hands, the sleeping face of his son. He reached out to trace a finger down the tiny cheek. So soft. He pulled back before the touch weakened his determination.

Next, he turned to little Nora, nestled in Ellen's arms. When he stepped closer, the woman reached up and pulled him down to plant a kiss on his cheek. Before she released him, she patted the spot and looked into his eyes. Motherly love radiated from her gaze. "God go with you, son."

Simeon swallowed and nodded, then dropped his focus. The sight of little Nora's face pierced his chest like it always did. He pressed a kiss to his finger, then touched her cheek, just as soft as little Reuben's. "My love."

And then, blinking against the tears, he turned away.

Ellen watched the strapping, broken man mount his horse and turn the animal toward the trail. Nora stirred in her arms, and she snuggled the child a little closer. She couldn't help the tears that slipped down her face. She could imagine what this poor man felt. Knew the pain that came from giving up something he loved more than life itself.

And even now, with joy filling her soul because of these precious gifts God had given them, her heart fractured a bit at the burden Simeon Grant would endure. *Lord, be with him.*

Quinn stepped beside her and slid an arm around her waist. She leaned into him, resting her head against his strong shoulder.

"The Lord has a plan." His voice rumbled in her ear, soothing away some of her tension.

Such a wise husband she'd been blessed with. And now these two precious babies. Their family was finally complete.

Chapter One

Though this journey frightens me, I can't help a strange anticipation. What plans does my Father hold for me?
~ Emma's Journal

5 YEARS LATER ~ SEPTEMBER 15, 1856
ROCKY MOUNTAINS, MONTANA TERRITORY

Emma Malcom stared out over the steep mountainside on her left and caught a glimpse of the river winding through the valley far below. Rising up in the distance beyond, a row of white-capped mountain peaks extended as far as she could see. The Rockies. God must have been in His element when He created this majestic part of the country.

A rock broke loose under her mare's hoof, jerking her forward in a stumble. Emma clutched the reins, pulling the horse's head up as a stone skittered off the path and down the slope to her left. They'd been riding for hours on this narrow mountain trail—really more like a mountain goat track—winding along the cliffside. It was hard to believe the pines rising up the hill to her right could grow in the steep, rocky ground.

"You all right?" Joseph, her twin brother riding just ahead, turned in his saddle to glance at her.

"All's well. Just a loose rock."

He faced forward again, giving her a clear view of his back and the contraption he'd strapped there. Even though she'd been staring at the same sight for at least a week, ever since they'd left Fort Benton to strike out on these mountain trails, any view that included Joseph would always be a welcome sight. Now, more than ever, he was one of the few good things left in her life. The only one she could count on, save her Father above.

Still, she couldn't resist a bit of teasing. "I can't believe you dragged that guitar up the side of this mountain. Especially since you barely managed to pack a change of clothes." Joseph cared for his guitar more than most men cared for their sweethearts.

"You'll be thankful when we reach Canada and all those cold winter nights around Aunt Mary's fire." He whistled a few jaunty notes, like a taste of what was to come. "Might even give you a sample of it tonight once we set up camp." He shifted in the saddle to shoot her a sideways grin. "If you'll help a fella out with chores, that is."

It was lucky for him her fingers were too numb from cold to snap off a branch and bean him with it. She'd done more than her fair share of the work on this adventure into the mountain wilderness. Not that she was complaining. Joseph had saved her life by dragging her up here.

As they rounded the bend in the trail, Emma breathed in a new scent. She caught sight of a thin stream of gray rising from the evergreens on a neighboring slope. A fire? That amount of concentrated smoke had to come from a chimney. A surge of relief flowed through her. People. They'd not seen a human in two days.

She straightened in the saddle, trying to get a better look. The movement shot a pang through her weary back, and she braced a hand under her swelling abdomen to relieve some of the pressure from her muscles. Even though her loose dress showed only a small bump at her midsection, her body was thoroughly aware of the baby growing within her. She'd never imagined bearing a child would take such a toll on every part of her.

"Looks like we've finally found human life out here." Joseph pointed toward the smoke.

Then his horse stumbled. Maybe Joseph's raised hand had thrown the animal off balance, or maybe it'd caught a hoof on the uneven ground. Her brother jerked the reins, leaning hard to his right—away from the steep descent on the left.

The hard shift of balance was too much for the horse, and the animal scrambled to regain its footing. It lurched forward and went down on its right knee.

Emma screamed as time slowed the scene before her. The horse falling. Joseph toppling to the rocky trail like a felled pine. Hitting the mountainside with an audible thud.

The horse landed on Joseph's leg, and then time raced forward with the thunder of her pulse. Emma slid from her own animal and sprinted toward her brother.

No, God! The gelding struggled as she neared, trying to rise from the rocky ground without sliding to the left, off the trail and down the steep descent. After several tries, it finally righted itself, limping free of Joseph's mangled body.

Emma sank to her knees by her brother as he moaned and gripped his shoulder. "Are you all right? Where does it hurt?"

"My arm." Joseph grunted through ragged breaths.

Emma's gaze scanned from his shoulder down, catching on what lay underneath the arm. A fist-sized rock.

"Let's get the guitar off." She reached for the leather piece that crossed his chest, securing the instrument to his back. She lifted it gently over his good shoulder, watching his face for signs she was hurting him. Finally, she pulled it free and breathed out a long breath.

With the contraption laid aside, she eased Joseph onto his back, then slid her gaze down the length of him, slowing on his right leg. Being pinned under the horse had to have damaged the knee, but the joint maintained a normal angle as he shifted.

Joseph gasped, and she brought her focus up to his face. Pale as an albino cat. He clutched his right elbow, and she studied the arm.

"Do you think it's broken?" She reached a cautious hand toward the limb but stopped just before touching it. She didn't want to make the damage worse.

"Either broken or going up in flames." Though the words sounded dark through his clenched teeth, at least he was trying to keep a sense of humor.

Emma glanced around at the trees and rocks surrounding them. What was she looking for? She'd never tended a broken arm, although Joseph had cracked a bone when they were kids and he'd fallen from an oak tree. She eyed his arm, trying to bring back the memories. It had been that exact bone, if she recalled correctly. Upper right arm. Back then, the doctor had built a stiff cast around the limb, then wrapped Joseph's arm close to his body.

She didn't have the doctor's fancy supplies on this deserted mountain, but she could try to secure the bones until they found help. "Wait here." She pushed to her feet.

Joseph's only answer was a sharp breath through his teeth.

Her own arm ached as she fumbled through the pack on her horse. Her extra set of pantalets should be sufficient to wrap around the break and hold the bones in place. And maybe her stockings could secure the limb close to his body. She grabbed the supplies and knelt beside her brother again.

Joseph yelped when she touched his arm at the injury. The area had already started swelling. Should she wrap it tight or leave the makeshift bandage loose? She pulled the woven cotton as tight as she dared, and he didn't cry out again, but his breath came in noisy gasps. At least his breathing was steady.

When she finished strapping the arm in a sling to his side, she sat back on her heels and studied him. "Is that any better?"

The pain pulled at all his features, forming weary

creases around his eyes and mouth. Red rimmed the amber color of his irises—the same deep reddish-brown as hers. The eye coloring was their most unique feature and one she'd always secretly been proud to share with him. But now, the striking hue was overpowered by liquid pain radiating in his gaze. She had to get him to a doctor.

"Do you think you can ride? It's probably less than an hour to the house where we saw the smoke." She hoped it would be that short anyway. Sometimes she had a way of softening reality a bit. But Joseph needed hope of relief from his pain.

"I can ride." His jaw clenched as he struggled to sit up.

She gripped his good arm and slipped a hand behind his back. Together, they got him to his feet, where he pulled away from her grasp.

"I'm fine." His tone was sharp.

Stubborn boy. Or man. Or whatever he was at twenty-one years. Sometimes, he was too pig-headed for his own good.

He glanced at the ground behind him. "Can you slip the guitar strap over my head?"

"I'll carry the guitar." She grabbed the instrument and fit the leather piece over her own head and left shoulder, adjusting the band so it didn't press on the gold engraved cross that hung from the leather strip around her neck. Jewelry may not be sensible in this wilderness, but the cross had been Gran's, and she'd worn it every day since her sixteenth birthday. Besides, around her neck was probably the safest place for the treasure.

Emma turned to the bay gelding who stood a few paces down the trail, watching them, head drooping a bit. "Stay here and let me see about your horse."

She approached the animal with her hand outstretched. "Hey, boy. You all right?" she crooned. He allowed her to run a hand over his muzzle and grip the reins. After a quick inspection, it appeared the horse only had a scraped knee, but he limped when she led him back to Joseph.

It looked like she'd be walking to the stranger's cabin. Her weary shoulders slumped at the prospect.

Simeon Grant tossed another log in the fireplace of his cabin, sending a spray of sparks from the small flames. He'd not been gone long enough for the coals to cool, so the fire would spring to life quickly and be warm enough to cook on soon. He'd best get the meat cut into chunks.

He turned to the fresh venison he'd laid on the table. A thick loin cut, tender from the summer's fertile grass.

A growl by the door brought him up short. Mustang, the rangy chestnut dog who deigned to share Simeon's company, had raised his head from the packed dirt floor. He fixed his gaze on the cabin door and released another growl.

Simeon didn't bother to silence him. Mustang didn't obey orders often, especially not when they went against his instincts. Instead, Simeon stepped to the door and peered through the inch-wide crack he'd cut into the wood as a sort of peephole. Winters in this country were too cold to make a wider window opening, and it wasn't worth the effort to obtain glass.

The threat was close enough for him to hear it now, something crashing through the woods. His muscles tensed. Only a handful of creatures would make that much noise. A bull moose, or maybe a bear. A buffalo wouldn't wander this far from open range.

But as he watched from the cover of his cabin, the worst of his suspicions came into view through the barren branches of the trees. People.

One on foot, leading a chestnut horse. Another rider on a bay was huddled over his saddle as he brought up the rear. The autumn air had grown nippy, but it didn't seem cold enough for a man to be curled that tight. Must be a newcomer to the mountains, not adequately prepared for the weather or the altitude.

As they drew closer and stepped from the edge of the forest, Simeon stared at the front man who walked beside the chestnut. The image took a second to focus in his mind. The man had something bulky strapped on his back, and his coat hung all the way to the ground.

No, not a coat. A dress almost the same blue color as the cloak covering the person's top half. It couldn't be.

A woman?

What was she doing walking? Why was she out in this mountain wilderness to begin with? And what did she have strapped on her back? Surely the man didn't make her walk and carry supplies like a pack mule. Was he holding her at gunpoint? All sorts of characters roamed these woods.

His eyes trailed back to the mounted figure. That one was certainly a man, but now that Simeon's focus was clearer, it looked more like he was slumped in the saddle, not huddled. Injured. They were probably decent folk who'd run into a bit of trouble, but he'd make sure they didn't have ill intentions before he let his guard down.

Simeon's hand wandered to the back of his waistband, where the revolver fit snuggly against his lower back. He didn't often need the pistol since his knife and rifle worked just fine for hunting. His cabin was far enough off the trail that he rarely had company unless someone sought him out.

Which they didn't.

The only visitors he'd had in the last five years were occasional trappers when they wandered into the area during a snowstorm. Otherwise, Simeon lived a solitary life. And that was how he wanted it.

He squinted at the pair as they reached the footpath leading to his door. These certainly weren't trappers. The woman's hair was pulled into a knot on top of her head, with windblown tendrils escaping down the sides of her face. She had a delicate look, both in her features and in the way she carried herself, like she'd been plucked from an eastern ballroom and dropped on the side of this mountain, smack in the middle of the northern Rockies. And the man…he had an honest face, despite the pain that was a little clearer now.

Simeon supposed he had to go out there. See what they needed—probably food. He'd give it to them and then run them off. He didn't want to be responsible for these people. Couldn't be. The man clearly had no sense, or he wouldn't have brought his woman into this inhumane wilderness. The harshness of it would swallow her up before he knew what he'd done. Before he had a chance to correct it.

Simeon's gut churned at the memories that still assaulted him. He couldn't be part of that again. He wasn't fit to have the responsibility for another's well-being. Especially not a woman's.

With a long, slow inhale, he stepped toward the latch, grabbed his rifle, and pulled open the door.

He held the gun loosely in both hands, pointed diagonally toward the sky. The stance was stern enough, in a somewhat casual way, to let them know this wasn't exactly a hotel welcome desk.

The pair pulled up in front of him, leaving about ten feet's distance between. He could see now that it was some kind of case strapped on the woman's back—the kind that would hold a guitar. A faint longing pricked his chest, but he pushed it aside.

He waited for them to speak. The woman's glance skimmed him, then landed on Mustang standing guard at his feet. The dog released another low growl—his idea of a proper welcome. If the animal thought there were cause for concern, he would have attacked long before now. The mutt didn't take chances on potential danger and certainly didn't wait for a handshake to take a man's measure.

The woman's eyes widened. Even from this distance he could see they were a pretty reddish-brown, like hardened amber resin from an apricot tree. Striking. She was younger than he'd first assumed, maybe not much more than twenty.

She seemed to drag her gaze away from the dog and back to Simeon. Her lips pinched, yet the action didn't take away from their fullness. "We need help, sir. Do you know if there's a doctor in the area?" Her gaze flicked back to the dog before she turned and motioned to the man on the horse. "Joseph's arm is broken, I think."

Injured, like he'd assumed. He couldn't run them off if the man was hurt. It'd be like tying them to a tree and planting a bloody carcass at their feet. The mountain lions and bears would have them half eaten before they made it to the next mountain.

He took in the slump of the man's shoulders, the way his eyelids drooped to half-mast. He'd been riding in pain for a while. Probably close to losing consciousness, as pale as he was. No wonder he let his woman speak for him.

Simeon kept his face impassive against the frustration building in his chest. "Bring him in. Leave the horses there for now."

He watched as the woman looped her reins around the lanky tree in the yard he used as a hitching post. Then she turned to the man. Joseph.

Simeon's body itched to step forward and help, but

he kept himself still by force of will. Let the pair try to come in on their own. It would show him the extent of what he was dealing with—both the severity of the injury and the tenacity of these people to persevere through trial. Because heaven knew they'd find trial if they spent any time in these mountains. Especially with winter coming on.

The man tried to slide from his horse's back without aid, but his groan probably woke any animals sleeping nearby. As Joseph's feet touched ground, he looked like he would have kept going to his knees if not for the woman, who caught his waist and slipped herself under his left shoulder. He leaned heavily on her as they walked, but she stood strong under the weight. At least she had some pluck.

Simeon turned and stepped into the cabin in front of them. He motioned to the pile of skins on the floor near the hearth. "Lay him there, and I'll look at his arm."

He strode to the fire and pulled the tea kettle from the ashes to refill it with water. He was halfway through the job when the stillness in the room made him pause. He glanced back toward the door.

The pair stood in the opening, unmoving. The woman stared at him.

He raised his brows. Was she waiting on an engraved invitation?

"Are you a doctor then?" She jutted her chin forward, her mouth forming another pert line.

"I've set a couple broken bones. The closest real doctor is two days' ride east of here, but I can give you directions if you'd rather find him." He refrained from mentioning the medicine man from the Apsaalooke tribe that wintered a couple valleys over. If she didn't want Simeon setting the arm, chances were good she wouldn't approve of a savage doing it. Not that there was anything savage about those good people, but she probably wouldn't stop to ask.

She held his gaze for a moment longer as her amber eyes flashed, then she pulled her husband forward and helped him lie on the furs.

Joseph groaned again as she eased him down, then he sank his head back against the bearskin fur on top. His eyes squeezed tightly while he clutched his right elbow.

Simeon set the kettle on the hearth and moved beside the man. He pulled his knife and sliced easily through the white wool sling, and again through the man's sleeve and something frilly wrapped around the upper arm.

Finally, he could see the exposed flesh. The angular lump above the elbow confirmed his fears. It must be a compound break, although the jagged edge of bone hadn't pushed through the skin. This was going to be painful.

He glanced up at the woman. "There's a rope corral in a clearing north of the cabin. You can unsaddle and leave your horses there."

Uncertainty flickered in her eyes, but then it disappeared as she narrowed them. "I'll help you with Joseph first, then see to the horses."

He tamped down another wave of frustration. He wasn't trying to steal her last dollar, just save her the grief of seeing her husband in pain. Setting this kind of break wasn't something a woman should see. "It would be best if you tend your animals now. These high altitudes are hard on them."

She took a step forward. "After Joseph is settled."

Simeon turned back to the husband. She could watch him then, if she was that stubborn. Maybe she *did* have the stomach to help, or maybe man and wife would both pass out, and he'd have peace and quiet again.

A pang of remorse knocked at his chest, but he pushed it away. Lucky for this woman, she wasn't his responsibility.

Chapter Two

Why does Fate torment me? What did I do to deserve the wrath of Providence?
~ Simeon

Emma fought a wave of protectiveness as the mountain man peered at Joseph's arm again. His face was hard to read, but she didn't like the way he'd tried to get rid of her. He either didn't know as much about doctoring as he'd made it sound, or the work ahead would be painful for Joseph. Either way, she would be here to protect and support her brother. She'd had more than her fair share of secretive men with hidden agendas, and she wasn't about to let Joseph suffer more than necessary at the hands of this one.

The mountain man rose to his feet, and she took an involuntary step back as his height towered above her. He was taller than Joseph. Taller than her late husband by at least six inches.

He strode to the other side of the room and opened a wooden box. After rifling through for a moment, he extracted a small cloth bundle and turned to face her. "I'm going to get a splint. Steep this in a tea for your husband." He tossed the parcel, and she barely caught it in the crook of her right arm.

"He's not..." She started to correct him about her relationship to Joseph, but the man slipped out of the cabin and shut the door before she could finish.

She held up the pouch, tied closed with a strip of leather, then glanced over at the pot warming on the hearth beside the fire. Should she make a whole kettle of the tea, or just one cup for Joseph? Her poor brother was pale as fresh milk, and his mouth was pinched in a tight line. If this was meant to help his pain, he'd need a whole pot full. She crossed to the fire and poured the contents of the pouch into the metal pitcher.

With the tea steeping, she knelt on Joseph's good side and stroked the hair from his brow. "How're you feeling, love?"

"Hurts." Joseph didn't open his eyes. And the fact that he didn't try to make light of his pain or sound reassuring gave truth to the intensity of his anguish.

"I'm so sorry." She combed through his curls, letting her fingernails skim his scalp in a way she hoped would be soothing. "I think we've found someone who can help you."

As if summoned, the door opened, and the mountain man stepped inside again. He wore buckskins like the frontiersmen they'd seen in Fort Benton. Except this man even wore them on his feet, laced up to his knees. She'd only seen Indians wearing shoes like that, and even then, she'd only seen drawings on flyers advertising Wild West shows as she and Joseph had traveled up the Mississippi.

Was this man an Indian? His dark hair appeared more brown than black, even in the dim light of the cabin. And those blue eyes… They'd been piercing as he'd stood in front of his home like a sentry, glaring at the two of them. No, he didn't look the way she'd heard the redskins described.

Although maybe there *was* something a little savage about him. No, not savage, just…wild. Something that made you take a second look at him. Something she wasn't sure if she should fear or admire.

The dog followed him in but stopped beside the door, circled twice, and lay down. It muttered another growl as it fixed its gaze on her.

She raised her brows at it. *A pleasure to meet you too, puppy.* Seemed man and beast were equally welcoming to visitors.

She turned her attention back to the man as he crouched by Joseph's other side. He held two sticks alongside the broken arm—comparing the length, possibly. Then he reached for the stockings he'd carelessly sliced apart, this time raising them so the full length hung to the floor. Suspended like that, it was impossible not to realize what type of garment they were.

His blue eyes rounded for a half-second, then he dropped the stockings to the floor.

She pinched her lips against a smile. Breaking through this man's façade was almost worth the mending she'd have to do to repair the underthings.

He stood again and stepped across the cabin to another crate. After rifling through it, he returned with a roll of leather strips. Once his supplies were positioned, he glanced up at her. He searched her face, his intensity making the skin on her arms prickle.

She held his gaze. "What is it?"

"This next part will hurt him." His scrutiny didn't let up. Like ice drilling through to her very soul.

Her defenses flared. "What will you do?"

"I have to straighten the bones. Put them back in place before I can splint them."

She swallowed, trying to restore a bit of moisture in her mouth. That sounded terribly painful. "What can I do to help?"

He shook his head. "Just don't swoon on me."

She stiffened her spine and glared at him. "I don't swoon." The man must think her quite a weakling.

With a nod, he dropped his focus back to Joseph's arm, his large hands working deftly.

Joseph jerked with the first touch, and Emma stroked his hair again. She murmured soothing words but couldn't keep her gaze from the mountain man's fingers as he worked.

He positioned both hands in a grip on Joseph's arm. With a grunt, he jerked.

Joseph screamed.

Emma flinched and pressed a hand to Joseph's cheek. He was breathing hard now, in short gasps. Like maybe his throat was closing up. "Breathe, Joey. Breathe." She focused on his face, willing his body to relax. *Father, breathe life into him. Peace.*

After an interminable moment, his panting seemed to ease. The muscles at his throat worked, his Adam's apple shifted up, then down. She tore her gaze from her brother to see what the mountain man was doing with the injury.

He'd positioned the sticks on both sides of the upper arm and wound a leather strip around all three. As he knotted the binding, he reached for the pantalets she'd originally tied around Joseph's arm.

Her fingers itched to snatch the fabric from his hands. But she forced herself to remain still. The garment was plain, without any lace. Maybe he wouldn't know what it was. Especially if he'd lived a remote life out here, far from any civilized ladies. Maybe he'd even think them a set of curtains.

He paused though, the cloth wadded in his hand. His focus wandered to the material, as if he were suddenly suspicious of it.

Emma couldn't stop the hot blush that surged to her face. She should have jerked them away when she'd first thought about it.

He dropped the wadded garment and again rose and strode to the box on the far side of the room. This time he came back with a piece of gray homespun cloth and dropped to his knees. "Think you can sit up?" he asked Joseph.

Her brother nodded and let the man help him to an upright position. Then he sat with his eyes closed while their host tied the sling in place.

"There." The mountain man sat back on his haunches and eyed her brother. "Feed him the tea while I see to your horses."

Emma opened her mouth to tell him she'd care for the animals, but the man rose so quickly, she couldn't snag his attention before he and the dog slipped out the door.

It was then she realized she'd never even asked his name.

Simeon stroked the diamond splashed across the chestnut's forehead before he slipped the bridle off over her ears. "Atta, girl. Take a good break." The mare shook her head and blew on his breeches, then dropped her muzzle to nibble at the remnants of brown grass left from summer.

He turned his focus to the gelding. Other than the nasty gash on his right knee, the horse seemed to be in decent condition. He'd come back later with a salve for the wound, but for now he pulled off the bridle and watched as the old boy meandered away to find a good patch of fodder.

The horses were decent stock, nothing extravagant, but hearty. Probably at least partial mustang. They didn't look as if they'd been pushed hard. Most likely, these newcomers had just purchased them in Fort Benton. That was the way most of these city people came into the mountain country. By steamboat on the Missouri to Fort Benton, which was pretty much the end of the river. Then on horseback, or by wagon if they were headed to one of the more settled mining towns. Eventually they all met the same fate, though.

Disaster.

If the wild animals didn't do them in, the hard winters usually finished the job. This land was too much for soft easterners. Especially women.

A surge of anger burned his chest. What was the man thinking bringing his wife into this country? It would be a death sentence for her. Experience was a hard lesson, and not one Simeon would ever forget. He'd made the same stupid mistake, and not one day passed that he didn't ache with the torture of it.

Nora would still be alive if he hadn't made the reckless decision to bring them west. And he'd still have his children with him.

He turned away from the horses and bent low to slip through the rope fence. Then he forced his feet to follow the footpath back to the cabin.

Maybe this Joseph had learned his lesson already. As soon as he was cognizant enough to understand, Simeon would talk some sense into the man and send them both back the way they'd come. He'd even deliver them to Fort Benton himself, if that's what it took. Maybe that one act of kindness could make a small dent in the penance he owed for his own poor decisions.

Maybe.

As he neared the cabin door, Simeon stiffened his resolve. He picked up their packs from the lean-to where he'd left the saddles, then inhaled several deep breaths. Pulling the latch string, he pushed the door open and stepped inside. He dropped the packs in a heap beside the door as he glanced at the man lying on the pallet in the corner. Sleeping.

The woman stood by the table in the center of the room and turned to look at him when he entered. Something caught his attention about the way the dress pulled at her figure when she turned.

His feet stopped midstride, and his mouth went dry. His pulse thumped in his ears. *No*. Not again.

God above, have mercy. She was with child.

Chapter Three

So many twists in the darkness, yet God is my light. Make clear my path, dear Father.
~ Emma's Journal

Emma eyed the mountain man as he stood in the doorway. His face had paled three shades, and he looked like he might turn and run. She'd not seen this much expression on his features since he realized she'd patched Joseph's arm with her undergarments. And she'd never imagined the emotion she'd see now would be fear.

But what was he afraid of? Her pulse leapt to her throat. Had he seen Indians while he was putting away the horses?

Her feet took a step forward before she could stop them. "What is it?"

He shook his head as if trying to clear away his thoughts. His gaze slipped to Joseph, then he turned and pushed the door shut behind him. He pulled the fur hat from his head and hung it on a peg in the log wall. The dog was nowhere in sight.

It was almost as if he avoided looking at her as he took purposeful steps toward the fireplace. What a strange man. Trying to figure him out was starting an ache in her temples.

She turned back to the meat spread on the table. "Would you like me to fry this beef for supper? I can whip together cornbread from our stock to go with it."

"It's venison." His words came out almost in a growl, and she turned to catch his expression. But his back was to her as he knelt and stared into the fire. Had she done something to anger him?

Gathering a deep breath, she tried again. "All right. Would you like me to fry the venison and cornbread for supper?"

"Sounds good."

Well. That was a more promising response than she'd expected. She set to work slicing the meat.

Her gaze kept wandering to the man as she worked. He still knelt beside the fire, unmoving. What thoughts ran through his mind? Did he hate strangers so much, or just her and her brother in particular? Should she try to break through his silence? Be sociable? It was worth a try.

She pasted on a smile and used her most chipper voice. "I don't believe I caught your name, sir. I'm Emma Malcom, and that lump on your floor"—she motioned with the knife in Joseph's direction—"is my brother, Joseph Malcom."

It felt strange calling herself by her maiden name

again. Like a distant memory replayed. But since that terrible night of the lynching, she was no longer Emma Carter. And even though her deceased husband was the father of their babe, she couldn't bring herself to give the child his name. This little one should have a fair chance in life, not be branded by the surname of a crook and a swindler.

"Your…brother?"

The man's words pulled Emma from the thoughts that had swallowed her too often these last few months. She met his gaze as he turned to stare at her. "Joseph is my twin."

When she said the word *twin,* the man gave a slight jerk. Almost as if he'd been slapped across the face. So much of the time he seemed like a detached mountain man, but he certainly showed emotion at the strangest things.

He turned away from her again, back to the fire. A ripple of frustration washed through her.

"And what is your name, sir?" Was the man simple-minded? Maybe that would account for his silence, his strange reactions, and the way he seemed to skirt around some of her questions.

"Simeon." The word was uttered so quietly, she almost missed it.

"Mr. Simeon?"

"Just Simeon."

Hmm… Was that his first or last name? Maybe he'd been raised by the Indians and they'd only given him one moniker. But he spoke perfect English, although he certainly didn't waste words.

She went back to work slicing the meat and laying strips in the frying pan she'd found. It was none of her business.

But she couldn't quite convince her mind to agree.

When the food was ready, Emma woke Joseph and helped him to a chair at the table. It wasn't until after she had him settled that she realized there were only two chairs.

Well, no matter. When Mr. Simeon came back in, she'd let the men eat before her. If she could get her hands on a bucket of clean water, she'd fill the time scrubbing the dust off the shelves around the place.

Overall, the cabin wasn't too grimy, despite the dirt floor, considering it was the abode of an uncivilized mountain man. There weren't food droppings scattered around or layers of grit on the dishes. It was mostly just…barren. No comforts of home whatsoever. It reminded her of the way Mama used to describe the priests' cells in the monasteries back in France.

Did this man enjoy the simple life then? His shadowed face didn't look like he enjoyed much at all. More like he was paying penance for something. A self-imposed penance? For what? Maybe if she watched closely enough, she might find a clue.

As she set a loaded plate in front of each chair at the

table, Joseph inhaled the aroma of fried meat. "Smells good, Emmy." He tried for a smile, but his weary eyes drooped to half-mast.

She ran her fingers through an out-of-place lock in his tousled hair. "The food will give you strength to recover, then you can rest."

The door opened, and Mr. Simeon entered carrying a large log. It filled both his hands and partially concealed his face. He strode forward and grunted as he lowered the piece to the floor beside the table. A tree stump?

He glanced at her and motioned toward the empty chair beside Joseph. "Sit." Then he plopped himself down atop the stump.

She couldn't help but stare. Had he gone out and cut the tree down just to have enough seats at the table? Or did he always keep a handy stump lying around the cabin. Neither option would surprise her at this point. This man was more than a little intriguing.

When they were all seated, Emma glanced from her brother to their host. "Do you mind if I say grace?"

He shrugged and bowed while she spoke a grateful *thank you* for God's mercy in sparing Joseph's life. She still trembled when she thought about how much worse the accident could have been.

As they started into the simple meal, Emma slid a glance toward the man sitting to her left. Maybe this would be a good time to get some information from him. As casually as possible, she asked her first question. "So, Mr. Simeon. Have you lived on this mountain long?"

"It's Simeon."

She forced a smile and took a deep, steadying breath. "Sorry, Simeon." She waited for his answer, but he just kept shoveling food into his mouth. Maybe he'd forgotten the question. She infused a pleasant tone into her voice. "Have you lived on this mountain long?"

"Five years." He took another bite of cornbread. He didn't look at her.

"Have you always resided in this part of the territory?"

"No."

He wasn't making this easy. "Where do you hail from then?"

"South Carolina." And now he did look up at her, a glimmer of wariness in his eyes. "What about you?"

She'd pushed too far, and now it had come back to prick her. But then, she could dance around a question as well as he could. She sent a bright smile Joseph's way. "My brother and I were raised in Baltimore."

"So you traveled from Baltimore to the Rocky Mountains?"

She forced her face not to betray her unease. Did he realize she hadn't given the whole truth? "Our parents moved to a little town in Texas a few years back." She swallowed. She had to say this next part, either speak the words or appear a loose woman. The babe inside her was becoming too obvious.

She allowed a hint of sadness to show in her eyes. "Texas is where our parents are buried, along with my husband." At least, she assumed they'd buried Lance. Right after they'd strung him up by the neck from the pecan tree at the edge of town.

A glimmer of sympathy flashed through Simeon's eyes. "I'm sorry."

Emma forced a weak smile but didn't put much effort in it. "Me, too." She was sorry about a great many things that happened during their time in Texas. Sorry she'd allowed Father to choose a husband for her. Sorry she'd refused to put her foot down, even when Mama wouldn't. Sorry she hadn't pushed Lance harder to tell her what sort of business interests occupied his time. She'd had no desire to be a simple socialite as Mama had been, happily shielded from anything that mattered to her husband. Papa had treated her as such, and she'd even allowed Lance to do it. But they were both gone now, and she'd never sit by in ignorance again.

If she'd only known what Lance was doing in his law practice, she could have saved the investments of all those hardworking farmers. Of course, her ignorance may have been the very thing that had saved her neck that night of the lynching. But by the looks of the *Wanted: Reward Offered* poster she and Joseph had seen in Memphis, her life might yet hang in the balance. Literally.

"So where are y'all headed?"

Simeon's question dragged Emma back from the dark memories. But he was looking to Joseph for an answer, so she sank into her chair, nibbling at a bite of venison.

Her brother raised his chin and tried to force his

eyelids open more than halfway. Poor fella. "On our way to Canada."

Simeon stopped chewing and raised his brows. "All the way north? This wilderness isn't suitable for women. It'd be wiser to go back to Fort Benton for the winter." He nodded toward Joseph's arm. "And you can find a real doctor."

And likely a sheriff, too. One who'd seen the poster with her description. Even in this wilderness, she couldn't trust that changing her surname alone would make her invisible if someone were hunting her. And the two-thousand-dollar reward offered for her capture would surely put someone on the hunt.

The next morning, it was harder than Emma expected to find a few moments alone with her brother. It seemed every time the mountain man left the cabin, Joseph was snoring loudly enough to chase away bears. What exactly was in that tea she'd been giving him? At least the sleep kept him from wallowing in pain.

So she spent the morning catching up in her journal, then scrubbing the cabin. The single room had only taken a couple of hours to scour.

Now, Joseph was finally awake, and she slipped a rolled fur under his head so he could raise up in bed for a few minutes. Of course, his *bed* was a little more rustic than any mattress she'd seen. They'd both slept on stacks of furs, layered eight deep and covered with coarse brown or black hair. Surprisingly, the pile had been as soft as her feather mattress in Lance's home.

"Are you hungry? You didn't eat much for breakfast. Shall I heat some gruel?" She sat back on her heels and studied Joseph's pallor. She'd feel better when he had some color in his cheeks again.

He shook his head, then winced.

Frowning, she brushed her fingers across his brow. "Did you hit your head, too?"

"Nah. Everything hurts a little."

She could feel the pain in his raspy voice. What would comfort him? She had no medicine in their pack. When they'd fled Westhaven in the dead of night, she'd not had time to pack more than a change of clothes and personal effects, money, her Bible, and her journal. So much had been lost that night.

Joseph's eyelids drifted downward again, a look she was becoming all too familiar with.

"Joey." She leaned closer and softened her voice.

His lids fluttered open, and his glassy gaze wandered to her face.

"I'm going to ask Simeon if he'll give us directions to the nearest doctor."

The eyes opened fully, and some of the haze cleared from his expression. "No, Em. That would mean going to town. We're not gonna do it."

Poor Joseph. He would rather suffer the pain of a

broken bone than risk her discovery. "Maybe not. Perhaps there's a doctor who lives on the outskirts, where we wouldn't be seen. It doesn't matter, though. A real doctor should examine your arm. At the very least you need something to ease the pain."

His chin jutted, and that stubborn streak flashed in his amber eyes. She returned the same glare. Not only did their eye color match, but they had the same oval face and strong chin that rounded softly at the point. Mama used to chuckle when they squared off like this. She'd say it was like looking in both sides of a window.

But Joseph's well-being was no laughing matter, and she didn't intend to lose this battle. Besides, in his weakened state, he'd back down soon enough.

"Em-my."

She couldn't tell if the slow cadence of the word was meant to display his frustration or was merely a result of his exhaustion. Either way, it softened her ire a touch. She didn't mean to make things harder on him. "What?"

"I don't need a doctor. The man splinted my arm fine, and this tea you've been feeding me makes things bearable."

She started to object, but he raised his good hand to silence her.

"What we need…is a guide to Canada. I plan to ask Simeon if he'll fill the job."

Every part of her body came to life—most of it in revolt at the idea. Even though the man intrigued her, the thought of anyone traveling with them raised a surge of panic in her chest. What if he heard about the reward? What if he were a mercenary, and this cabin was merely where he spent downtime between jobs? That was probably unlikely, but who knew?

If she'd learned anything through the mess with Lance, she'd learned to trust her intuition and never assume a man was what he seemed at face value.

She met her brother's gaze. "Joey, I don't think it's safe to trust anyone else. We don't know what kind of connections he has. And really, why do we need him? You've done an excellent job guiding us so far. You have your topographical map, right?" He'd been so excited to find it in Fort Benton, so proud when he finally learned how to read the thing. And it had seemed fairly accurate so far.

Something glimmered in his eyes, but their cloudiness covered it before she could catch the emotion. He was in so much pain.

"Emma, we're going to need help. There's no way I can take care of the horses and hunt with this broken arm. And you know we don't have enough food to last the rest of the way without catching meat as we go."

She forced a smile through her tight jaw. "I see your motive now. You're just trying to get out of work. Well, don't worry, baby brother. I'll do your chores for a while until you feel better."

He sank back against the furs with a faint chuckle. "You know me." His eyes drifted shut, and his breathing filled the space between them.

Hopefully the argument hadn't worn him out too much, but at least he'd seen her side. It wouldn't be easy to take on Joseph's work, too. Despite her teasing, he pulled more than his fair share. But she'd do whatever it took to get them safely to Alberta. From then on, they'd have the protection of Mama's sister and her husband. They could build a whole new life in that country.

"Emma?" The word rasped from Joseph's reddened lips. She should find something to help with the chapping.

"Yes?"

"I don't think I can get us there without help. We don't have another choice." Joseph whispered the words, but they had an icy finality to them. He never opened his eyes though, and part of her wanted to pretend he hadn't spoken.

"What do you mean?" A tightness pulled in her chest. "We can do it together."

He raised one eyelid, the cloudiness gone, replaced by clear focus. "I can't, Emma. I didn't tell you, but we already lost two days when I took us down the wrong mountain pass. According to the map, the elevations are going to be high enough to make us sick if we don't handle it right. I don't know if there's a way to avoid the worst or not. And I won't take chances with you and the baby."

The baby. She couldn't risk her child's safety either. But did Joseph really think the trip would be so bad? Why hadn't he spoken his concerns earlier? She hated when men kept secrets. Even if he thought he was protecting her, she could handle the truth.

She forced herself to loosen her clenched jaw. "What else aren't you telling me?"

"The terrain we've traveled so far was already worse than I'd expected." He had both eyes open now. "I have a bad feeling about what's ahead. This man is our only hope, Em." His earnest gaze tightened the knot in her chest.

"You don't think I can help you?" She sounded like a belligerent child, but she didn't care at this point.

"Please, Em. Let's just ask him. If he says no, we'll know it's God's will."

God's will. The words took the starch out of her corset. Yes, that's what she wanted more than anything on this trip. It didn't matter if she were frustrated with secrets and untrusting of strangers. They had to follow God's leading. But surely He wouldn't want their unusual host to guide the rest of their journey, and He would make that clear when the man refused. "All right. We can ask him."

She watched Joseph's eyelids drift shut again and his breathing regulate. If God opened the door for the mountain man to guide them the rest of the way, so be it. But the idea still left a tingle in her chest that had nothing to do with the cool autumn air.

Chapter Four

This force drags me where I don't want to go. I once thought myself a man, but it was a naïve deception.
~ Simeon

Simeon's gaze scanned the room as he stepped into the cabin and shucked his gloves. He tossed them in their usual spot on the chair, then frowned. He should keep things a little more orderly while he had guests. Especially a woman. Who knew what she thought about his little abode? The least he could do was keep it tidy.

He looked around again, trying to see the place as she would. Dirt floor, log walls. He'd spent time chinking so no wind could blow through but hadn't worried overmuch about appearance. The inside was sparse, maybe even gloomy. No window openings, which helped keep the cold out and the fire's warmth in. But it offered precious little natural light. Even the stack of furs that had formed his bed—and now served as mattresses for his guests—seemed dark and depressing shoved against a far wall.

He stepped toward the fire, pulled a stick from the

blaze, and used it to light a candle from his stash on the hearth. There was no sense in wasting his lanterns inside the cabin when candles would do the trick. He could make oil for the lantern from animal fat, but the wicks were harder to come by. It would be spring before he made his yearly trip to town for supplies, so what he had needed to last.

The lone candle didn't do much to brighten the place, though. He carried the metal holder with him as he stepped closer to Joseph Malcom. The man's steady breathing seemed more labored than it had earlier that day. His sister was outside sorting their supplies. When was the last time she'd checked him?

Simeon lowered to one knee beside the man. He still couldn't fathom the fact that these two were twins. But he saw their similarities now. The shape of their face and the color of their eyes. And he'd caught a few of the same expressions.

Having the constant reminder of his own babes had tightened a ball of pain in his chest that wouldn't release. A boy and a girl. Born together. Two gifts when only one had been expected. The ache for his children almost cut off his breath. How could he have given them away?

He squeezed his eyes shut against the burn that always assaulted him. He'd been so foolish back then. So lost in his grief over Nora, he'd not even realized the extent of what he was giving up.

And now they were lost to him. The little girl, lost truly. Gone the way of her mother when she was just six months old. That first letter from the Scotts giving him the news had almost pushed him over the edge. The only thing that kept him going was the image of his Nora in some faraway heaven, rocking their baby daughter. They were together now, as they should have always been.

And the boy. Reuben must be five years old now. From the letters that came every year, he was a strong, independent spirit. Quinn Scott had written a story about how the boy sneaked away early one morning, riding atop one of the plow horses. Mrs. Scott had thought him merely sleeping late until they found the animal missing. After a two-hour search, they discovered the pair sitting at an overlook on the mountainside, staring out toward the distant peaks. The child had defended himself by saying he'd only wanted to go exploring.

Simeon could understand the feeling. The same yearning resided in his own chest. It was what drove him out into the wilds for days or weeks at a time. He'd been all over these mountains in every direction.

But he'd never gone back to see his son. He'd honored his promise to the Scotts when they'd taken the children to raise.

It was best, really, that Reuben believe them his own parents. He didn't want the boy to feel like he'd been given away, that his father didn't love him enough to keep him close. He never could have given two tiny infants the love and care they needed to sustain life. Not in this wild country when he'd not even had a home to shelter them. And when his heart had been ripped in two by Nora's death.

Yes, the Scotts were doing right by his son. He had to

believe it. Otherwise he truly wouldn't be able to live with himself.

Joseph stirred in front of him, pulling Simeon from the memories. The man's head tossed back and forth, and he murmured something.

Simeon leaned closer to hear.

His patient didn't speak again, but his lips were awfully red against his pale skin. Simeon touched his forehead. Warm.

He straightened and studied the length of the man. The bone hadn't broken through the skin, so he didn't expect infection. Maybe the fever was just the body's way of working to heal. Still, they should try to help it along. Knitbone tea would do the trick. And maybe a garlic poultice just in case there was some infection trying to take hold.

As he was chopping the garlic, Mrs. Malcom came into the cabin in a flurry of cold air. "The temperature's dropping, I think."

He nodded but kept at his work. Her presence in the cabin still unnerved him. Had it been so long since he'd been around a female? He'd interacted with the Apsaalooke squaws plenty over the last few years. And some of the miners' wives when he went to town for supplies.

But Mrs. Malcom was a lady, through and through. From the way she carried herself, poised and regal, to the smooth cadence of her voice. Her presence crept under his skin, as if he were an imposter in his own cabin.

And what of her surname? She'd spoken of a

deceased husband, and the child she carried seemed to confirm that, yet she used the same last name as her brother? Something wasn't right there. The look in her eyes when she'd mentioned her husband's death was enough to put him on edge. It hadn't been sorrow, exactly. More like…anger, and maybe a touch of fear.

"Joseph is still sleeping?" She hung her cloak on a nail and padded over to examine her brother.

"He has a bit of fever.."

She jerked her gaze to him. "Fever? What does that mean?"

This woman hadn't done much nursing apparently. "Fever means his body's fighting something, which makes his skin hot. We need to keep him drinking. I'm making a garlic poultice, and there's knitbone tea in the kettle."

Her demeanor changed, and that pert chin came up. "I know what a fever is. I meant, what relation is it to his arm? Is there infection, do you think?"

He shrugged. "It's possible. The garlic will help. Could just be his body trying to recover."

She sank to her knees beside her brother and took his hand between her long, delicate fingers. They were probably soft, too.

The urge to touch them itched through his own hands. He tightened his hold on the knife and pressed hard on the garlic clove. The blade sliced through with a thud, and both chunks flew off the table.

He leaned down to snatch up the pieces. Time to get his reactions under control.

Simeon knelt beside the bay gelding the next morning and applied a fresh dose of salve to the skinned knee. A branch snapped behind him, too loud to be the step of a forest animal. Joseph's fever had been lower this morning, but he still looked ill. So ill he shouldn't be out in the cold unless the man really was insane. Which was still a possibility, considering where he planned to travel with a woman thoroughly unfit for the conditions. A woman *with child*.

His jaw still clenched at the thought.

"Mr. Simeon?"

He focused on taking in even breaths, despite the way her voice made his pulse race. "Call me Simeon." She seemed like a decently intelligent woman, but that simple concept had proved hard for her to grasp.

A soft laugh laced the air like the bubbling of a clear stream over rocks. "I'm sorry, Simeon. I suppose you should call me Emma then."

He nodded but kept himself crouched beside the horse's leg, his back to her. The salve was in place, but he stroked the animal's thick winter coat, running his hand down the bones and tendons. Anything to keep from turning to face the woman.

The name, Emma, seemed to suit her softer side, but maybe not the stubborn streak he'd seen rear its head with every jut of her chin. He wasn't sure he could obey her request, though. Using her Christian name allowed too much intimacy. He was barely able to stand her presence as it was.

She'd lapsed into silence, and the quiet thickened in the air around them. What had she come here to say? Surely she wasn't going to stand there for hours watching him.

Finally, he could endure it no longer. He straightened and turned to face her. "Is your brother worse?"

Her mouth formed a soft smile. "No, I think his fever may be gone. He's certainly sleeping a lot—which is good, I suppose."

Simeon eased around to stroke the gelding's shoulder, his side to her now instead of his back. This way he could watch her from the edge of his vision. And maybe it wasn't quite as rude as keeping his back to her. "The willow bark can make him sleepy, especially if it's steeped for a while."

She nodded but didn't speak. Surely she would leave soon. He was a patient man. Had learned to live in silence, to sit and watch the animals for hours on end if he needed to. But standing under her scrutiny made his neck itch against his buckskin collar.

At last, she broke the silence. "Simeon, my brother and I have a question for you. We're in need of a guide to take us to Canada, and we'd like you to fill the role."

She said it in a rush of breath as if trying to push the question out of her mouth before it caught there. And the flurry of words charged at him with a powerful force, smacking him hard in the gut.

Take these people to Canada? Not in a thousand lifetimes.

He schooled his features and turned back to the horse. "I'm sorry, Mrs. Malcom. I'm not available."

"Please, call me Emma. And are you sure? You seem to know this country and how to get by out here. We think you'd be the perfect guide."

He pinched his eyes shut, forcing his breathing to stay even. Take another woman into the deep wilderness? And with winter coming, the land they'd traverse would be more treacherous than what they'd been through so far. It could be deadly to her, especially in her condition.

"Mrs. Malcom—"

"Please, call me Emma."

He inhaled a breath. "Emma. The only place I'll take you is back to Fort Benton. This country is dangerous. No place for a lady. You should go home while you still have the chance." He softened his voice at the end. He didn't want her angry, but she needed to know the truth of it.

He heard an intake of breath behind him. "We're not going back to Fort Benton. We're going to Alberta, Canada." The words were forced, almost clipped.

Yep, he'd made her mad.

"We'll be going north whether you go with us or not, Mr. Simeon." She paused for half a second. "But we'd like you to go." Her tone eased with those last words. "Joseph won't be able to do much, but if I know him he'll still try. I don't want him to reinjure his arm, and if someone else is along to help, I hope he'll let it rest."

Simeon whirled. "If you plan to leave before his arm is healed, you'll both be proved touched in the head. It'd be certain death out here."

Her chin came up, but as she paused for a moment, a flash of uncertainty touched her eyes. "I agree it would be better to wait, but I thought it best not to impose on your hospitality."

Hospitality? This was a matter of life and death, and she was worried about manners? He threw up a hand. "That's exactly what I mean. You need to stop being stubborn and listen to someone who knows before you do something foolish."

Her chin jutted a little farther. "That's exactly what I was doing when I asked you to come along." She spoke through her teeth. Though the way her eyes sparked, she looked like she'd rather use them to bite something. She reminded him of an injured cougar lashing out.

Her chest rose in a long breath. "We can pay you for your trouble."

Pay him? She thought money would make up for leading her to an early grave? He spun back to the horse and gritted his own teeth. "No, thank you."

Silence reigned for another long minute. Then the rattle of leaves filled the void as she turned and walked away.

Chapter Five

Every moment of peace. Of joy. A gift from the One I can trust.
~ Emma's Journal

Darkness had fully enveloped the land for several hours before Simeon finally forced himself back to the cabin. He had a string of mountain whitefish and a few larger trout to show for his time away, but he couldn't stay gone forever. He'd just drop off the fish and grab his blankets, then head for the lean-to behind the cabin where he'd bedded down the last couple of nights. If he was lucky, both brother and sister would be sleeping, and he wouldn't have to face them.

Wouldn't have to face *her*.

Heat still surged up his neck when he thought about the way he'd spoken earlier. She'd asked for help, and he'd called her crazy. Foolish, too. Even he knew he'd messed up. And his long-ignored conscience wouldn't let him forget it.

But it still irked him that she seemed so set on traveling north.

Was it truly just stubbornness, like he'd assumed earlier? Or did she have a stronger motivation? Maybe it had something to do with the shadow that had touched her eyes when she'd mentioned her late husband.

Perhaps she was running *to* something. *Someone*. Did she have a man waiting for her in Canada? She could be one of those mail-order brides the trappers spun yarns about. Ol' Dan Weaver had even sent for one, although Simeon had yet to hear how the matter played out.

He paused at the cabin door, his hand hovering over the latch string. If he couldn't convince his visitors to turn back, the least he could do was try to get them through safely. Although the thought churned bile in his gut.

He pressed his eyes shut and pushed into them with his thumb and forefinger. Twin brother and sister. The woman with child. Was God taunting him? Forcing him to relive his past failures?

Or maybe this was the chance to redeem himself. He could only hope.

Emma found herself humming a simple tune as Joseph picked one-handed on the guitar. It was such a homey feeling, sitting at this rustic wooden table, working her needle as she mended the ragged quilt squares. She'd found two blankets hidden among the stack of furs Simeon carried outside with him each night, and both quilts had apparently been well-used, worn around the edges with some of the seams separating. Since she had her sewing kit in the pack, the least she could do was re-stitch the unraveling areas.

This first quilt had piqued her interest with its interlocking circles in blue-and-yellow floral cloth. She'd made the same design for her trousseau, although her colors hadn't been as fetching. But why would a bachelor mountain man have a double wedding ring quilt? Had it belonged to his parents? That much age would explain the excessive wear.

The cabin door pushed open, and Emma's muscles tensed as she eyed the man who stepped inside. This was his first time home since their little dispute earlier. Was he still angry?

The flickering light from the lantern illuminated the strong features on his face, including the day's growth of stubble on his jaw. She would have expected a man living this far from civilization to be more unkempt. Shaggy beard and long tangled hair. After all, why worry about social niceties? But maybe assuming the man disdained culture wasn't fair to him.

If that wasn't the reason though, why *did* he live so far from people and town? Surely good trapping and hunting could be found closer to one of the mountain villages. And it'd be worlds easier to get supplies. If he didn't hide out here to snub society's strictures, what else drove him?

He closed the door behind him, and the room seemed to shrink against the weight of his presence. She could feel his stare and raised her gaze to meet it.

But he wasn't looking at her. Instead, his focus was aimed at the quilt in her lap. His eyes narrowed, and the

Adam's apple at his throat bobbed.

Her grip on the fabric tightened. What did that expression mean? It certainly wasn't a look of thanks. Had she been presumptuous?

She opened her mouth to apologize, or at least explain, but he turned toward the fire. Emma forced her gaze not to follow him, to ignore his magnetism. Instead, she focused on her brother.

Joseph had caught his tongue between his teeth as he worked the frets and strings with the fingers of his left hand. His right knee was bent around the body of the guitar to hold it in place as he picked the final bars of an old Irish folksong. It was a simple tune, one of the first he'd learned to play from their neighbor back in Baltimore. Mr. Finnegan had loved music as much as he'd loved the customs from the land of his youth, and he'd filled their imaginations with his stories. Emma had never learned to play the guitar, but the words to each song would be forever ingrained in her mind.

After the last choppy note, Joseph raised his head and rested it against the wall behind him. His weary eyes took away some of the joy in the smile that curved his mouth. At least his fever hadn't come back. He rolled his head to the side to watch Simeon, who was still standing by the fire. "You like music, Simeon?"

The man turned to face Joseph, a mug of tea in his hand. His answer was slow in coming. "Some."

Joseph nodded toward Emma. "You should hear when me an' Emma get goin'. She can sing up a storm. Sometimes I'm hard pressed to keep up with her on those

Irish jigs."

Simeon turned to her with a single raised brow. One side of his mouth twitched. "She can, huh?"

She shot Joseph a glare before ducking back to her sewing. It'd been years since she'd sung around anyone other than her brother, and that was not a tale she wanted him spreading. Especially not to this man.

The tingles on her neck told her Simeon's scrutiny stayed with her for several moments as the room quieted, but Emma didn't dare look. What did he think of her? She couldn't begin to imagine. A stubborn tender-foot not capable of enduring tough conditions? He thought her foolish—he'd made that clear enough.

The clearing of a throat brought her head up. Simeon's gaze flicked from Joseph to Emma, his blue eyes locking with hers. "If you're still looking for a guide to Canada, I suppose I can do it."

The breath seeped out of her. After his adamant refusal earlier, she'd assumed God was closing that door, telling them to proceed north without this mountain man. But did this mean God was now saying *yes*?

She studied the look in Simeon's eyes. Intensity. Earnestness?

Did she and Joseph dare trust him?

"That's great." Joseph's voice forced its way into her awareness, like a hammer and chisel cracking through ice. It seemed her brother trusted the man.

She did her best to scrutinize the mountain trapper, to see beneath the fierce outer façade of his leathers and hardened expression. Was the man underneath as honorable as part of her wanted to believe?

Apparently, God must have thought so.

Simeon tightened the cinch on the bay gelding and pulled the strap in place. The scrape on its knee had healed well over the last week, leaving only a scar where the black hair would likely grow in white. Too bad Joseph's arm couldn't heal as quickly.

He eyed the low, thick clouds above them. If they could, he'd wait longer to let the man recover before they set out, but winter would hit hard any day now. The trip to Canada could take anywhere from two weeks to two months, depending on the weather. The sooner he got these two to their destination, the better for them all.

He'd drilled Joseph last night about Emma's condition. The man had said she should have at least three months left before her time, according to the doctor she'd seen in St. Louis. But why had she seen a doctor in that transient city? Why not the family physician back in Texas where they claimed to have lived? Were they running from something? So many secrets seemed to surround them, especially Emma with her maiden surname and expectant condition.

If they were escaping to another country, should he be helping them? He couldn't imagine either of them had done anything too serious. Neither the man nor the woman looked like a vicious killer. But the territories' affiliation with laws of the proper states was loose, at best.

Still, maybe he should insist on answers before he took them farther into the northern mountains.

His mind wandered over the impending trip. Had he missed anything in his packing? The Malcoms had brought a few dry goods, and he'd stocked plenty of smoked meat for the meals he wouldn't have time to hunt fresh. They had matches, candles, two lanterns, dry firewood, salt for the meat he'd hunt, furs for bedding. His gaze flickered to the pack under Paint, the mare whose chestnut and white markings fit her name. He'd packed the letters, of course. They were tucked in with the medicinal herbs. And Nora's quilts were with the bedrolls. He couldn't quite bring himself to leave them behind for a wandering, lice-ridden trapper to snuggle beneath. It had been hard enough to see them in the hands of his female houseguest a week ago.

That old, familiar vise clamped around his chest. Nora had loved those quilts, especially the one with all the blue and yellow flowers sewn into circles. And when he'd walked into the cabin and seen Emma's needle working through the fabric, his first instinct had been to snatch it from her. No female hands besides Nora's should be allowed to stroke the soft material. But it would have been rude to jerk the blankets away when Emma had been performing a kindness. Turning aside had been the hardest thing he'd done in years.

A whistled tune drifted through the early morning

air, snapping him from his thoughts. Joseph appeared through the trees, ending his song as he reached the gate of the little rope pasture. "Thought maybe you'd like a hand bringing the horses down to the cabin." He raised his left arm, splaying his fingers. "All I have is one, but you're welcome to it." A grin tugged the corners of his mouth.

Simeon's own lips twitched. As much as he didn't approve of the man bringing his sister into these mountains, it was hard not to like Joseph Malcom. He had a quick wit and a way of setting a person at ease.

After gathering the bay gelding's reins, Simeon led the horse to the gate and pulled the rope off the hook he'd mounted to fasten it. "You can take this boy. I think his knee should hold up, but we'll go easy on them all." He nodded toward Pet and Paint. "My girls are both due to foal in the spring, so they'll appreciate a slower pace."

Twin lines formed between Joseph's brows. "Do you think the mountain heights will be too taxing for 'em?"

Simeon followed the man's gaze and scrutinized his mares. Both were rounded, with some extra weight obvious beneath their thick winter coats. "They were raised in these peaks. Got them from a band of Apsaalooke several years back. They're good breeding stock with thick enough blood to handle the altitudes." He brought his focus back to Joseph and couldn't help driving his point home one more time. "I'm more worried about other members of our caravan. Your sister is also in the family way."

Joseph met his look squarely. "I understand the concern, Simeon. I do. But we need to go. Emma's strong."

No hint of merriment lingered in his eyes now. Only stark determination. A look strongly reminiscent of the one Emma had glared at him the day of their dispute…in this very place.

Simeon worked his jaw as he turned away. Maybe it was time to get on with things.

With Emma's mare on one side and Pet on his other, Simeon followed Joseph and his gelding down the trail to the cabin. Paint ambled along behind Pet, her tether strap keeping her close. He'd rotate the mares throughout the trip, but with Pet's easy disposition, she would be a more pleasant ride as they started out.

Speaking of easy dispositions, he kept an eye out for Mustang, but the dog hadn't appeared again since Joseph and Emma first arrived. Not that Simeon was worried. Mustang managed his own affairs, wandering off for days at a time before appearing again on the cabin stoop. He'd eat a meal and take up his spot beside the door as if he had no doubt of his welcome. Must be nice to be so certain. A niggle of concern wove through Simeon's mind. If Mustang showed up while they were gone, would he wait for Simeon? Or move on to a new resting spot?

The cabin came into view. Emma stood in front, the guitar case perched at her feet. A stab of longing hit his chest. Every time he saw the guitar, his fingers itched to take it in his hands and let the music flow through him. It had been so long.

He swallowed the feeling. All these emotions hadn't warred inside him before his visitors arrived. He'd been fine living on his own with not much more to sustain himself than what he could find or make. He'd fit seamlessly with the wild things in these mountains. Perfectly content. Well…maybe not content. But at least no one depended on him.

Joseph tied off the gelding in the yard and slipped past his sister into the cabin. Simeon pulled the three mares to a stop in front of her. The way the light shone from behind, it framed her in a glow that seemed to radiate from within her soul. Especially when she flashed that smile. She had uncommon beauty, no doubt about it.

Tearing his gaze away, he turned to stroke his horse. He had no business thinking like that. Had he been secluded from people so long he couldn't control his own thoughts? He'd already been given one wife and proved himself unworthy. Incapable of one of the most basic duties assigned to man—protection.

"Thank you."

Simeon turned as she tugged her mare's reins from his hand. With the case strapped to her back, she gripped the saddle and prepared to mount.

"Wait." He strode forward before he could stop himself. Surely this woman didn't intend to carry the awkward thing all the way to Canada, especially in her expectant state. She'd have her hands full just managing her horse on some of the trails. "Take off that instrument."

She looked at him, chin jutted and brows raised in that stubborn expression he'd already become acquainted with. "Joseph can't carry it yet. I'm fine. No need to worry."

He clamped his teeth against his reply and reached to lift the guitar off her back. "You can't carry it either. Take it off." She twisted away, the motion stretching her dress tight over the swell of her abdomen. Even with extra bulk in front, she was lithe and slid the instrument from his grasp.

He forced himself to still. And breathe. "Mrs. Malcom, you can't carry it over the trails we'll travel. It's too much." He started to reach for the guitar again, but the look in her eyes stopped him.

"Mister…." She propped a hand at her waist. "What is your last name, anyway?"

Something about the way she stood, hand fisted, stubborn jaw cocked, made him fight a grin. "Grant."

Confusion clouded her eyes for just a moment. Like she was surprised he'd given in so easily. Then it disappeared, and all her righteous indignation flooded back in. "*Mis-ter Grant.*" She drew out each syllable like a schoolteacher chastising the scoundrel who hid the frog in her desk. "My brother carried this guitar a thousand miles to get it here. There's no way I'll leave it behind now."

This woman had more pluck than a runt rooster. He eased out a breath, then extended his hand.

She eyed it, backing up another few inches until the horse's mass stopped her.

"Don't worry, *Mis-sus Malcom.*" He drew out her name the same way she'd done his. "I'll carry the confounded thing."

She arched her brows, then propped her chin even higher and raised the instrument over her head.

Simeon slipped his arm through the strap and turned as Joseph stepped from the cabin. "Mount up."

When they rode out, Simeon took the lead. Emma followed next, and Joseph brought up the rear. This first bit of the trail was a slight incline around the mountain. An easy ride.

The guitar on Simeon's back took some getting used to, especially the way its size restricted his movements. He had to shift his balance to compensate for it as Pet maneuvered the rocky terrain. No wonder Joseph's horse had stumbled. A man and horse unaccustomed to riding these parts didn't need extra bulk. And a woman in the family way shouldn't try to carry the thing.

The image of Emma with her fists clenched flitted back through his memory. He hadn't planned to give his last name. It made him more…identifiable…in a world where he'd prefer to fade into obscurity. But she'd been so all-fired cute flustered like that. She was a feisty one, no doubt about it. So unlike Nora, who'd always been sweet and strong in her quiet way.

He didn't doubt Emma Malcom was strong too. But different than Nora. Maybe that difference could keep her alive out here.

The gentle murmur of Emma's voice drifted up to him as she spoke to her mare. He couldn't make out the words, but the cadence eased the tension in his muscles. She had a nice sound. Musical. Joseph said she liked to sing.

That longing rose up again in Simeon's chest. He hadn't heard good music in years now. What would it take to get her to sing a ballad around the campfire one night? Joseph couldn't play the guitar one-handed, but maybe the man wouldn't mind loaning it for a song or two. But it had been so many years since Simeon's fingers pressed guitar strings. Would he even remember the chording? Did he have the nerve to try?

Chapter Six

Even when my actions are right, the Fates plot against me.
~ Simeon

Emma eyed the dog as she poured water into the pot of beans and settled it among the logs on the fire. The animal had shown up midway through the day, falling into step behind Simeon's horse like it had trotted there all morning. Simeon seemed to take little notice of the mutt, and it responded in kind. Such a strange connection between them—if you could even call it that.

Now it watched her, lying on its belly with its head resting on its paws, eyes shifting with every one of her movements. At least it didn't growl at her anymore.

She pulled a sliver of smoked meat from the supply in her pack and held it out to the dog. A low snarl drifted from its throat. So much for not growling.

"You'll like it, you untrusting cur." She kept her voice soft and welcoming and her hand steady.

He eyed the meat, then shifted his big brown eyes to her face. She kept her gaze soft on the animal. Their pet dog in Baltimore had always responded to her body language, especially the way she held her eyes and shoulders.

After several long minutes, the animal still hadn't moved. The men would be back soon from settling the horses and securing their supplies for the night, and they'd expect food. She'd planned to have flapjacks cooking by the time they returned.

She dropped the meat on the ground where her hand had been. "You'll still have to come get it."

The dog's spotted ear twitched, but he never shifted his gaze from her.

She turned back to her work and scooped a dab of lard into the frying pan to melt. Flapjacks would be filling enough with the beans, and she could make plenty, so they'd have some to eat for breakfast tomorrow and sandwiches on the trail.

She'd expected Simeon to press on longer than they had today, pushing them for prolonged, weary hours in the saddle followed by exhausted nights. But even with the shorter autumn days, they'd stopped at least an hour before nightfall. Surprising, considering his comments about reaching Canada before the worst of winter hit.

He seemed to know what he was doing, though. He'd been quiet on the trail, only speaking when he had some warning or important instruction to impart. Yet each command—and his bearing in general—bespoke an innate confidence. It was impossible not to trust him.

"Here's meat for supper."

She spun to find the object of her thoughts standing right behind her. How had he approached so close without her hearing? Those leather stocking-shoes he wore made almost no sound. She pinched her lips to stop the heat surging to her cheeks.

He extended his hand, displaying a limp bird hanging upside down, a little smaller than a chicken. She raised her gaze to his. "What is it?"

"Grouse. You can fry it in flour or roast it on a stick." He raised the fowl before her. Did he expect her to take it? And do what? The thing still had feathers and blood oozing, for goodness sake.

His brows lowered, and he glanced down at the bird as if seeing it for the first time. "I'll, um, get it plucked for you."

As he turned away, awareness sank through her. He'd meant for her to ready the bird. Was that what a frontier woman did? She'd never even imagined such a thing. Mama had always bought fresh meat from the butcher. And in Lance's home, the chef took care of such things. She could cook a decent meal and hadn't done bad these last weeks making meals over an open fire. But they'd been eating packed supplies, not slaughtering animals that had to be de-feathered and cut open and... A shudder slipped through her. *Lord, give me strength.*

The problem was, even if she found the strength, she had no desire to apply it. *Lord, if you could make me willing, too. Please*. She let out a breath. Her Father above had His work cut out for Him.

Emma scrubbed the bottom of the frying pan one last time and dumped the sooty water into the creek. Then she scooped clean water to rinse it. Her hands had long grown numb from the icy stream and the chill in the air. It would be nice to settle into her blankets near the fire. But first, she needed to wrap up the last of the food supplies for Simeon to pack away.

He'd been very clear on that request, even though it would be easier to keep the food out that she planned to serve for breakfast. From the looks of his cabin, she hadn't realized the man was so fastidious about everything being in its place. Of course, his dwelling had been rather sparse. There wasn't much to put away, nor many places to store them in the single open room.

As she approached the campfire, the soft strum of a guitar drifted through the chilly air. That was the best she'd heard Joseph play since his accident. It was a gentle tune, and not one she'd heard before. Yet with the combination of picking and strumming, he must be using his injured hand. A surge of concern tightened her muscles. The last thing they needed was for him to reinjure the limb because he pushed too hard.

She stepped into the circle of light to chastise him but drew up short at the sight of her brother lounging on his bedroll, his good hand stroking the dog's head. Her gaze stalled on the animal, but she'd focus on the ungrateful mutt later.

Instead, she turned to Simeon, who sat propped against a tree with the neck of Joseph's guitar resting on his bent knee. That relaxing melody continued as his fingers worked the strings with a familiarity that made the scene feel perfect. Like a picture of home.

His gaze wandered up to hers but lacked focus as his mind worked the chords along with his hands.

She couldn't quite bring herself to move. Didn't want to spoil the serenity that seemed to hover in the space like a morning mist.

But then his eyes sharpened. She was staring. She forced herself to look away as she stepped forward and crouched beside the pack that held her cooking supplies. If she stayed quiet and unobtrusive, perhaps he would keep playing.

That song ended, and he started into another, this one with a stronger, more haunting melody as he picked at the strings. She had the last of the supplies put away, so she unrolled her blankets and eased her weary body down to listen. She was directly across from Simeon now, as their bedrolls formed a U shape around the fire with Joseph in the middle. Flames flickered between them, and the distance and the barrier gave her courage to watch the man of so many unexpected talents.

Where had he learned to play a guitar? She hadn't seen an instrument in his small cabin, so he must have gained the skill long ago, yet learned it well enough for the memory to still be ingrained in his fingers. Did he sing too?

She could imagine a deep baritone rolling from his throat. A sound that would mix perfectly with the sadness of the haunting melody.

His eyes had sunk deep into shadows now, but she could imagine the look there. The aura that seemed to touch him every so often. A pain that now exposed itself in his music.

A burning sensation pricked behind her eyes, but she swallowed it down. It must be the music making her overly sympathetic. She didn't know his story, but her heart told her it was a tragedy.

He picked the last few notes, and their sound lingered in the night air before settling into silence. Without a word, he placed the guitar inside its leather case and fastened the buckles to close it.

She wanted to speak, to tell him how much she'd enjoyed the music. But the tension that seemed to shroud him warned her off. What was it that seemed to form a protective armor around him?

With the guitar safely stowed, Simeon rose to his feet with a grace that would have made an English princess look on with envy. He stepped toward the food pack, then turned a glance to her. "Is all the food in here? Nothing left out?"

She scanned the ground to make sure she hadn't missed anything. "Yes, that's everything except the tea kettle. You said we could use that still, right?"

He nodded as he hoisted the pack, then turned away and disappeared into the darkness.

She turned toward her brother. "Joey, you want more

tea?"

But her brother's chin rested on his chest as it rose and fell in a steady rhythm. Poor fellow. Riding all day had to be hard on his weakened body, although he hadn't complained. He'd even helped build her cook fire when they first set up camp. She'd seen the lines of pain around his eyes then and brewed tea for him from the willow bark powder. That must have eased his pain enough for sleep to take over. She crawled closer.

The dog let out a warning growl, and she sent him a glare. "You found a new friend, huh? Well, he was my brother first, so back off." The animal didn't move but allowed her to approach Joseph's other side.

Why did the animal distrust her? She'd been nothing but pleasant to it. Had tried to feed the beast this evening. Even after she'd left the meat on the ground, it'd taken well over an hour before she saw him slink back for it. And now, here he lay snuggled into Joseph's side. Something about this picture was cock-eyed.

She stooped low and extended her hand toward the animal, reaching over Joseph's leg. "Hey, boy. It's all right. I won't hurt you."

The animal eyed her like he might attack any moment, but at least he didn't growl. Should she be worried about it? Surely Simeon would have said something if the dog were dangerous.

Still, she withdrew her hand and straightened Joseph's covers. Leaning over his face, she planted a kiss on his forehead. "Sweet dreams, love."

Then she straightened and used a nearby sapling to pull herself to her feet. It seemed like the baby had grown more than normal this last week, and maneuvering was becoming harder each day.

She sank onto her quilt and laid her saddle pack at one end for a pillow. As hungry as she'd been lately, she'd probably need the smoked beef inside for a midnight snack. She eased down with a sigh as the aches in her body came alive. Now that they no longer carried a load, the muscles in her back screamed their complaints. She focused on steady breathing as they quieted, one by one.

A spasm in her abdomen brought a smile to her lips. She touched the spot with her fingers. *Lord, bless this little one. Make her strong and healthy.*

With the prayer in her heart, Emma turned onto her side to enjoy the warmth of the fire on her face. She'd only close her eyes for a moment until the mountain man returned.

Simeon's muscles coiled as his eyelids jerked open. He forced the rest of his body to keep still as his senses strained.

Mustang growled low in his chest from his spot at Joseph's side. Not the playful sound he seemed to tease Emma with. This snarl meant business.

A noxious odor slipped into Simeon's awareness. It pricked at his memory, and he scanned the recesses of his mind to recognize the smell. A high nicker drifted from the clearing where he'd tied the horses as the scent registered in his brain.

Bear scat. The odor was unmistakable.

He'd hung the food pack in a tall tree some distance away from their camp, in the opposite direction from the horses. Had a bear found it? It should be high enough the animal wouldn't try for it, but as long as it kept the creature away from their camp and animals, he wouldn't quibble over the supplies.

Simeon eased himself up to a sitting position and grabbed his Sharps breechloader in the same movement. He'd cleaned the gun and filled the breech with bullet and black powder after taking down the grouse for dinner, so the weapon should be ready. He rested it in his lap and waited.

His ears would do most of the scouting now, and he kept himself tuned to the forest noises. It was still early in the night, and the fire kept a steady blaze from the wood he'd loaded on before bedding down. His gaze wandered beyond the fire to Emma.

Her hair had pulled loose from its knot to feather around her face, and the glow from the fire illuminated the softness of her features. Like an angel. A feisty one. Even in sleep her chin formed a stubborn jut. Something tightened in his chest. He shouldn't be here with her. Shouldn't be thinking how beautiful she was.

A sound from the woods jerked his attention that direction. The crunch of leaves and branches echoed in the distance as the bear lumbered along. He stilled his breathing to listen. Was the noise growing louder? Maybe.

Simeon raised his rifle and sighted it in the direction of the noise, then squeezed the set trigger so the gun would be ready to shoot. The animal had to be fifty feet or so away, but it didn't sound like it was traveling very quickly. Maybe it would smell their campfire and move on.

His gaze darted to the flame. Should he throw on a few more logs? He tightened his grip on the rifle barrel. There wasn't time now.

"What's wrong?" Joseph's sleepy voice rasped in the quiet.

Simeon didn't take his focus from the darkness beyond the trees. "Bear."

A gasp sounded across the circle, and something moved at the edge of his vision. His gaze darted over before he could stop it, and he saw Emma sit up in her blankets.

"Joey, where's your rifle?" Her strained whisper resounded in the unnatural calm. Even the popping of the fire had stilled as the forest waited in expectation.

Joseph reached behind himself to the scabbard on the saddle he'd been using as a pillow. His angle was awkward using only his left arm, and Emma crept over to help him.

"Here. Let me have it." Did she even know how to shoot a gun?

Simeon tore his focus from the pair and scanned the woods again. The tromping sound was louder now. Why was it coming toward them and not the food pack? Maybe the animal hadn't smelled the supplies. But surely a bear wouldn't be hungry enough to kill a live meal this late in the season. Most had already gone into hibernation, although he'd seen a few grizzly tracks earlier that day.

The noise from the trees seemed to be moving faster now. Closer. Should he go toward the animal? Cut it off before it reached their camp? The lighting was better here, and he had the best chance for a clean shot. And seated, he could keep a steady aim. He still couldn't believe the beast would approach their campfire when they had no food in the area for it to smell. It should have gone for the pack hanging in the tree a hundred yards away.

He glanced at Emma, perched on her bedroll with her rifle positioned to fire. Its barrel rested on her bent knees as she sighted. Maybe she did know how to shoot. But it would be best to avoid it if at all possible.

"Let me shoot first," he said, "but aim for the chest if you have to."

"All right." She didn't move as she squinted through the sights.

He turned his full attention back to his prey and fingered the front trigger. He couldn't let the beast get past him. A wounded bear was even more deadly than a hungry one.

The animal was close now. From the amount of noise, it had to be a grizzly, not just a black bear.

A motion flashed through the trees. He focused his aim and inhaled a slow breath. Brown fur appeared. The animal was lumbering on all fours.

It paused just inside the edge of the tree line, where several saplings and a pine blocked an open view. Simeon's muscles strained. He had to wait for a clear shot.

The animal rose up on all fours and waddled forward a step. There.

As a mighty roar escaped the beast, Simeon squeezed his trigger.

Chapter Seven

I know not the dangers of this land, but I know the One who does.
~ Emma's Journal

The gun exploded, lighting up the night with the spark from the barrel. A scream ripped the air as the echo of the bear's cry faded.

Simeon dropped the gun to his lap, opened the breech, and reloaded with quick movements he'd practiced a hundred times. He darted glances at the bear. Any moment it could rise up from the brown heap and charge again.

With the gun loaded, he pulled the set trigger, then pushed to his feet. He pressed the butt of the rifle into his shoulder and sighted the barrel but kept his finger off the front trigger.

Still, the animal didn't move.

He eased forward, sidling around to get a better look at the fallen creature. It lay not ten feet from the fire, and the dancing flames flickered golden across the fur. He stepped close enough to kick one of the huge, furry front legs. Still no movement, save the shifting of hair where he'd touched.

Emma's footsteps shuffled behind him, and he turned

to meet her gaze. She was probably terrified, and he expected to see shoulders curled as she clutched her rifle in defense.

But there was none of that in her outline as she stood in the firelight, her shoulders squared with a quiet dignity. Yet, there was a softness in her posture.

"You got him, then?" Her voice didn't quiver, only held a gentle frankness.

He swallowed. "Got him." The silence stretched, and suddenly he wanted to say so much. But…what? "Are you all right?" Yes, that was good.

Her mouth pulled at the corners, and the side of her face shone as the fire illuminated her profile. "Yes. We're fine." She nodded toward the carcass behind him. "What do we do with it?"

He turned to where she motioned, and reality sank back in like the dousing of a mountain creek. "We clean it."

He stepped forward to inspect the carcass. The bear spanned almost to his height, and stretched impossibly long as he dragged the thing toward the creek to skin it. Joseph tried to help, but Simeon waved him away. The man was still weak from his wounds and should rest through the night to recover from their day on the trail. The last thing they needed was another injury.

Once he had the animal far enough away from camp, he strode back to ready his tools. The moon would be bright enough for him to see without a lantern.

Emma met him at the edge of their little clearing. "What can I do?"

"Lay back down and get some sleep. I won't be far." He knelt by his saddle and withdrew his long skinning knife from its sheathe.

"I can help. Just tell me how." She hovered a few feet away.

He glanced up at her. She'd looked tired after dinner, yet the weary lines were gone now. Still, an expectant mother needed her rest. "I'll take care of it." He fumbled through his pack for the oilcloth he could use to wrap the meat.

"Simeon."

He looked up again.

This time she had her hands propped at her waist. "I need to learn how to do this. Please. Let me help."

By George, but she was stubborn. "Fine. We'll need a pan of cold water from the creek."

He rose and started to turn back to the bear, but Emma still stood there. "What is it?"

"You have my pot in the food pack." She nibbled her lip.

Ah, yes. A lot of good it had done to hang the food that far away. "I'll go get it." His gaze scanned their campsite. "I still don't understand why the animal came here instead of where the food was. Maybe he smelled the remains of our dinner in the air. It's hard to believe he was hungry enough for a fresh kill this late in the season."

"You…think he was after our food?"

He eyed her. "Our food's hanging in a tree a hundred yards away. He walked right past it."

The air was thick with her silence, but she turned so her face was mostly shadowed. He couldn't catch her expression.

"Well, there might be a little smoked meat in my pack. You don't think he could have smelled that, do you?"

A surge of anger whipped through him. "You have food here? After I told you to pack it all?"

"Only the meat I've been carrying with me. There are times I need it."

The bear had been coming after her then. A picture of the possible carnage flashed through Simeon's mind. If he'd been away checking the horses, or even down by the creek, it would have attacked her without a second's regret. Within moments, she would have been a bloody mass. Her and the baby.

Simeon turned away, shaking too hard to hide it. Not even a full day away from the cabin and he'd almost lost Emma and the baby.

What was he doing out here?

Emma watched the mountain man turn away as her heart seized in her chest. Part of her wanted to curl up in her blankets and hide from his anger, but the other part of her wanted to reach out to him. She'd had no idea he was worried about bears when he said to pack all the food away. The meat in her bundle hadn't occurred to her, really. But she saw now the danger in her naïveté. They'd never thought about their food attracting bears, which meant it was a miracle they hadn't been attacked long before now. She was beginning to be very thankful the Lord had brought this man to guide them.

Even if he was furious with her. His shoulders shook with rage, or maybe those were just deep breaths to control his temper. She should apologize.

"Simeon?" She took a tentative step toward him.

He didn't move, but the quivering stopped. Did he no longer breathe?

"I'm sorry. I didn't realize the meat would be a problem. I keep it for snacks and I…didn't think."

Still no response. She laid a hand on his forearm.

His muscles were solid under his buckskin sleeve. Tension radiated from the set of his shoulders. Still, no response. The man talked less than a deaf-mute.

She dropped her hand and turned away. She'd apologized. It was all she could do. "If you'll tell me where the food pack is, I'll go get the pan and bring you water."

"I'll get it." He turned and almost vaulted toward the woods.

As she watched him fade into the blackness, her chest squeezed tighter. Even with the danger they'd just been through, she hadn't expected that much of a reaction over her mistake. Was he still angry they'd asked him to accompany them on the trip? She couldn't shake the feeling there was more.

The next day, they made even less progress than the first. Emma covered a yawn as she gathered her cooking utensils by the creek that evening and headed back to their camp. She'd woken bleary-eyed that morning and hadn't been able to shake her exhaustion since. But Simeon had slept even less after tending the bear carcass, so if he could persevere, so could she.

They'd spent several hours that morning cooking and salting the meat. Simeon was fastidious about using every bit of the animal they could. In just that small amount of time, she'd learned so much about preparing the meat, which parts were edible, and how they were best cooked. The steaks she'd fried tonight had been the best meat she'd tasted in a while.

Joseph was stoking the fire when she sank onto her knees beside the food pack and began securing the supplies inside. Simeon was nowhere to be seen.

"How's your arm?" She glanced at her brother's face to gauge his pain.

Deep lines etched around his eyes as he looked at her. "I'm holding up. How about you?"

She reached for the pot of willow tea she'd left brewing. "Drink some of this and relax now."

He let out a snort. "All I've been doing is relaxing. You and Simeon do all the work around here."

With a steaming mug, she turned to face him. "That's

why we asked him to come, remember? So you could let your arm heal. I've given him strict instructions to alert me if you try anything." She hadn't, actually. But it was a good idea. Joseph's body needed time to recuperate.

He took the cup with a weary smile. "I'm not so fragile." But he scooted back to where she'd stretched out his bedroll and sank against a tree.

Simeon stepped into the ring of light from the fire, materializing from the darkness. The man moved without sound as if he hovered over the ground.

"Let me know when you have all the food stuffs packed." His eyes met hers. "All of it."

She nodded. "Of course."

That twitch at the corner of his mouth surely couldn't be from amusement. And the gleam in his eye must be a trick of the fire. He'd been so angry last night.

Simeon picked the strings of the guitar in a Spanish tune he'd learned in his early teen years. The music flowed through him as his fingers found their rhythm.

Joseph snored faintly from his blankets, and Emma had left for the creek to wipe away the day's grime, he supposed. Although the icy water would surely chill her to the bone. Snow would be on them soon.

But for now, he had nothing to worry over except his thoughts. They'd made it through a second day with no further incident. They probably hadn't traveled more than forty miles from his cabin, but he could content himself with the slow pace as long as his charges stayed safe.

Light footsteps sounded through the trees, drawing closer. He forced himself not to turn and watch Emma approach. She had the power to captivate him if he allowed his eyes and thoughts to wander.

But he couldn't let himself be affected.

She sat on her blankets and fumbled with her saddle pack for a moment, then set it aside. After pulling one of his furs around herself, she leaned back against one of the trees that lined their campsite.

He moved his gaze to the fire as the burn of her focus seared his skin. What did she see when she watched him? A man who'd grown rough and bitter in this remote wilderness? He'd not always been this way. But it was the life he chose now. The only life he could stand.

The song came to a close, and he ended with a slow strum, then allowed the sound to slowly fade into the night. The quiet seemed right as he stared into the flickering flames.

"You play well." Emma's voice didn't break the stillness but fit inside it.

He shrugged, not moving his focus from the fire as his mind wandered back to the days when Reverend Sanders allowed him to slip into the church and practice on the man's guitar in his spare time. Occasionally, the good pastor would break from his sermon-making and demonstrate a few chords. But mostly Simeon taught himself. The songs they sung in services. Music he heard from taverns. Songs sung by the housewives through open windows as he wandered along the outskirts of town. He planted each melody in his mind, then relived it on the strings of the instrument when he could slip away to the church.

The older he grew and the more mouths he had to help feed at home, the harder it was to find time alone. That only made the moments more precious.

"Did you learn as a child?"

He glanced at her. He could just answer with a *yes,* but something in him wanted to say more. He'd not talked of those days in so long, he wasn't sure he could. Her face was gentle, curious, not demanding. Her eyes bright, mouth gently curved. He looked away from that mouth.

With a deep breath, he forced out the words. "When I was seven or eight, the reverend at our church let me use his instrument. Taught me some chording. I haven't played in years, though." Six years, to be exact. Not since he and Nora left South Carolina to chase his dreams of a ranch in these mountains.

"Sounds like the way it was with Joseph. Our neighbor taught him a few songs, then Joseph spent every waking moment practicing. You could hardly pull him away for studies. Tested Mr. Hampton's patience many a day." Her voice held tender memories, a pleasure that drew him in.

"Mr. Hampton?"

"Our tutor. He came a few hours a day for lessons. I

studied with them until I was thirteen, then I attended Mrs. Livingston's School for Girls until we left Baltimore." Her voice took on a strain with the last few words, and he glanced at her face. The softness had left it, replaced by a pinch of her lips.

"Texas wasn't to your liking?"

She shook her head, her eyes focused on the fire. "No."

A single word, yet it dripped with emotion and meaning he couldn't begin to decipher. He wanted to press for more, but something stopped him. He wouldn't wish the same were their conversation reversed. If she wanted to tell him more, she would.

He took up the guitar again, and an old melody drifted through his mind. One he'd not thought of in over a decade. His left hand found the chord, and his right hand started the tune, a combination of picking and strumming as the longing in the song settled into his soul.

When the final strains faded away, he allowed silence to take over again.

"That was beautiful. I haven't heard it before."

He met Emma's gaze across the fire. "I wrote it around the time my youngest brother was born."

Her brows rose the smallest bit. "I didn't know you had siblings."

Should he show her more of himself? He'd come this far, and wasn't sure he could stop now. "There were nine of us."

Now her eyes opened wider. "Nine? Where did you

fit in the order?"

"The oldest." And that said it all, really. The eldest. The one always expected to work and be responsible. The one never seen, but always counted on.

"That must have been hard." Her words were tender, and she met his gaze with an expression that matched her voice. It didn't look like sympathy, but he couldn't tell for sure.

He thumbed the guitar's strings. "What's a song you know?"

She tipped her head, a glimmer shimmering in her eyes. "Do you know 'Arthur MacBride'?"

He thought back through the recesses of his mind. "I'm not sure. Can you sing the tune? I'll try to pick it up."

She started into a haunting song, and his fingers found the frets as he strummed each new chord. Her voice was clear and achingly beautiful, just like the woman herself. He found the melody line and picked each note, then improvised a decorative flourish as she moved from the chorus to another verse.

The passion in the music came alive within him, and he lost himself in it. The purity of it. The chorus again and another verse. He would have played on forever with Emma's clear soprano giving life to the sound from the strings. He'd not breathed in such perfect harmony with another person in years. The feeling clenched tight in his chest as she held out the final words. He played the last line again, rising up the frets in a descant that reflected the state of his emotions.

As his hands came to rest, he allowed his eyelids to close for a final perfect moment, then raised them to sneak a peek at Emma. Had the music affected her as much?

She watched him, meeting his gaze with a hint of wonder glassing her eyes. Her mouth eased into a smile, then she said, "That was the most beautiful thing I've ever heard."

And it was. Her voice had a power he'd never dreamed of. A power that would draw him in if he allowed it. But he had to resist.

With an effort that took all his strength, he laid the guitar back in its case, then fastened the buckles. He rose and loaded more logs on the fire, then lay down again and covered himself with several furs. Without glancing at Emma, he closed his eyes and forced them to stay that way.

If only he could shut down his mind as easily.

Chapter Eight

There is a melody that pulls me. A tune that haunts my waking moments.
~ Simeon

The next few days fell into a steady rhythm, although there was nothing steady about the country they traveled. At times their path would wind through pine and fir, up steep inclines with boulders strewn about the woods. Those were the more boring rides compared to when the trees would open up and their trail became little more than a crevice on the side of the mountain. The views often stole her breath as Emma stared out over deep valleys and snow-covered peaks. Lakes snuggled in between the mountains, with water as green as spring grass. One time they even passed a waterfall careening down the mountain to the west.

The horses seemed to tire more easily than before, and Emma could empathize with them. It was harder to catch her own breath when she worked by the campfire each morning and evening or scrubbed dishes in the streams Simeon always camped near. The growing baby pressed against her ribs and lungs, and even the air she took in seemed thinner. Less satisfying.

Simeon had proved an excellent guide, strong and sure in his direction. He was always certain their campsite was as comfortable as he could make it. He was thoughtful in ways she'd not expected from a mountain man. Like when he held her horse while she mounted each morning and allowed plenty of breaks throughout the day—which her expectant body much appreciated. Of course, his considerations shouldn't surprise her anymore. She'd caught a glimpse the other night of a man far different from the loner he tried to appear.

Nine children? She couldn't imagine a family so large. And it seemed he'd been well-acquainted with the church his family attended. Yet he showed little sign now of an intimate connection with the Father. Had he ever known the joy of a living faith? Or was his experience head knowledge only? He bowed readily enough when she or Joseph said grace before their meals, but that was the only time she'd seen him acknowledge God. Not that it was her place to judge.

Emma snuggled deep under the extra furs Simeon had handed out that night. He'd also stretched an oilcloth over their shelter. He must expect rain or snow. It was certainly cold enough for the latter. Joseph's gentle snores drifted from his bedroll, but Simeon still hadn't returned from hanging the food pack.

He'd not played the guitar again since she sang the other night, although truth be told, she'd been so worn out the last few nights she was thankful to sink into sleep almost as soon as she rested on her blankets. Growing new life was exhausting.

The babe inside squirmed, pressing her abdomen in two different directions. She touched a hand to one of the bulges. "Settle down, sweet one. Rest now." The pressure eased, and she couldn't help but smile. Her arms ached to hold the child, but that time would come. Soon.

Emma squinted against the brightness of the fire as she glanced around the campsite. The dark weighed thick outside the ring of their campfire. What had awakened her?

She struggled to sit up without pushing the blankets off her shoulders. Still, cold air seeped onto her neck and arms. She glanced toward the woods again.

A layer of white coated the leaf floor, and more fluttered through the air. She sucked in a breath. Snow?

A sensation prickled the skin along her shoulders, and she glanced around the campsite again. Simeon sat on his blankets, his gaze on her as though he'd been in that position all night.

"It's snowing." She offered a smile, and his face softened, but he didn't return a comment.

It must be awfully hard for joy to break through that façade he kept wrapped tightly around himself. What had happened in his life to cause such pain? Every so often she caught a glimpse of hurt, but he shored up his defenses too quickly for her to break through.

She tried again. "Has it been snowing long?"

He looked like he'd taken root there, sitting propped against that tree. Did the man not need rest?

"About an hour."

"Couldn't you sleep?" Let him think her pushy. Maybe she could help.

"No."

"Would you like a cup of willow tea?" She motioned to the kettle she'd brewed for Joseph that evening. "It helps my brother within minutes, every time." She tipped one side of her mouth higher than the other. Joseph had succumbed to slumber right after dinner each night of their trip so far. Honestly, she'd never seen him nap so much. His body must've been struggling to mend itself with the added strain of travel.

One corner of his lips pulled. "No. But thank you."

Well. Maybe he was finally softening.

The chill pressed in around her shoulders with a shiver, and she leaned forward to stack another log on the fire. Her abdomen had grown large enough now that it was a struggle, and she sank back to watch the flames lick the new wood. As she fingered the cross at her neck, her mind wandered to the man across the blaze. What would it take for him to share his thoughts? Was he worried about the trip? Something else? There were times his blue eyes were as clear as a summer sky. Yet other times, like now, when they swam in so much mystery it pulled at her soul.

She raised her gaze from the fire to meet his. "Are

you worried about the snow? Or another bear?"

He shook his head. "Bears should be in hibernation by now. I think we just found a late sleeper." His lips pinched in a grimace. "Much to its peril. The animals have a rhythm and an order of things. I try not to mess with it, and we usually get along just fine."

So was it the snow that had him stewing? The way his brow was knit in a soft V, it seemed like it must be more than that. But what worries could a man like him have? He lived such a remote life, his only concerns should be securing enough food and warmth. And Simeon Grant had proved himself more than capable of accomplishing both.

Was there something else that haunted him? Maybe he was a fugitive, hiding from the law. He didn't seem malicious, but perhaps his crime had been a single act of uncontrolled anger, or even desperation. So many possibilities could push a man over the line of violence.

Of course, perhaps he'd never committed a crime at all, but had been unjustly accused. She knew all too well how the passions of fear and desperation could target the innocent, slandering with untrue accusations in a tidal wave so strong it swept away any thought for objectivity.

Was that what concerned him now? Had he been treated unjustly, forced into this life so far away from other people? If only he would share.

Maybe if she told some of her story first. People usually responded to openness. But no. If she gave any hint of the reward on her head, he could just as easily turn them south and collect the two thousand dollars for himself.

No. She couldn't imagine that. As she studied the man across the campfire, the light cast a sadness around his features. The angular cheekbones and strong jaw, the straight nose and firm set of his lips. All of those features seemed to soften now in a way that tightened an ache through her chest. If only she could break through to him. Talking about his troubles would surely help.

Could she tell part of her story without naming anything that would incriminate her? Maybe. But how to lead in to it?

"Thank you again, Simeon, for helping us get to my aunt's in Alberta. When my husband died, Joseph and I decided the best course of action would be to find our remaining family. Start fresh in a new place." She forced as much of a smile as she could muster. "A very different sort of place from Texas, I would imagine."

His gaze penetrated. She'd have to be careful not to give too much away under that scrutiny.

"I'm sorry for the loss of your husband."

She bit down on the edge of her lip. "I wouldn't wish his method of death on anyone. He was…not well liked at the end." How much disclosure was too much? "Due to his own actions, that is. I didn't know about everything until just before..." She couldn't say the rest. It would give away too many details.

The lines on his forehead deepened, and twin grooves formed between his brows. "I'm sorry." The words were softer this time. More than just a patronizing response.

"I am, too." She couldn't help a wistful tone. In truth,

she was sorry for a great many things from the past few years. "Our family had only known Lance a few months before Father presented the idea of marriage to me. I was wary. Father had so much ambition, sometimes it colored his perspective when he made decisions. But I do believe he thought I would be happy in the match." At least, she clung to that belief when she remembered her parents. It was one of the ways she'd kept bitterness at bay when she sat in her fancy parlor, where loneliness pressed in like poisoned air. Surely Father hadn't known Lance's true character.

She swallowed. "Lance had a smooth polish that tended to sway people. And he was just generous enough with his wealth to let others know he had plenty of it." If only they'd known it was really their own hard-earned cash he was squandering. "Father saw only the good in the match."

Simeon stared at her, not speaking a word. His face gave away nothing, and he'd shifted his position so his eyes sank into shadows. Should she go on? No. She'd said enough, maybe too much.

And maybe she was distorting the picture anyway. Life hadn't been completely miserable in the Carter home. At least Lance hadn't been violent. He didn't drink too much or fall into fits of rage. He was just…distant. And deceptive. And a dirty, lying swindler.

Simeon soaked in the story until the woman across the fire drifted into silence. The picture that formed in his mind was just a charcoal sketch, an outline of a wasted life. How could her father have trusted a treasure like this woman in the hands of the man she described? Even if the suitor had enough charm and money to fool most people, wouldn't her father have tried him through fire to prove the man's worth before gifting Emma into his charge? Of course, Simeon didn't have a lot of experience with overly ambitious or corrupt men. Yorkville had been a quiet town with hard-working citizens whose biggest ambition was to build quiet, comfortable lives.

He couldn't fathom how any man who'd taken Emma to wife wouldn't do his level-best to live up to what she deserved. Between her startling beauty, the loyalty and kindness she'd shown even to him, and the strength of her determination, she far exceeded the kind of woman most men dreamed of.

A pang pinched his chest. Should he really be having thoughts like these?

But he couldn't bring himself to regret them.

Chapter Nine

In every beauty, there is a trial. But on the other side is the best yet.
~ Emma's Journal

They rounded the rocky mountainside, and a lake came into view. Emma leaned forward on her mare and fought the urge to push her horse faster as the pretty picture stretched before them. In a level part of a gully between two mountains, a placid lake lay nestled with snow surrounding it on all sides. The water held a white film over the surface, mottled with grayish patches in some areas. Not the crystal blue or startling green of the other two lakes they'd seen. Had something tainted this water?

But as they neared, she squinted harder at the surface. Ice? Yes, the entire lake was covered in a layer of ice, with a thin coating of snow blowing and swirling across the top like a skater's pattern.

They neared the edge, and Emma pulled her hood forward, covering as much of her cheeks as she could from the bitter wind. Simeon reined to a stop, so she and Joseph did the same.

"How thick do you think the ice is?" She studied the section nearest them.

"Hard to say without cutting through. Especially with snow blowing across the top. The areas where the ice is clear when you look down, they'll be the strongest."

She scanned the frozen mass. "Like there?"

His gaze followed her finger to a spot about a third of the way across the lake. The wind had blown its surface clear, and she could see the blue crystal even from here.

He nodded. "Probably. Better not to trust it unless we have to." He reined his horse away from the edge of the lake. "Which we don't."

Were they leaving then? Surely he would let them stop and enjoy the scenery for a while. It was almost lunchtime anyway.

"Simeon. Could we stop here to eat? The view is breathtaking."

He halted his horse and turned in the saddle to scan the scene. "It'll be warmer in the woods."

The wind did have a sharp bite, but they'd been riding in trees for days now. They could all handle a half hour of the chilly air. "It's worth it to enjoy the open water. Maybe we can sit near that tree." She nodded toward a massive tree at the edge of the lake, overhanging the water.

"I'm game if you both are," Joseph volunteered, and she sent him a thankful look.

Simeon shrugged and reined his horse toward the spot.

He was right about the cold. They'd barely sat to eat

her simple meal of johnnycakes and smoked bear steak when the temperature seemed to drop ten degrees. The wind whipped her hair around her face, slipping under her hood and through the woolen fabric of her coat.

She ate faster, and it seemed like the men had the same idea. Within ten minutes they'd scarfed the food and she was refastening the straps on the food pack that Pet carried. Emma huddled close to the mare to block the wind, and once she had the buckles secured, she slid her gloved hands under the horse's mane, then lowered her face. "Can you share some of your warmth, girl?" The mare seemed to inch closer. Either she understood the English language or even she was eager to conserve body heat.

After a few moments of blessed relief from the wind, Emma pulled herself away from the horse and turned back to the men. Joseph hunkered down by the lake's edge, and she stepped toward him. "Where's Simeon?"

"He took a little trip to the woods." Joseph answered without taking his focus from the ice. "How thick do you think it is? A foot?"

She leaned down, peering through the frozen layers. A few bubbles had been caught in the ice, preserved by the cold. It was hard to tell where the ice ended and the water began through the depths. "I'm no expert, but I think I see at least twelve or fifteen inches of ice." She lifted her skirts and touched the frozen surface with the toe of her right boot. "Solid."

He fisted his good hand and knocked on the ice. "Yep."

Carefully, she shifted weight onto her right foot, testing the strength of the support. Even with the extra weight she carried from the baby, the ice held sturdy without any give. She inched the other foot onto the frozen surface. "Look, Joey. It's holding." A frisson of excitement rippled through her. "Reminds me of that time we went ice skating at that farm outside of Baltimore. Remember?" She took another step forward, but her boot slipped and she threw her arms out to balance.

Joseph jumped to his feet and gripped her hand until she stabilized. "Come back now."

"All right." But as she turned toward him, the wind whipped his fur hat from his head and tossed it down on the ice a half dozen feet away from Emma. "I'll get it." She headed toward the cap.

"No, leave it. I'll see if Simeon has an extra."

"You need it, Joey. Let me just grab it. I'll be fine." In baby steps, she crept out further. She was near enough now and lowered herself to reach the last few inches. Her fingers gripped the fur, and she clutched tight to it, then slowly rose and turned toward the bank. The extra weight at her midsection skewed her balance, and the last thing she needed was a fall on the ice.

As she headed back toward the edge, Joseph reached out for her, closing on her fingers when she came near enough.

At that moment, the floor dropped out from underneath her. For a terrible second, she was suspended in midair.

Then, *cold*.

Icy water gripped her legs, sending spasms through them. Her arm jerked hard, and she struggled to grasp at something as her skirts ballooned in the icy water. But she sank down…lower…

From behind hands clamped around her upper arms, a vise that lifted her like a pulley out of the water.

Her skirts hung limp, dragging her down in a fierce tug. She tried to raise her legs up, to help remove herself from the water, but her limbs wouldn't respond. Nothing.

She was tugged onto the ice, then dragged across it. A million pinpricks pierced her upper body, but her legs seemed limp and heavy as if they were stuffed replacements with no sensation or power to move on command. She was lifted into the air, and she curled into herself to fight against the shivering. Pain and marrow-deep cold fogged her mind.

Something warm pressed her right side, and she burrowed toward it. Squeezing in and clutching tight around the heat. A faint scent tugged her nose, but she couldn't decipher it. She pressed her eyes closed as she soaked in the warmth.

Simeon charged through his earlier tracks as he clutched Emma and dragged his packhorse behind him. They'd almost made it to the tree line, at least two hundred feet or more. Maybe he should've started a warming fire right under that cottonwood by the lake, but the forest would provide a buffer from the wind.

What had she been thinking to go out on the ice like that? Would frostbite harm the baby? Anything that hurt Emma surely couldn't be healthy for the little one inside her.

He reached the woods and dropped to his knees just a few feet into the trees. He lowered Emma to the ground as Joseph puffed up behind them, pulling the three saddle horses in his wake.

"Get these wet clothes off her while I find blankets and start a fire." Simeon tried to disentangle himself from the frozen woman, but she clutched tightly around his ribs. He'd stripped open his buckskin coat to tuck her into his warmth, and she nestled in, snuggling as close as his own skin.

For a second, he allowed himself to slip his arms around her shoulders and hold her, the softness of her body awakening something inside that seemed so foreign. Like he was feeling it as another person, someone very different from the man he'd become.

Craziness.

"Emma. I need to find blankets so we can get you warm." He loosened his hold on her and reached behind his back to unclasp her hands.

She made a little mewling noise, and her shoulders quivered. The shivering was a good sign, her body generating heat.

He slipped away from her hold and stood as Joseph knelt beside her. After tossing the softest of his animal skins and the blankets to Joseph, Simeon unstrapped the dry wood Pet carried and worked on the fire.

He kept his back to the brother and sister to give her some privacy, but it was impossible to drown out their words. Rather, Joseph's words.

"Here, Em. How do you get this thing off? There, all right." A moment of silence. "Can't I just cut it?"

The steady monologue formed an all-too-clear image in Simeon's mind, no matter how hard he tried to suppress the thoughts. His muscles wound tighter the longer he waited.

"There, now wrap this around you and move closer to the fire." Finally.

Simeon stood and stepped away from the flame, which was finally starting to put off heat. He dared a glance at Emma as she scooted toward the blaze. Her hair was thoroughly mussed, but not wet. He was pretty sure she'd only been submerged to her waist, but he couldn't be positive. Had it been enough to harm the baby?

He'd need to check Emma's feet for frostbite, but it might be best to get something warm in her first. He turned toward the horses. "I'll get water from the lake for tea." Shouldn't be hard now that they had a nice hole in the ice.

"I'll go."

He paused and glanced at Joseph, who'd jumped to his feet and was already headed toward the water. "Take something to carry it in."

Joseph halted, then shifted toward the packhorse without acknowledging his lapse. The man must be as worried about his sister as Simeon was.

Emma pulled the furs and blankets tighter as she huddled in front of the fire. It didn't seem like the flame's heat would be able to penetrate the mass of covers around her. She was…so…cold. She sank deeper into her cocoon, balling as tight as her bulging midsection would allow. But still she shivered, her teeth clattering over the snapping of the fire. The inside seemed to be doing flips, poking and churning inside her. Probably doing everything the little one could to keep warm.

"Let me see if I can rub some heat into your arms." A strong presence settled behind her and applied gentle pressure to her upper arms.

She didn't look at Simeon but sank into the touch as he rubbed up and down through the furs. She could hear his steady intake of breath, and its warmth feathered her hair. Everything about his touch soothed.

Too soon, his movements stilled. And his hands fell away, leaving a chilly void in their place.

She groaned. "Don't stop."

The warmth returned, stroking more slowly now. "Your teeth aren't chattering anymore." His words graveled so close to her ear, sending a skitter down her spine.

If she hadn't been shivering before, she was now.

Joseph appeared by the fire, tucking the kettle into the

flame. Then he rose to his feet again. "I'll settle the horses."

It didn't matter what he did as long as Simeon didn't stop his warming ministrations on her arms. Who knew this man's touch would be so incredibly comforting? Her eyes drifted shut, and at some point, he shifted from rubbing her arms to sitting beside her, tucking her into his chest. She'd never felt so protected. So cared for.

"Can you drink some of this tea?"

She forced open her eyes to find a cup in front of her. Simeon gripped it, still holding her tight in the crook of his arm. She turned to look up into his face, cataloging the worry lining his eyes. "Yes, of course."

Biting back a groan, she pulled into a more upright position. But leaving her nesting spot against him brought a chill that washed away her grogginess in a hurry.

She sipped the tea as Simeon moved onto his knees beside her. He reached forward and pushed a stick farther into the fire, then brushed his hands. "Anything else you need?"

She forced a soft smile. "I'm fine now. Just sorry to cause such a fuss."

"That's my baby sister. Always has to be the center of attention." Joseph stepped into the circle around the fire and plopped on the ground across from her.

She shot him what was supposed to be a withering look, but her cheeks wouldn't cooperate. He returned the effort with a grin.

"Can you feel your limbs? Your feet?" Simeon's words were quiet, still carrying some of that earlier worry.

Turning her gaze back to him, she wiggled her toes under the blankets, trying her best not to grimace at the needle pricks shooting up her legs. "Yes, I'll be fine. You got me out so quickly, there's no damage."

His eyes narrowed, darkening in their intensity. "What about…the baby?" He hesitated. Apparently he knew it wasn't proper to speak of an expectant woman's condition.

She didn't mind, though. His voice had gentled with the words in a way that tightened her chest.

Under the blankets, she slipped her hand to cup her belly. A sharp poke pressed her palm, and she couldn't help but smile. "The baby seems fine. Still feisty as always."

His face softened, and faint creases formed at the corners of his eyes. "Good."

Such gentleness. Who would have thought this was the same rough man who'd greeted them with a rifle and a growling dog just a few weeks ago?

Speaking of the dog, where was he? She glanced around. "I haven't seen Mustang since we started out this morning."

Simeon raised a brow. "He comes and goes as he pleases. He'll be back when he's hungry."

She searched his gaze. "Don't you worry about him?"

"Mustang? He knows how to handle himself better than humans do in these hills." The smallest hint of a smile touched the corners of his mouth. "It wouldn't be fair to try to control him. He makes his own way. But he's kind enough to check on me every so often."

The sparkle in his eye was contagious, and her heart

couldn't help a little flip in response.

Chapter Ten

The pain is in the knowing. Take me back to my blissful ignorance.
~ Simeon

Simeon carried another load of firewood to the overhang he'd found under the boulders growing out of the mountainside. The rock protruded about six feet over their heads, leaving a shelter protected on two sides—the best they were likely to find tonight.

Dense snow clouds had threatened low in the sky all afternoon. They'd get another foot at least, unless he missed his guess. He piled the wood on the waist-high stack already under the shelter.

Emma turned from stirring something in the pot over the fire and eyed the logs, then raised her skeptical gaze to him. "You think we're staying here 'til spring?"

He glanced at the stack. "Never know how long the snow will last." A smile played at the corners of her mouth, but changed to a grimace as a sneeze shook her body.

He frowned. She seemed to have recovered from her dunking yesterday except for the sniffles that had harassed her most of the day. They needed to keep her warm so it didn't develop into something far worse.

She turned back to the pot. "The stew's almost finished."

He nodded. "I'll check on the horses and Joseph first." The man seemed to have regained some strength in the past few days. Tonight, he'd even offered to settle the animals under the oilcloth covering Simeon had tied up in the nearby trees.

With the animals secure and the supplies laid beside the stack of firewood under the rock overhang, he and Joseph joined Emma, where the three huddled in the remaining space around the fire. The wood and their packs took up over half of the protected area, so there wasn't room for them to do much more than sit side by side before the fire. Stuck in this position, with a steady curtain of white falling in the darkness, it looked to be a long night.

Simeon accepted his bowl of stew from Emma, then raised the spoon to his mouth as he sank against the rock wall. The warmth of the soup eased down his throat, spreading its comfort through his belly. She did well cooking with the limited supplies they carried and what he found on the trail. Winter wasn't exactly a peak time to find produce in the higher elevations, but she made do with what she had. It was probably nothing compared to what she'd been used to in Texas, what with her wealthy husband.

Or maybe she hadn't even needed to cook there. Perhaps she had servants to prepare the food and clean the house. A far cry from what he offered her in this wilderness. No wonder she looked at him like he'd grown three noses when he presented her with the grouse to cook that first night.

His gaze wandered over to her, but she was staring into the darkness. Intent on something. All his senses went on alert, straining to discover what had caught her attention.

A motion. Something small, not much bigger than a raccoon.

Mustang.

His body eased as the dog faded from the night, padding into the ring of firelight. He headed toward Simeon's side then circled once. He perched on his haunches and eyed the group, waiting patiently for his own bowl of stew. Spoiled rotten, this mutt.

Simeon gulped a few more bites of his soup, preparing to let the dog lap up the remainder. But Emma beat him to it. She spooned a fresh helping into her own bowl, then pressed her skirts close as she moved around the front of the fire, easing toward the dog. The animal growled as she neared. More mouthy than was good for him.

But Emma stopped an arm's length away, crouching low. She extended the bowl toward the dog, placed it in front of him, and backed away. Once she was settled again in her spot on the other side of Joseph, Simeon eyed her.

"You're going to spoil him. He'll think he's even more special than he already does." He meant it as teasing, but she huffed.

"That dog is incorrigible. I'll win him over if it's the last thing I do."

It was awfully hard to hold in his grin at the glare on

her face. That stubborn jut of her chin, the flash in her eyes. If she turned even half of her charm on poor Mustang, the dog was doomed to fall in love.

The rest of the evening passed quietly enough, the falling snow dampening their conversation yet giving the mood a more intimate feel. Joseph drifted to sleep first, as usual. Simeon cut glances at Emma periodically as she scribed something in a book. He'd seen her writing in it before—must have been a journal of some kind.

But locked in this tiny shelter now with nothing to do and no one to talk to, his mind started imagining. He tried to rein it in, but it seemed his self-control had suffered when he'd met Emma.

Had she journaled the events that brought the intense sadness when she talked about her husband and life in Texas? He itched to ask more. Had almost done it when she was talking the other night. What he wouldn't give for a glimpse of the words in that book. Of course, he'd never read it unless she offered, and what were the chances of that? Still, maybe she'd tell if he asked.

"How did your husband die?"

Her head jerked up with a startled glance. That approach might have been too direct. If only he could retract the question.

She worked her mouth, though, like she would answer. So he waited.

Then her expression changed, and she met his look head on, her chin coming up a hair. "He was hanged."

Simeon worked hard not to let his surprise show.

Hadn't she said they lived in East Texas? He'd been given to believe folks were more civilized in that part of the country, but apparently not. He nodded slowly. "That's a hard way to die."

Something glimmered in her eyes. "I wouldn't have wished it on him, despite his sins." Her gaze changed again. Determined, maybe a little wary.

Simeon braced himself. From her expression, it didn't look like she'd said the worst of it yet.

"They thought I was involved in Lance's deceptions. After the mob strung him up, they came back for me, but I was already on my way out through the back garden. I found Joseph, and we left town that night."

She was watching him like a judge scrutinizing an unreliable witness.

He met her stare. "Were they right?"

She stiffened, locking her jaw. "They were not."

He held her gaze for a long moment and schooled his features. He'd learned the patience of a hunt. If you waited long enough, the prey came out of hiding and showed their true nature. It couldn't be much different with people.

Finally, she eased out a long breath, her shoulders relaxing. "Lance never talked to me about business. A fact that brought me no end of frustration." She sank back against the rock wall and cupped her belly with a hand. Her gaze sank into the fire. "He never really talked to me about anything, so you'd think I would have become used to his silence. Still, it bothered me…the not knowing. I caught snippets of conversations when people came to visit him at home. Something just didn't…seem right. I wish I'd tried harder to find out why."

His muscles itched to reach out to her. To ease the sadness that thickened the air around her. But with Joseph slouched between them, touching her would be awkward. And what could he do that would make a difference anyway?

"Those poor people. If half the things they screamed at Lance that night were true, my heart breaks for their losses." She paused for a moment, then blinked. "When we arrived in Memphis, Joseph saw a *Wanted* flyer with my name on it. That was when I knew my life would never be the same."

A surge of anger burned through Simeon's chest. "Why didn't you go back and set the record straight? Tell them you had nothing to do with your husband's misdeeds."

The expression she raised to him was the bleakest he'd ever seen. Eyes so weary they pressed a smothering blanket over his soul. "Would they have believed me? The wife of the man who cheated them? I wrote a letter to the sheriff telling everything I knew. Or rather, didn't know. Then we set off for the North. I just wanted to be through with the place. Leave Texas behind and start over. My parents were gone. The mess with Lance was in the past. I had God and Joseph, and they're all I need." Her gaze drifted to her brother's sleeping face. His mouth hung open, jaw slack as steady breaths slipped in and out. "He's the best gift God ever gave me."

The love in her voice matched what shimmered in her gaze, and it raised a stinging sensation to the back of Simeon's throat. He'd never seen or felt that kind of love until Nora, and he never wanted to experience it again. Love hurt too much.

Simeon blinked as something stirred to his right. He raised his head, sending a shot of pain through his neck. Joseph shifted beside him, twisting toward something on the man's other side. Simeon forced his senses to come awake. "What is it?"

"Got to find an outhouse. Trying to get Emma off my shoulder so I can move." His whisper echoed off the rock wall behind them. "Trying"—he grunted—"...not...to wake her...up." With his good hand under Emma's shoulder, Joseph scooted forward. She slouched sideways, her relaxed posture too much for his braced arm.

Simeon leaned over and cupped her shoulder, then shifted closer to fill Joseph's spot. "I'll sit with her."

As Simeon eased her against his shoulder, she let out a little mew and snuggled closer. Too close. Her warmth penetrated his coat, her softness quickening his pulse. The scent of roses brushed his nose, and he breathed it in. How did she smell so good out here in the mountain wilderness—in the dead of winter, no less? She spent time at the creek each day, but never came back with wet hair. He'd have told her not to take such a risk in this weather. Yet, even in this majestic, barbaric place, she managed to maintain the feel and smell and look—even the sound—of a lady.

He ached to slip his arm around her, turn and pull her close to his chest. Stroke the hair that had slipped from her braid. Run his fingers through the thickness of it. Touch her cheek.

He swallowed and pressed his eyes shut, willing his body to calm. What was he doing? How could he allow himself to feel so much attraction? Even though this woman was more than desirable, he should make himself immune to her.

He focused on deep breathing. He had to give his mind a problem to sort through. Like the story she'd told before drifting off to sleep. So many pieces had fallen into place as she'd spoken.

No wonder the secrecy. If she were a wanted woman, it made sense they would avoid towns. But if her statements were true, she was innocent. Innocent of everything except marrying the scoundrel, and being the man's wife was hardly an unlawful offense. Besides, it didn't sound like she'd had much choice in even that.

His feet itched to take action. He would take them to Canada. Help her start the new life she craved. But part of him burned at the injustice. How dare they run her out of town—out of the country, really—when she'd done nothing wrong? Someone should take a stand for her. Clear her name. Why hadn't her brother done it?

His gaze dropped to Emma's head resting on his

shoulder. The richness of her hair, auburn in the firelight. The feathering of her long lashes on her pale cheeks. Her straight, delicate nose. She didn't deserve to be dragged into an assault on her character. She should be allowed a fresh start, a life far distant from the awful events she'd spoken of.

If her words were true. She could tell him anything she wanted, after all. How could he know for certain? He swallowed down the lump in his throat. He could still see the loneliness in her eyes as she'd spoken of her husband's secrecy. The desolation when she mentioned his character and the losses of the people he'd wronged. Growing up with so many siblings, he'd learned early how to spot a lie. And living in the wild, where strangers—both trappers and Indians—stopped by his cabin at random, he'd honed the instinct. Talking a little too fast, the exaggerated innocent look, a flickering gaze—Emma had shown none of those. Everything in him wanted to believe her.

Could he trust that instinct? The more he saw of her, the more trust seemed possible.

The snow outside crunched, and Joseph slipped through the falling flakes into their shelter. Simeon started to straighten, but the man crouched down in Simeon's old seat.

"Don't disturb her. My shoulder's just now waking up anyway." Joseph rotated his arm with a grin, then he sobered. "Unless you mind, that is."

Simeon swallowed, turning his gaze to the fire. "I don't mind." But with her pressed up against him, her hair brushing his cheek, there wasn't a chance in all the Nebraska Territory he'd be able to sleep.

Chapter Eleven

I am resigned to the changes within me. And now love for this gift overwhelms my heart.
~ Emma's Journal

Emma tucked the last of her hair pins into the chignon and sat back on her heels. The freshness of the mountain streams always awakened her senses, bringing her to life better than any cup of coffee could. Which was good, because their supply of the brew had dwindled to almost nothing, even though she and Joseph only drank a small cup each morning.

Interesting that Simeon didn't drink the stuff. Only tea made from any number of leaves or roots. He was always bringing in a handful of something to steep in the kettle. She nibbled her lip against a smile. Coffee beans probably didn't grow on the flora in these parts.

It was a nice way to live, though. In harmony with the world around him. Only introducing a few extra necessities, but mostly sustaining himself from the gifts God placed before him. Like the Israelites and their manna. His daily bread.

She reached for a sapling to help pull herself to her feet, then grasped the pot she'd scrubbed clean from breakfast. The baby shifted inside her, pressing a solid limb against her abdomen. Who would have thought a tiny babe could be so active? And strong.

Heading for a stand of cedars, she huffed in the thin air. Just one more stop to relieve herself, then she'd finish packing up. Simeon had said he wanted an early start while the falling snow lessened. He hoped to reach a cave he was familiar with before another thick blanket of white clouded their vision and shrouded the trail before them.

As she fumbled through her mass of skirts and woolen stockings, a crimson stain in the white fabric caught her eye. Blood? That was impossible while she was in the family way, right? Her pulsed thumped harder in her chest. Did it mean something was wrong?

Her hand cupped her abdomen and stared down at the way her blue dress hung over the bulge of the child within. "What is it, little one?" A firm kick pressed her palm, and she stroked the spot with her thumb. But the racing of her heart wouldn't be denied. She inhaled a deep breath through her nose, then released it from her lips. She had to stay calm.

If only there were a doctor around. How could she know if the baby was safe? She leaned back against a tree trunk and cradled her arms around her belly. "God, I really need you this time. *We* need you." The whispered words left her heart, replaced by a gentle peace. God had them in His hand. She had to believe it. Otherwise the fear gnawing at the edges of her peace would consume her.

Later that day, Emma ducked against the snowflakes as they tangled in her lashes and pricked her face. The snow fell thicker now.

She glanced at Simeon's tall form on the horse ahead. Joseph had insisted on carrying the guitar today to give Simeon a break, so the lines of his profile were no longer encumbered as she watched him. She'd ridden behind those broad shoulders so often these past weeks, they'd started appearing in her dreams. Two nights before, her dreams had formed an image of Simeon driving a wagon, her parents sitting in the back as it rolled away from their Texas home.

And in her sleep last night, she'd glimpsed him in the doorway of Lance's home, holding off the lynch mob as she escaped through the back. She could see only the shadow of his outline, gripping his rifle like a sentry, the same as when he'd first met them in front of his cabin.

What did it mean that she saw him even in her dreams? It meant she was going batty, that's what. Too much of this man filled her senses. It was high time she occupy herself otherwise.

She glanced around at the thick blanket of white spreading every direction. Snow and more snow. The bareness of it left too much room for her mind to wander back to the sight that had occupied her thoughts much of the day. Another piece of white, with a crimson stain smeared in the center. How could she not be concerned? But was the danger enough that she should brave finding a town with a doctor to get help? Of course, they may be so far into the remote wilderness a doctor wouldn't be possible.

Pinching her lips, she catalogued the aches throughout her body. Her back rarely stopped throbbing these days, but the pain often stayed in the upper portion. And at the moment, it didn't hurt as much as it had the first day they'd started on this trek.

The baby squirmed in her belly, thrusting itself toward her right side. The child seemed lively enough. Was that good? If only she had someone to talk to.

"How you holding up, Em?"

Joseph's call drifted toward her, and she turned in the saddle to send him a smile. "Probably better than you."

Joseph actually looked more recovered than he had earlier in their travels, but the lines around his eyes showed the arm still pained him.

He offered a weak grin. "I could stand some grub. Simeon, you gonna let us stop or do we have to chew the leather on our saddles to hold us over?"

A grunt issued from the man in the front.

Joseph raised his brows. "I hope that means yes." Then he sent her a wink.

She turned to face forward. Her brother was a clown, but she couldn't help loving him for it. Maybe she could find a moment alone with Joseph to ask his advice about the baby.

Joseph dropped to his knees by the creek and pushed the pot under the icy water with his good hand. It would be tricky toting it back to their little camp, but the last thing Emma needed right now was to carry heavy loads. It was bad enough she'd prepared their midday meal. Hopefully she was taking a moment to rest before they took to their saddles for the afternoon.

His stomach churned around the knot growing there. What should he do about the concerns she'd shared? She said she thought they should wait and see if more symptoms arose before they sought a doctor. But by then it might be too late.

Entering a town to find a doctor would expose her to possible discovery, but that wasn't as big a risk right now as the danger to her and the baby. Besides, surely any place this far north would be too removed from the states to be concerned about a little gal wanted in Texas. When he got back to camp, he'd pull Simeon aside and ask him to find a town straightaway. The man would wonder, but he didn't need to know why.

He pressed one edge of the pot into his left side and gripped the other with his good hand, then lurched forward onto his knees and struggled to his feet. This sling got in his way more than it helped. If Emma weren't such a mother hen, he'd have taken it off days ago. But where his sister was concerned, it was awfully hard not to give in. She'd had too many lousy situations forced on her these last few years. The least he could do was let her dote on him if it made her feel better. And soon enough, she'd get the fresh start she deserved. They both would.

Joseph ducked under a low-hanging pine branch and cut left around a Douglas fir. Something darted out near his feet and he stumbled trying not to step on the thing. A sharp pain pierced his left calf, drawing a gasp as he kicked out. A black furry creature clung to his leg. He gave it another kick and sent the thing flying through the air in front of him.

It landed on the ground with a hiss and spun to face him, teeth bared. The animal looked like a skunk—black with wide white stripes down both sides. But a skunk that attacked? He didn't have time to consider further, because the animal charged again, its lumbering gait propelling it quickly.

He swung the pot toward it, splashing water and delivering a hard blow to the animal's face. It bounced backward, landing in a heap. The animal sat for a moment, shaking its head. Surely it would retreat into the woods now.

"Go on." He took a threatening step toward it. "Git."

The thing hissed again and crouched low, snarling as if it would attack again. Was it rabid? An icy chill shot down his back. If so, it would be better to put it out of its misery, not scare it away to infect someone else. If only he had the rifle with him, but it was mounted in the scabbard on his saddle.

He raised the pot again, then heaved it as hard as he could at the animal's head. A yelp filled the air, and the mass of fur darted away, its stump of a tail flowing out behind it. The strangest skunk he'd ever seen.

He stopped for a moment to catch his breath, bending over to rest his hand on his thigh. The bite in his leg ached, but he tried to push the thought from his mind. Striding forward he scooped up the pot hurled into the snow. He'd have to go fill it with water again.

Emma could feel Joseph's stare through the thickness of her winter coat, but she didn't turn in the saddle to face him. He was worried. That was obvious from the way he'd scrutinized her since she told him of her concerns. He'd gotten so upset, she'd almost told him she was teasing. After all, it was only a tiny bit of blood. A little spot that had grown larger when she'd checked after lunch.

But still, she had no other unusual pains that might be symptoms of a problem. It may be nothing. After all, as perfect as God's handiwork was, she'd never quite understood why he made the female body such a messy thing. And being with child—she'd have never imagined what a trying business this was. Her little concern was probably perfectly normal.

"Ho." Simeon's voice called from ahead, and his right hand came up to halt them. He peered over his horse's shoulder at the snow in front.

"What is it?" She leaned forward to see what caught his attention, but the pack horse shifted up beside his mount, blocking her view.

"Tracks. Looks like a group came through here yesterday."

"A group of what? People?" They hadn't seen a soul since they left Simeon's cabin. Honestly, it had come to feel like they were the only three people in the world.

"Indians."

A shiver ran up her arms. "How can you tell? Are we in danger?"

He was quiet for another moment as he studied the ground. She itched to ride up beside him and see for herself, but snow-covered rocks lined their right, and the left side of the trail dropped in a steep descent.

Simeon finally looked up, his eyes scanning the path before them as it wound upward around the mountain.

She could stand the quiet no longer. "Simeon?"

He turned to meet her gaze. "It's not a war party. Looks like squaws and young ones, too. Most of the tribes in these areas are friendly."

But his face didn't look as unconcerned as his words sounded. His lips pinched in a thin line.

"Should we turn around? Find another route?" Every muscle in her body tensed, but she forced her shoulders to relax.

He scanned the trail again. "There's a cave somewhere near here I wanted us to spend the night in. Let's push on. We might be able to barter supplies from the band, too."

Without another word, he nudged Pet forward, pulling the tether line tight until Paint fell into step behind.

Emma's mare did the same, but she couldn't summon a happy feeling about the prospect. Barter with Indians? Did Simeon really know what he was doing?

Simeon strained to listen over the horse hooves crunching in the snow. The fresh pile of horse manure they'd just passed meant the band was close. There was a good chance they were Apsaalooke, a friendly tribe whose groups roamed throughout these mountains, but he couldn't be sure until they met the group. And then it could be too late.

Maybe he should have turned back to find a different trail, but that cave had to be close. And it would be perfect cover until the storm passed. The flakes falling now were thicker than in the last hours. The low, gray clouds overhead would open up any moment, and the wind had already picked up. They had to push harder or they'd find themselves stranded in a blizzard.

Should he ride ahead and scout things? Probably.

He reined Pet to a stop and turned in the saddle to study his companions. Both wore the same pensive expression, highlighting the similarities in their features. His heart squeezed, as it always did when he thought of his own twin babies. He pushed the feeling aside and started untying Paint's tether strap from his saddle.

"I'm going to ride ahead. Can you keep this girl?"

"Of course." Emma caught the leather when he tossed it to her, and Simeon studied her one last time. So beautiful. What was he doing bringing a woman like her out in this country? With Indians and blizzards, and more ways to die than faced a soldier in battle.

The thought burned his throat, and he turned away, nudging Pet faster down the trail.

Chapter Twelve

No matter what I do, the nightmare comes to life again.
~ Simeon

Emma pushed her horse forward as the incline steepened. "You all right, Joey?" She didn't dare glance away from the path but strained to catch his response through the wind blowing around her hood.

"Right as sun in the summer. You want me to take the pack horse?"

"She's fine." Emma had almost forgotten the mare was tied to her saddle, the horse trailed behind so quietly. Besides, all her focus was on the snowy tracks and watching for dangers ahead. For a while, she'd been able to distinguish Pet's hoof prints from those of the Indian ponies. But once she lost them, she hadn't been able to pick the mare's tracks out again. But surely she would have noticed if Simeon's prints broke off from the others. He would have left some kind of sign if he wanted them to turn off the trail.

A noise ahead brought her focus upward, and she glimpsed a horse rounding the bend to meet them. The tension in her chest eased when she recognized Pet's wooly head, then Simeon's fur coat. And those broad shoulders. *Lord, thank you.*

She reined in her mare when he reached them, then scanned his face. No hint of what he'd found, good or bad. She'd learned to read through his façade most times, but at the moment, he'd moved back into that emotionless place.

"The good news is, they're Apsaalooke, as I hoped. A band of about a dozen, plus a handful of children. They agreed to barter some of our salt for grain for the horses."

That all sounded good. So why didn't he look relieved? "What's wrong, Simeon?"

He met her gaze squarely. "They're holed up in the cave I was hoping we could shelter in for the storm. We'll have to find someplace else."

She studied him. "We can find another campsite, can't we?"

He let out a breath, his shoulders sagging. "We'll have to. In a hurry. The storm'll be on us within a couple hours."

A knot tightened in her stomach. "God will lead us to a better place."

His face blanched, but he looked past her, reaching out a hand. "Let me have the pack horse and let's get moving."

"She's all right with me. Lead on."

In less than a half hour, they rounded a bend to see a huge hole in the face of the mountainside. Its opening yawned dark, at least a horse length across and the same in height. A figure appeared at the entrance, so bundled in gray animal furs he would have blended with the rock and snow were it not for the dark brown of his face. So this was an Indian? She'd expected him to be shirtless, with paint on his face and feathers in his hair like the sketches she'd seen. Of course, he'd freeze to death dressed like that out here.

Simeon reined in his horse about a dozen feet in front of the man, then slid from its back. He spoke to the Indian. The sounds had a rolling, high-low cadence. Words, probably, although they could have been gibberish for all she knew.

The other man nodded, then answered with half as many words. He didn't move from his post, but Simeon turned to Paint and worked at the rawhide lacing that strapped on a bag of salt.

"Can I help you?" She whispered the question to Simeon but kept her eyes focused on the Indian at the cave. Another man appeared beside him, dropped a leather satchel at the first brave's feet, then disappeared again into the darkness.

"Just stay put." Simeon muttered the words barely loud enough for her to hear. His tone wasn't nervous, just firm.

Fine with her. The sooner they got out of there the better. She fingered the cross hanging around her neck as Simeon made the trade with little ceremony. He swapped another few words with the Indian, then returned to Pet and mounted in a smooth motion. Without a glance behind, he turned his horse toward the trail and started off. Emma nudged her mare to catch up, and Joseph fell into stride behind her packhorse.

She caught Simeon's sideways glance as the animals formed a line on the trail, but it wasn't until they'd rounded the curve in the mountain that Simeon turned in his saddle to face them. "You all accounted for?"

Emma glanced at Joseph, then nodded. "We're fine. Did he say something concerning?"

Simeon's brow knit. "He wasn't as friendly as the other Apsaalooke I've met. Made it clear they'd not be sharing the cave with us."

An image formed in her mind of sitting in a dark cave across from a row of Indian braves, only a small campfire separating them. She'd rather ride on in the driving snow.

Several more hours passed before Simeon called for a stop in front of another rock overhang. The protected area spanned farther than their shelter the night before, but the dry ground looked to be only three feet or so from the rock wall. They'd have to huddle close again to be near the fire.

If she closed her eyes, she could still feel the strength of Simeon's shoulder under her cheek in the night, the warmth of his arm against hers. It had been so strange to wake up sitting beside him. Especially when she'd looked up and seen his deep blue eyes watching her. The heat surged to her face even now.

The three of them worked to unpack the supplies they'd need for camp, then Simeon and Joseph led the horses to find shelter while she started their fire. What she wouldn't give for a mug of hot cocoa right now. Wouldn't that be nice with the snow falling in huge flakes around her? Mama had loved that treat on snowy days in Maryland, and even though it had been years, she could almost taste it now in the icy air.

If only Mama were here for her to ask about the baby. She would know if bleeding were normal at this point in the pregnancy. Emma probably shouldn't have mentioned it to Joseph. He didn't need the extra worry when she wasn't even sure there was cause for concern.

She had flapjacks frying in the pan when the men returned. Joseph took a seat by the fire and extended his good hand toward the heat. Behind her, Simeon dropped a load of wood in a heap. She turned to offer him a smile. "The food should be ready in about five minutes. Just need to brown the meat."

He didn't offer a responding grin. In fact, his look was more of a glare. A scrutinizing one, at that.

She raised her brows at him, turning more fully. "What's wrong?"

"You tell me." His gaze dropped to her rounded middle, and awareness sank over her. Joseph must have told him. Heat crept up her neck. Surely her brother wouldn't have shared something so private with a stranger. Of course, Simeon wasn't exactly a stranger, but the matter was so…*personal.*

He gripped a log in each hand and strode forward to place them on the fire. "You should lie down." He didn't meet her gaze now, just toed one of the sticks farther into the blaze. "I'm going to get help. I'll be back in a few hours."

Help? From where?

He spun and headed toward where they'd staked the horses.

"Wait, Simeon."

He'd only made it a few feet when he paused and slowly pivoted. He didn't answer, just stood with brows raised for her to speak.

"Where would you go? I don't need help. I'm not even sure it's a cause for concern."

His eyes narrowed into dark slits. "It's a cause for concern." The words came out with such intensity, almost ferocity. "I'll be back." He spun on his heels, and she sat there like a statue, watching him go. All powers of speech slipped away in the wake of his passion. What had Joseph told him exactly?

She turned on her brother, whose amber eyes were studying her as he still held out a hand to soak in the warmth of the fire. "What did you say to him?"

His brows raised. "Only what you told me."

A surge of anger rippled through her. "Why? Didn't you think I'd want to keep my private concerns…private?"

Then his eyes narrowed as Simeon's had. "We need help, Em. If there's something wrong with the baby, we have to find a doctor. Simeon needed to know what was going on." His chin came up. "I'm glad he's going for help."

She turned back to scoop the flat cakes from the pan. What was done was done. And she wouldn't admit it to Joseph, but having a doctor to talk with would be a godsend. She'd have to get past her present embarrassment.

Moments later, a thudding sound caught her

attention, and Simeon rode into sight. Pet stepping high as she trotted through the snow. He reined in beside the fire. "I'll be back by morning. Keep the fire strong and stay put." His eyes locked on Emma's. Such intensity there. His throat worked, and she waited for what else he would say. But then he turned away and pressed his horse into a trot.

She almost called out to him to be careful, but the words seemed pointless. If anyone knew how to handle himself in these mountains, it was Simeon Grant. But should he be riding that fast over cliffs in the darkness and snow? *Dear Father, please keep him safe.*

If anything happened to him because of her, she'd never forgive herself.

Simeon's breaths came in shallow gasps as he struggled to see the trail ahead through the darkness. They must be higher in the mountains than he'd thought. If he was having this much trouble breathing, Pet would likely be struggling, too. Especially in her expectant condition. He should have taken Joseph's gelding.

He eased back in the saddle to let her slow to a walk. Yet, his muscles itched to move faster. What had those two been thinking to wait all day before telling him there was a problem? That day could mean the difference between life and death for Emma *and* the baby.

His heart pounded faster in his chest. How could this

be happening again? Sweat trickled down his back as that old feeling of helplessness pressed in on him. He should have taken Emma back to Fort Benton when he'd first realized she was with child. God gave him a chance to redeem himself, and he'd made the same stupid mistake again. He tried to swallow down the lump in his throat, but it grew larger, threatening every breath he took. But he savored the pain. It was the least he deserved for his faulty decisions. Now if he could only get Emma help before it was too late.

As Simeon neared the cave entrance, the cloudy sky made the night seem even bleaker. The snow had stopped—he could be thankful for that, at least.

He forced himself to relax as he rounded the corner and the opening came into view. He called a greeting, even though he was still a good thirty feet away. The last thing he wanted was for the Indians to think he was trying to sneak up on them. They probably had half a dozen braves watching him even then.

A shadow flickered beside the black hole in the rock. A man stepped to the side bundled in white furs so he almost melted into the snow.

Simeon spoke the greeting again as he reined in his mare about a dozen feet from the brave.

No response.

"I seek help." He was pretty sure those were the right Crow words to make his request known.

The man shifted.

That wasn't a command to leave, so he pushed on. "The woman in my band is with child. She's having trouble. Is there a medicine man among your people? We're camped about three hours' ride from here."

Still no answer.

Desperation surged in Simeon's chest. If these people wouldn't help, where could he find someone else? As far as he knew, the closest town was several days away. That would likely be too long for Emma.

He scanned his memory for something he could do to encourage them. All the Apsaalooke he'd ever met were friendly. Wary sometimes, but willing to help or trade when he asked. Maybe this band didn't meet with many white people. "I can trade for the help. Another bag of salt and bear meat." He held his hands about ten inches apart to show the size of the bundle of meat. They weren't carrying many extra supplies, but he could always hunt more game as they traveled. But he *had* to get help for Emma. Now.

The brave spoke low to someone in the cave, then louder to Simeon. "She will come."

The relief that flowed through him sapped a bit of strength from his muscles. Relief slipped into his chest, but he bit back a smile and nodded instead.

Within minutes, two figures stepped from the cave, bundled in furs. One was squatty and hunched while the other stood tall. The shorter must be the squaw the man had promised. Her braid peeked from the furs and hung down one shoulder, the thick gray strands giving testament to her years of experience. Yes, she was what Emma needed.

The old squaw approached him, but the man turned aside, jogging into the woods. He must have gone for their horses.

The woman didn't give Simeon a second glance as she stood waiting, and thankfully, the brave reappeared within a minute, leading two spotted Indian ponies.

The young brave mounted his horse first, and Simeon almost dismounted to help the old squaw up onto hers, but she swung up easily.

Turning Pet the direction they'd come, he pushed her into a trot as he led the way. Hopefully, these Indian ponies could handle a fast clip. Emma needed him, and for once, he might actually be able to help.

Chapter Thirteen

God's grace to me is a gift I must pass on.
~ Emma's Journal

Simeon paced in front of the tie line, straining to hear any sound from the direction of their camp. How long would it take the old squaw to help Emma? It must have been at least an hour. Was her condition that bad? Fear pressed harder on his chest, and he spun and stomped the other direction.

His gaze connected with the brave who'd accompanied the squaw, now sitting at the base of a cedar—watching him. Even though the man's face held no expression, that gleam in his eye was enough to start a burn in Simeon's gut. He fisted his hands and twisted the other direction. What was taking so long?

He'd left Joseph stationed near the women in case Emma needed help and brought the brave out here where the horses were tied to allow the women some privacy. But maybe the squaw had overpowered both brother and sister? Perhaps this particular band held a grudge against white men, and they'd sent the squaw to poison them. Had he put

Emma in danger? His muscles pulled even tighter.

"She's asking for you."

Simeon spun to face the voice, his right hand reaching for the knife strapped at his waist. He had it out of the sheath and poised to throw before his gaze landed on Joseph.

Joseph.

He forced in a breath, lowering the blade. "Is she all right?"

Joseph shrugged, a gesture that seemed too relaxed for the situation, but the deep lines in his brow hinted at worry. "We can't understand the squaw, but I think she's saying she wants you to come back."

He strode forward before Joseph had the last words out of his mouth. Pushing past the man, he broke into a jog as he wound through the trees to get to their camp. Privacy be hanged. He shouldn't have left Emma alone with an Indian. Even an old woman from a tribe known to be friendly.

When he reached the rock overhang, Emma sat next to the fire with the squaw kneeling beside her. He crouched in front of them, his gaze sweeping first the Indian, then Emma. The older woman ignored him, stirring something in a cup.

Emma met his gaze though, and he studied her. For the most part, she looked hale and hearty. Maybe a bit tired, judging from the dark half-moons under her eyes. But she didn't appear pale or as if she were struggling to breathe.

A corner of her mouth eased up, drawing his gaze to

her lips. He forced it back to her eyes, but they were almost as intoxicating. She may not be breathless, but she had the power to make him so.

He turned to the squaw, summoning his mind to find the right phrase in her language. "What is wrong?"

She spoke a string of sounds, her hands gesturing in broad strokes as she talked. He focused on the hand motions to make sense of what she said. Something about being high. Was the baby high up inside Emma? Not yet dropped into the birth canal? In a horse, that would be a good thing if the mare hadn't gone to the end of her term.

His face must have showed some of his confusion, because the squaw spoke again. This time he caught the Crow word for *mountain*. That didn't make sense with the other.

She motioned again, and her face showed a bit of her impatience as she repeated some of the earlier words.

He squinted as he turned the expressions over in his mind, matching them with her gestures. *High in the mountains*. He straightened as the words finally fell in place. "She's having trouble because of the high…" He searched for the Crow word for elevation, but his mind came up empty. Finally, he used the English version, scooping his flat hand up and down like a mountain peak.

She flashed a toothy grin and nodded. Then she held up the cup. "To make blood thick. Baby strong." She clenched her fist and shook it.

He eased down on his knees. "So that's all it is?"

The woman turned away from him, stirring the cup,

then handed it to Emma. It took a moment before he realized he'd spoken in English, so the squaw hadn't understood his question.

"What did she say, Simeon?" Emma's gentle question brought his full focus back to her face.

"She said it's the altitude that's causing the…concern." Could she see the heat creeping into his face? This wasn't the type of conversation he was accustomed to having with a lady. Not that he talked to ladies much these days. Except for her.

"You're joking."

He inhaled a deep breath, willing his pounding heartbeat to slow. "No. I've seen the heights do funny things to people and animals. I knew it could be a problem, but didn't expect…" He scrubbed a hand through his hair, the greasiness of it pricking his awareness. He must be a sight. Up all night. Hadn't shaved in two days. And most likely in dire need of a haircut.

His hand slipped back down to his knees and clenched his thigh as his gaze roamed over Emma's face. What must she think of him? He was pretty sure he didn't want to know. But for the first time, it seemed to matter. It shouldn't, but it did.

The squaw pointed to the mug in Emma's hands, and she sipped obediently, but her gaze never left Simeon's face.

The warmth of her eyes penetrated him, making him desperate to fill the silence. Anything to distract her from the rough image he must make. "She said that drink will make your blood thicken and the baby grow strong."

Her brows lifted as she took another sip. The delicate tendons in her throat shifted when she swallowed. So beautiful, every part of her. She turned to the Indian woman with a gentle smile. "Thank you."

The squaw nodded, then looked at him and spoke in her throaty voice. "Need rest."

"Yes." He would make sure she got it.

"I've been resting all day. Throwing together a simple pot of stew is not going to hurt me." Emma propped her hands as close to her hips as her wide girth would allow and glared at her brother. Her *younger* brother, even if only by a few minutes.

"The squaw said to rest, Emma. And I agree with her. Besides, Simeon'll have my head if I let you do any work. And if it's a question of you or him, I think he has a better chance of blackening my eye." He cupped a hand over his right eye with a cheeky grin.

"Then you think wrong, little brother." She stalked away and picked up the bundle of dried herbs and her stew pot. "I'll sit while I put the stew together. Will that make you happy?"

She ignored his "harrumph" as she eased herself down beside the fire. She'd been resting all day, but they couldn't expect her to sleep forever.

Thankfully, Simeon had finally gone hunting after

lunch, a reprieve from the pacing he'd done all morning. He'd worn a muddy path in the snow outside the rock overhang.

So unlike his usual unruffled demeanor. Was he chafed because they were losing precious travel time? He'd said he wanted to reach Canada before the worst of winter hit, but from the two feet of snow surrounding them, it seemed they were already experiencing it. She hoped so, anyway.

That must be the source of his frustration.

Well, she would be more than ready to set out again the next morning. He could ease his mind on that score.

She had a thick, savory stock simmering in the pot by the time Simeon appeared through the trees carrying a leather-wrapped bundle the length of his forearm. He halted mid-stride when he saw her standing beside the pot stirring the broth.

With a wary step, he moved forward, circling the fire to approach her head-on. "What are you doing?"

She gave him a cheery smile. Maybe she could disarm his concern. "Is there meat in that package? I have the herbs simmering."

He nodded but didn't unwrap it. "Why are you up?"

She almost gave him the same glare she'd used on Joseph but caught herself just in time. Instead, she inhaled a steadying breath. "I've rested all day. I feel wonderful. And preparing a simple stew won't hurt me." *Lord, grant me patience.* The men in her life were awfully overprotective.

The men in her life... Her mind flickered back to

Lance. It could never have been said he'd been overprotective. Or that he'd bothered much with her at all. Maybe there was something to be said about men caring enough to worry.

She smiled at Simeon again, but this time the expression grew from her heart. "I'm all right, Simeon. Honest."

He rolled his lips, but then nodded once. "If you're sure."

Yes. The bleeding hadn't shown up today, and lying around all day had rejuvenated her spirits. Her breathing came easier than it had for several days now. The Lord was taking care of them.

After the meal, Joseph and Simeon left to feed the horses, then Joseph came back alone for his nightly cup of willow bark tea.

"Where's Simeon?" She handed him the mug once he'd settled on his pallet.

"Oh, you know him. Always has to check and recheck everything. I can't tell if he's really that particular or if he simply can't bring himself to sit down and relax." Joseph eased back against the rock wall, inhaling the aroma of the tea with a satisfied sigh. "Me? When the work is done, I don't have a problem settling in for the night."

She raised a brow. "I've noticed that."

He gave her an impish look, and the way his hair fell across his forehead in a swoop made him look just like he had fifteen years ago. Add a few more freckles, and she'd feel like she'd gone back in time. "How's your arm feeling?"

The sass left his expression as his face pinched. "Better, I think, if I could ever get away from this chill. The cold stings all the way through the bone."

Her heart ached for the pain he'd endured every moment. If only she could take it on herself and free him of the burden. "They say old injuries can tell when the season's about to change. In another year or so, you'll be forecasting the weather with that arm. Might make some money off you if the farmers'll believe it."

He winked, the old Joseph. Her hero, fighting through pain.

Her brother's eyes had drooped by the time Simeon padded into camp with his usual silent tread. She'd been reading some of David's Psalms but couldn't keep her gaze on the page as the mountain man gathered a load of logs from the stack and laid them one by one on the fire. His height didn't feel as overwhelming as it once had, but his presence still unnerved her.

Not from fear, or even curiosity. Not anymore. No, when he came into sight, it was like her very soul took notice, drawing near to him.

He finally eased down onto the bearskin he used as a bed, then leaned against the rock wall and clasped his hands around his knees. He hadn't yet looked at her.

Not once.

She knew because she'd not been able to take her eyes from him. The stubble that had flecked his jaw earlier had disappeared. He'd pulled his fur cap off, and even his hair looked shorter. But it wasn't like he could have visited a barber out in the middle of the mountain wilderness. It must be a trick of the light. There was no denying his attractiveness. Strong features proportioned so perfectly. And those blue eyes.

Her chest squeezed as those eyes turned to her, and for a moment her breath cut off. She wanted to look away. Wanted to never look away. The penetration of his gaze stirred emotions she couldn't begin to fathom.

Then he broke the connection turned back to the fire and stared far away, stared into another world. Grief was etched in the lines of his face. Not just concern or frustration like she'd convinced herself earlier.

And she could stand it no longer.

"Simeon, what's wrong?" She kept her voice just loud enough to reach him.

He didn't move. Didn't speak. His eyes turned glassy. Was he so deep in that other world that he hadn't heard her?

"It's happening again." The words were so quiet they may have been only the rustle of the flame, but her heart captured them.

"What's happening?"

The silence fell again. She wanted to prod, but he would answer when he was ready. To make herself wait, she listened to her own breathing. In. Out. In. Out.

Then he turned his eyes on her. The deep blue of them had hollowed into a thick gray. "My decisions put you in danger. I'm sorry."

Her mind stammered. His words made no sense. Danger? Her hand slipped to her belly. "Simeon, I'm fine.

The squaw said it was just the altitude, right?" But then a surge of panic sluiced through her. Was there more? Had he withheld some of the Indian's words from her? The news was so bad he'd been afraid to share it. "What else did she say? Tell me." Her heart thudded in her chest. "Please, Simeon. Now."

He jerked back, eyes widening. "No, there was nothing else. At least, I don't think so. Not as far as I understood."

She studied him, squinting as her pulse gradually slowed. "What danger then?"

He nodded toward her midsection. "The baby. I shouldn't have brought you out here. I knew better. I should have taken you straight back to Fort Benton where you could go home. This was my chance to get it right."

She should have been peeved at the words, but the anguish in his voice pressed on her soul. If Joseph hadn't been snoring between them, she'd have reached out to touch Simeon's arm. Anything to reassure him. To still his pain.

Instead, she willed the truth to shimmer in her eyes as her gaze locked with his. "Simeon, if you hadn't brought us here, we'd have come anyway. We're much safer with you than without. Besides…" She pressed away from the rock to lean forward. "I'm fine. The baby's fine. We're already adjusting to the heights. We're not in danger."

He regarded her with a bleary gaze. Her words hadn't changed a thing in his mind. Had he even heard her? "I knew better."

Something must have happened in his past to instill

this fear. Hadn't he used the word *again*? If she could get him to talk about it, maybe she could help combat his worry.

She gentled her voice. "What happened before?" The worst he could do was be angry with her for prying, but something in his demeanor gave her hope.

He still stared at her, but his eyes had glassed over, his mind far away.

She waited.

"My wife was pregnant when we came to the mountains. The trip took so long, but I thought we still had time. Months." His voice rasped and he paused. "We hadn't even reached Butte when the labor pains hit. But there was a cabin, and a woman. She whisked Nora in and seemed to know what to do. The labor took so long and the pain was so awful. But finally, there was a little boy." The break in his voice stopped him again, and Emma had to fight the burn in her own eyes. The story he described seemed so incongruous with his tough façade. But she could see it. The scene matched the Simeon she was coming to know underneath. The man who felt and worried and cared…really cared.

"He was so tiny." His voice broke again, and his eyes slipped down to his hands. Did he remember holding the child? He dropped his hands between his knees and stared into the fire. "The pain didn't stop. Then Mrs. Scott said another babe was coming."

Her breath caught. Twins? The ache in her chest pulled even tighter.

Simeon released a shuddering breath. "The girl was

even smaller than the boy. And everything so perfect. But Nora…" He paused. "I was trying to feed the boy and didn't realize how quickly she slipped. Mrs. Scott said the bleeding…" His voice shuddered.

She'd never heard such raw pain from a man. The ache pressed through every part of her. Tears slipped down her cheeks, but she ignored them. He'd watched his wife bleed to death? No wonder her small concern had struck him with such force.

What could she even say in the face of that story? His experience had been horrific. No wonder he wanted her to head back east. Could she make him believe she would be all right? Did she believe it herself? She inhaled a breath. *Lord, give me the words. Your guidance.*

But before she could summon a response, he spoke again. "I was so lost without Nora, I barely noticed the little ones. If it hadn't been for the Scotts, I don't know what would have happened. We still had days to travel before we reached the land I'd purchased, and then nowhere to stay until I built a cabin. I didn't know how I could manage. And the babes were so small. I just couldn't see the way." His voice broke again, and dread slipped into Emma's chest.

"The Scotts agreed to take them as their own. They'd been unable to have children themselves, so they were eager." The words fell flat, fell as if they were a line he'd forced himself to memorize.

She swallowed. "It sounds like God placed them there for a reason." But why had Simeon had to endure so much pain?

He pivoted, landing a hard gaze on her. "I gave away my children. What father does that?"

Tears pressed harder in her eyes. Hadn't it felt like that's what her own father did? Gave her to Lance and wiped his hands of her. But with one glance at Simeon, it was clear he'd never wiped his hands of his children. Their memory haunted every part of his thoughts. He carried the burden in all his features.

Lord, show him grace.

She didn't have any words to still his anguish. He didn't look ready to hear them anyway. But maybe talking about it helped. Perhaps now the healing process could begin.

She swallowed past the lump in her throat. "My heart aches for you, Simeon. For all you lost. I'll be praying God shows you His peace."

His throat worked, and the muscles in his jaw flexed.

Joseph's light snores stopped with a snort, drawing their attention. He shifted in his bedding, but his eyes never opened. Finally, steady breathing raised his chest again.

Simeon turned back to the fire. "It's late. Better get some sleep."

He didn't shift positions, but it was clear he was done with the conversation. He'd bared his soul enough for one night, and the revelations still had her reeling. So much of his brooding made sense now. The flickers of grief he'd shown in rare moments. He carried a weight on his shoulders no man should have to bear. *Lord, help him forgive himself.*

She settled under the heavy stack of furs and blankets but couldn't quite force her eyes to close. The fire danced before her as her mind replayed Simeon's story again and again.

Then words from Isaiah crept in. *He was a man of sorrows, and acquainted with grief.* Though they were written to describe Jesus, they just as aptly fit the mountain man sitting mere feet away, staring into this same fire. Did he know how much God loved him? How could he, and not accept the grace that was his for the taking? A surge of determination flooded her. She would show Simeon the Father's love, live it out in word and deed. *Guide me, Lord. Give me opportunities.*

With the peace that settled over her, her eyes drifted shut, but sleep was still a long time coming.

Chapter Fourteen

I want to shed this fear, but it haunts me.
~ Simeon

Another day? Emma swiped the branch aside as she stalked through the woods following Simeon's tracks in the fresh coating of snow. Talking about his past the night before had apparently not alleviated his fears.

He'd been gone when she awoke that morning, but Joseph had been there, sipping a mug of tea with sleep-tousled hair. Her brother had shared the news that they would stay another day in this spot and had only offered a shrug when she'd told him she was more than healthy enough to move on.

"Go see Simeon," he'd said. "I think the man's probably right."

So that's exactly what she was doing.

Except she hadn't counted on him traveling so far. She'd been following his trail now a half hour, at least. Although why she'd thought he would stay close, she couldn't say. He was a mountain man and probably planned to be gone all morning. Of course he would travel easily over the territory, exploring like a mountain goat. Maybe she should turn back.

But sunlight shone through the trees ahead where they must open up to a cliff edge or some kind of change in the mountain terrain. She'd go that far and look around, then head back to camp.

When she stepped past the last of the trees, a line of boulders edged the woods. The land dropped in a steep descent beyond the rocks.

Standing at the brink beside the largest stone was a single figure clad in buckskin and furs. A lone timber staring out at the vast mountains beyond.

Her breath lodged in her throat. Were it painted in oils, the scene would be enough to inspire tears. But seeing it live, feeling the intense loneliness of the single man in such a vast wilderness—it was almost more than she could bear.

She stepped closer, stopping when she was a few feet away. Part of her hated to disrupt the beauty of the scene, but the rest of her craved to step inside it, to become a part, to maybe relieve his loneliness.

She could fit there, beside him. She knew it instinctively. She could become part of this place. This wild beauty.

For a long time, they stood that way, the wind whipping against them as it soared through the peaks and gulches, unencumbered by trees on the rocky cliffs. Her woolen coat was no match for the chilly force of air, and her frozen nose began to run. But that was a small inconvenience compared to the opportunity to stand here at the edge of the world.

"I didn't expect to see you here." He didn't turn, and his voice gave no hint of whether he was glad she'd come or not. Probably the latter or he wouldn't have headed out before she'd risen and prepared breakfast.

"I thought we'd be in the saddle by now. Trying to make up ground." She slid a sideways glance at him, but he wasn't looking her way.

"We'll wait another day." The words were casual, but the tension in his jaw said otherwise.

She turned to fully face his profile. "Simeon. I feel fine. Really. You don't have to worry about me." Although she had a feeling that was like telling a lion not to be hungry.

He turned to her then, and the power of his gaze almost felled her. She swayed a bit but couldn't tear her focus from his.

His hand gripped her wrist, his eyes deepening their blue intensity. He must have seen her sway. Then saved her, as had become his habit. He was such a good man. Even the burden he still carried for his lost family proclaimed it. When this mountain man determined to protect something, he spent every last piece of himself to accomplish it.

His eyes roamed her face, releasing her from the power of his gaze. But she still watched him, feeling the heat of his scrutiny everywhere it touched. What did he see when he looked at her? A burden? A responsibility?

Suddenly, she wanted more than anything for him to *not* think of her as a responsibility. Was it too much to wish he might come to care for her? Did she want that?

"Your cheeks are red from the wind." His hand came up to her face, the texture of his leather glove a strange feeling to her frozen skin. It was warm, though, and she leaned into it, finding his gaze again.

A shiver ran through her, but the chill barely registered. What was she doing so close to him? But she couldn't bring herself to step back.

Twin lines formed between his brows. "You're cold." His voice came out husky, although the sound could have been distortion from the wind. She slid her gaze to his mouth even as she struggled not to. He moistened his lips. Not a good idea in this chill. And not a good thing when her stomach already fluttered from his nearness.

She forced her gaze back to his eyes, and the desire in their depths drew her even more. Before she knew what her traitorous body planned, she rose up on tiptoes, slid her hand behind his neck, and pressed a kiss to his lips.

They parted underneath her touch, and the hand still on her wrist pulled her closer. Before she could think, he had a hold on both her elbows and was kissing her back with an intensity that took her breath.

And pulled her in deeper. She melted into his touch, breathing in the strength of him. The vulnerability.

He was so fragile, his pain still so fresh. She shouldn't have given in to her desire, no matter how right it felt. With every bit of her strength, she pulled back. But only a few inches.

He rested his forehead on hers.

Her breath came in ragged gasps, mixing with his in a

foggy swirl around them. For long moments they stood like that, although her weak knees may not have supported her without his grip on her upper arms.

"I need to get you out of this cold." His words spoke a warm caress on her face.

"I'll be all right." She wasn't ready to move. Not yet. Not ready to break the connection between them. She hadn't realized how much she'd longed for it. Care for this man had sneaked up on her so completely, and she was surprised at the depth of the emotion that now pressed in her chest.

"I'm not sure I will."

It was several heartbeats before the meaning of his words filtered through the muddle in her brain. Did he…? Could he…care for her?

Releasing a long breath, he stepped back. He turned for a final scan over the panorama around them. Then he looked at her again, a soft gaze crinkling the corners of his eyes. "What say we head back?"

Simeon could feel Emma's gaze on his back as their horses wound over the mountain trail. She'd asked again on their way back to camp that morning whether they shouldn't get in at least a few hours on the trail today. And after that kiss…it seemed he'd lost his ability to tell her no.

Heat flamed up his neck even now. How could he have kissed her? At least he'd not been the one to initiate the contact. Did that mean she felt something for him? How could that be true? How could a woman like her—a woman so…so special—ever want a man like him? He was broken. Irredeemably flawed. She shouldn't trust herself to him. He couldn't trust himself with her. The only sensible thing she could do was to stay far away from him.

He tightened his jaw. He'd have to make sure of it. No matter how much her kiss had brought him to life.

Emma laid the meat in the frying pan that evening and listened to the sizzle as the grease touched the hot iron. She glanced up when Joseph stepped into their clearing, sledging through the snow that almost came up to his knees.

Weariness weighted his shoulders, and he dragged his feet as he approached the campfire.

She frowned. It actually looked like he dragged one foot more than the other. The left, if she wasn't mistaken. Had the cold become too much for him? Maybe he was suffering from frostbite.

She pointed to a spot she'd cleared of snow beside the fire. "Sit and warm yourself. Are you in pain?"

He shrugged his good arm. "No more than usual."

But there was something different about him tonight. The way his mouth pulled down. The dullness in his eyes. Joey always fought hard to keep a cheery spirit even through the worst of his pain. Was it all finally getting to him?

She flipped the meat over in the pan, then reached for the kettle. "I'll get water for tea. Tonight, you're to eat and go straight to bed."

A slight nod was his only acknowledgement as he slumped against a tree, legs spread out before him.

Joseph didn't eat much at dinner, and he seemed to melt into the blankets when he laid down. Poor fellow. Maybe it was the altitude getting to him, too. She'd noticed her own breathing took a little more effort as the horses had climbed upward this afternoon. Of course, she'd never tell Simeon. He'd barely had them in the saddle a half day as it was. But every little bit helped, getting them closer to Alberta. Closer to Aunt Mary. And a new life.

Although somehow, that life didn't shimmer as brightly as it once had.

Traveling through the beauty of these mountains, so far removed from Texas and everything tainted by the mess there, it felt like she'd already stepped into her new world. And she was quickly coming to love it.

Did the man sitting across the fire have anything to do with this new affinity? She glanced at Simeon as he strummed absently on the guitar. He'd not played in a week or more, but the music worked its magic in her soul now as it had before.

It was good he played tonight, because she'd been a little nervous about how they'd pass the time with Joseph sleeping. Their kiss that morning still lingered as a clear memory, both in her mind and on her lips. From the times she'd caught him watching her, the kiss didn't seem far from

Simeon's thoughts, either.

But there was something else there. Something she'd sensed when they'd stopped midafternoon to let the horses blow. He carried a tension in his shoulders and in the set of his jaw. It wasn't just when he looked at her, but her presence didn't appear to soften it either.

Did he regret their kiss? Did she? Yes, part of her. That part still flamed at the memory that *she'd* been the one to initiate the act. What kind of floozy had she become? Certainly not the lady of breeding Mama had raised her to be.

But the kiss had awakened so many emotions within her. It had brought clarity to her thoughts and illuminated the state of her heart. She was growing to care much too deeply for this mountain man. In a matter of weeks or less, they'd arrive in Canada, and Simeon would leave them. He'd escape back to his hiding place, abandoning her with what pieces of her heart she could guard from him.

But the image of his retreat squeezed her chest even more. If there was one thing she wanted to do for Simeon, it was to help him forgive himself. Help him grieve the past and find hope in what was to come. The tricky part would be to do that without dimming her own future.

A life without Simeon Grant.

Chapter Fifteen

You've not let me down before, Lord. Please don't let this be the first time.
~ Emma's Journal

They kept a steady ascent the next day, the horses stepping around icy rock formations and trekking beside steep drop-offs. Many times, Emma forced herself not to look to the left or right but to keep her focus on the broad shoulders leading their caravan.

Thank You for letting Joseph talk me into inviting the man. How would they have made it through this treacherous land without him?

Simeon paused every hour or so, and at times it seemed they rested more than they traveled. But they all breathed hard, horses and humans alike. Joseph seemed to be taking it the hardest, though. His skin had paled, and by the time they stopped for the evening, a thin sheen of sweat glimmered across his brow. He seemed to struggle through chores too, and he slumped on his bedroll during dinner.

He'd already drifted to sleep by the time she returned with a pan full of clean snow to wash the dishes. And he hadn't even drunk his willow bark tea.

After finishing her chores around camp, she settled on her bedroll with the Bible and her journal to occupy herself until Simeon returned from scouting. The man had spoken little that day, and, in truth, she was relieved. The more distance she kept between them, the easier it would be to stop herself from growing to love him. If it wasn't already too late.

But tonight, concern for Joseph weighed heavier than the need to guard her heart. Her brother's struggles may be nothing more than his body trying to adjust to the higher altitudes. But she had to ask Simeon's thoughts on the matter. He would know for sure.

She jerked awake when Simeon stepped into the ring of light around the campfire, blinking to clear the sleep from her eyes. She'd not meant to doze, but the child within her seemed to drain so much of her energy these days.

Simeon lowered himself to his furs, and Emma pushed to a seated position to address him.

"The animals bedded down for the night?"

He glanced up at her, a flicker of surprise touching his eyes before they shadowed. "Yes."

"We've climbed high in the mountains today."

He shifted forward, clearing the shadow from his gaze as he studied her. "Is the altitude bothering you?"

Heat crept into her face before she could stop it. She wasn't planning to have another conversation with this man about *personal* things. "I'm fine. It's Joseph I'm worried about." She turned to her brother. "He's been so tired these last couple days. Do you think his body could be struggling to adjust?"

Simeon's gaze drifted to Joseph and wandered the length of him. Then he focused again on Joseph's face. Her brother was still so pale. "It's possible. I haven't looked at that arm in a while, though. We'll check it in the morning."

A small weight lifted from her chest. "Good." If anyone could tell if something were wrong, it would be Simeon. She raised her gaze to his face. "Thank you."

His eyes found hers, and she glimpsed the pain even through the mask he'd tried to place over it. She wanted to look away. To save herself from the ache of the connection, knowing he would be gone soon. But she was like a wild horse lured into a pen, knowing it would be held captive, yet willing to step forward for the draw of the carrot. If only she had the strength to turn away.

Emma's gaze fell on her brother's sleeping form as she returned from her morning ministrations the next day.

He still slept.

Her emotions warred between concern and relief. She typically held to the belief that sleep helped one's body heal itself—a good thing, especially with Joseph's broken arm and the changes in elevation that affected them all.

But the uneasy churn in her stomach had swelled into a tempest, and fear now pressed firmly in her chest.

Something was wrong with her twin.

A pain shot through her left calf, the twinge making her step unsteady as she stumbled over a rock hidden in the snow. She threw out her hands to balance and grabbed a tree to steady herself, then paused to gather her wits.

Should she wake Joseph now or get Simeon first? Creeping closer to her brother, she watched him sleep. Still as pale as the snow piled around the edges of the space they'd cleared. His lips were a bright red, and as she leaned closer, a sheen of sweat beaded his forehead and just below his nose. A trickle of moisture dripped down his temple.

Her heart hammered in her chest. This overheating was more than just one too many blankets. He must have been feverish, yet why? His breathing was loud and raspy in a way that sounded painful. A stark contrast to the twitter of a bird somewhere in the trees.

She lowered herself to her knees beside him, holding in a grunt as her back complained against the awkward position. She ignored the grumbling of her muscles, though, and reached to stroke Joseph's brow.

She jerked back at the heat that assaulted her skin. But then she reached out again, brushing his forehead. "Joey, wake up. What's wrong, love?"

He stirred but didn't wake.

She used her other hand to nudge his good shoulder. "Wake up."

A soft groan broke from his lips, drawing her focus there. The skin had turned crimson and chapped, and a spot on his lower lip was puffy and red where it had split.

"What's wrong with him?"

She jerked at Simeon's voice. "I don't know. He's burning up with fever, and I'm still trying to wake him."

Simeon crouched on Joseph's other side, and the weight of his calming presence eased the edges of her fear. He reached for the tie that held Joseph's broken arm close to his body. "Keep trying." Simeon's voice was steady, intense.

She glanced at his face and saw the focus knit in his brow as he worked to unwrap the splinted arm. *Thank you, Father, for bringing this man to us.*

Then she turned back to her brother. "Wake up, Joey. Now." She shook harder on his shoulder, eliciting another groan. "Come on. Get up."

An eyelid flickered, parted, then dropped shut again.

"Nope, you have to wake up and tell me what's wrong." She shook the arm again, then patted her brother's face with enough effort to annoy.

"Egg."

She almost missed the word and leaned closer.

Nothing.

She squinted at him. "Egg? You're hungry?" That was a good sign. She glanced at the bundle she'd set aside from breakfast. "I have Johnnycakes for you. Can you sit up to eat?" Broth would probably settle better on his stomach. Maybe she should stoke the fire and put some meat on to boil.

A slight motion drew her focus back to her brother. He shook his head. "Leg." The word came out a little stronger than the last one, but the effort seemed to exhaust him. His ragged breaths grew louder. Shorter.

She looked at Simeon, meeting his gaze, and saw the same question in his expression that raced through her own mind.

"His arm looks fine. No redness, and the swelling is almost gone."

Then why was he so ill?

Simeon's glance turned to her brother's legs, buried under the stack of blankets and furs. Simeon pushed the pile aside near Joseph's feet.

Her brother had removed his boots before going to sleep the night before. Something they didn't usually do as a measure to fight against the cold. His stockinged feet stared up at them, a sight she'd seen many a time. Simeon pulled the covers back further, exposing Joseph's trousers to the knee.

A moan slipped from her brother's lips, pulling her attention back up to his face. His mouth pinched, and pain lines etched deep beside his lips and eyes. Her heartbeat picked up speed. Something was very wrong.

She looked again to his legs as Simeon worked at the left hemline. He pulled it up, exposing the under pants beneath. Emma gasped. The wool cloth bulged against the swollen limb it encased. Joseph's calf had expanded to almost twice its normal size, and a dark, wet patch larger than her hand covered the top and outer side. "What's wrong with him?"

But Simeon didn't answer as he tried to pull up the bottom of the stretched material. It clung so tightly to the leg, he couldn't budge it farther than an inch. He reached for the knife sheathed at his waist, and the metal gleamed as he adjusted it in his hand.

Emma bit down on her lower lip when Simeon slid the knife between the fabric and Joseph's flesh. He knew what he was doing. He'd be careful. She had to believe that.

She did believe it.

But she didn't breathe again until he'd sliced the material up to Joseph's knee. The cloth sprang back, splitting to reveal a sight that churned bile in Emma's stomach.

Swollen flesh mottled red and purple, and brown puss oozed from four gashes in the calf muscle.

She clutched a hand to her mouth as a bitter taste rose up into her throat. "What is it?"

"Looks like an animal bite." Simeon peered close. "You can see the upper and lower teeth here." He motioned toward the gashes, then glanced up at Joseph's face and raised his voice. "What bit you, Joseph?"

No answer, just the steady rasp of his breathing.

Emma inched back to her brother's head. "Joey, did an animal bite you? What was it?" She stroked the hair away from his brow, the sweat dampening his locks. They had to get his fever down. Had the infection reached his bloodstream yet? It must have, from the looks of his leg. The burn of tears pricked her eyes, but she willed them back.

"Skunk." He spoke the word so quietly it took Emma a moment to realize what he'd said.

"Skunk?" She studied his face, leaning close in case he corrected her interpretation. He only managed a slight nod.

She looked at Simeon, asking the question with her face so she didn't have to say it aloud. Had Joseph lost his senses? *Lord, don't let the fever affect his mind.*

Simeon's brows furrowed. "Was it big for a skunk? With the white stripes down each side, not on top?" His voice held an urgency.

Joseph didn't answer, although the line in his forehead deepened.

"Do you remember, Joey?" She stroked his temple with the back of her fingers, fighting the urge to take action. But they had to know what they were up against, and only Joseph could tell them.

"I…think. Maybe." So much effort for just those three words. She wanted to cradle his head in her lap, drop her forehead to his, and sob. But it would have to wait. For now, he needed help.

"Was there foam at its mouth?"

Cold dread numbed a circle in her chest at Simeon's words. He thought the animal was rabid? *Oh, Father, no!* She jerked her gaze to Simeon's, and he met it with a softening of his eyes.

Then he turned back to her brother. She did the same, slipping her fingers through Joseph's sweaty hair.

"Don't…think." Joseph's words loosened a flood of relief in her chest, and tears welled in her eyes again. But when her gaze wandered back to the disfigured leg, the sight broke through her feeble strands of joy. Even if he'd not been bitten by a rabid animal, the infection could easily take his life. Especially out here with no doctor or medicines.

She had to fight the infection with every fiber in her being.

Simeon blew out a breath. "I hope that's right. In these parts, it's more likely you ran into a wolverine than a rabid skunk. We'll treat the cuts accordingly."

She tried to catch his gaze, but he studied the mangled leg. "What can I do?"

He glanced at Joseph. "Try to get his fever down. Get some water in him. I'll find something for the infection."

With that, he pushed to his feet and strode toward the horses.

She did as Simeon asked, wetting a cloth in the snow, then wiping Joseph's face. He drank a few sips of icy water but tired too soon. She'd let him rest and try again.

Simeon reappeared while she refreshed the cold cloths on Joseph's burning head and neck.

"Good thing I brought a supply of this. He needs to eat two or three cloves. Think he can chew or should I crush it into powder?" He held a small plant bulb in his palm.

"Garlic?" She'd heard Doctor Turner back in Baltimore mention using garlic to fight infection. But how had Simeon known to bring it? God's leading, certainly.

She glanced at Joseph's languid form. He'd not opened his eyes when she'd doused him with icy cloths. "We should probably do the powder. He could only swallow a few sips of water, so I doubt he can chew."

While Simeon pounded the root into dust in the frying pan by the fire, she scooped more snow onto the cloths cooling Joseph's face. His skin melted the ice so quickly, yet the effort didn't seem to lower his temperature much, if any. She tried her best to ignore the bile churning in her stomach.

Heal him, Lord. Please. She'd been repeating the words over and over since she'd first found her brother, yet they seemed so insufficient. "Simeon, please pray for him. God has to heal my brother."

She didn't turn to look at the man working behind her, so she couldn't tell his reaction to her words. But the drumming of his knife on the cast iron didn't stop. Did he pray of his own accord, or just when they said grace before meals? Did he know God as his Father? *Lord, be what Simeon needs, too.*

Her emotions were so tied up in knots, her chest ached with the strain. One thing at a time. For now, Joseph needed all her energies.

"Here. Mix this with enough water to get it down his throat without choking him. I'll crush more to make a salve for the leg." Simeon handed her a cup of tiny chunks, no bigger than poppy seeds.

And so went much of the day, sitting by Joseph's side, cooling him with snow and attempting to get some of the garlic mixture in him. She'd suggested steeping a tea to make the stuff easier to swallow, but Simeon said heating it diminished the strength of the plant. Better not do it unless they had to.

Joseph stayed in a semi-conscious state, shifting every few minutes as he drifted in and out of troubled sleep. Her heart ached, the exhaustion from his battle seeping all the way through her bones.

How could she have not realized he was so weak? She'd always felt everything Joseph did. They were twins, connected long before birth in a way that was difficult to put into words. And now, watching her brother battle this invisible foe—a foe that manifested itself in such a gruesome sight… It was a good thing Simeon had covered the salved leg with a loose cloth. She couldn't have managed all day with that angry, swollen limb glaring up at her.

Chapter Sixteen

How painful it is to be helpless. To have nothing to offer.
~ Simeon

Time passed in a blur as Emma alternated between caring for Joseph's physical needs and attempting to stir him mentally. She talked to him, chattering on about anything—and sometimes nothing. She read from Scripture, picking up where she'd last studied in the book of Psalms. Some of David's cries hit a little too close to home, but she kept on, even as tears leaked down her face.

It was at one of those moments that Simeon eased onto the ground beside her. He'd been tinkering around the camp all day—grinding more garlic, refilling her water supply, appearing any moment she had a need.

But this was the first time he'd positioned himself next to her, settling in as if he planned to stay a while.

She sniffed, but the effort did little to stop the moisture seeping from her eyes and nose. She dabbed at them with her sleeve, then cleared her throat and sniffed again. No matter if she looked a mess. The more important concern lay before them.

"Does he seem any better?" The rumble of Simeon's steady voice settled in her chest, undergirding her feeble emotional state.

"No change that I can tell." She gazed at the Bible in her lap. "I thought maybe I could boost his spirits." Or at the very least, find an essence of peace in God's promises.

It had been impossible to focus on the words with all the *what if*'s clamoring through her mind. What if the fever rose higher? What if it affected his eyesight, blinding him? What if the garlic wasn't enough to fight the infection? Would they have to amputate the leg to save the rest of him? Could Simeon do such a thing? Would it be best if he rode back to find the Indian squaw? Was there anything she could do at this point?

But amidst all the questions, there was one she refused to consider. There was no need to even think it. God wouldn't take her brother from her. Not Joseph. Her loving, faithful Father would grant this mercy. *Please, Lord.* She couldn't let her mind imagine otherwise.

"Do you ever wonder if God can see us out here? So far from civilization." Simeon's words took a moment to push through her thoughts.

She looked at him to make sure she'd heard right. His brow knit, and his eyes narrowed as he stared at Joseph. Almost as if he weren't aware he'd spoken aloud. She played his words through her mind again. *Do you ever wonder if God can see you out here?* He'd not said *Do you wonder if there is a God* or *if God cares.*

Give me the right words, Lord. She paused to gather her

thoughts. "There are times I think I should wonder. Especially moments like these." She motioned toward Joseph's chest, rising in shallow, rasping breaths. The sight lodged a familiar lump in her throat. "There are times I want to blame God for everything that goes wrong."

She tried to swallow past the lump. "But I can't." How could she convey the certainty in her soul? "I know beyond any doubt that God has me in his hand. Has us." She motioned to Simeon and Joseph. "He's proven it. He's been there in my darkest days." And there had been some very dark days. The pain of them pricked her eyes even now.

She pressed her lips together and stared at her clasped hands. What else could she say? God's love was a truth her heart knew. A fact written on her soul. It was hard to put such certainty into words.

"I came out here to hide from Him," Simeon said. "To find myself. To stand on my own after my family was gone." Simeon's voice strained, a roughness dragging it low.

Emma held her breath, praying he'd go on. And praying for the right words to answer. But nothing pressed itself in her mind.

"I think the only thing I accomplished was to lose myself."

She looked up then, turning to face his profile as certainty filled her chest. "Even when we are lost, we aren't lost from God." The thought left her mouth even before her mind formed it.

He turned to meet her gaze, his eyes probing. Absorbing, maybe? Could he accept the idea that God loved him? That the Father would pursue him anywhere just to show him that love?

She touched his arm, resting her hand on the thick leather of his coat. "God loves you, Simeon. He'll never stop trying to show you. All you have to do is accept His never-ending love."

He dropped his gaze. The tendons in his throat worked, the Adam's apple bobbing.

Would he respond? Or had she pressed too hard? She didn't regret her words. They'd been God's message to him. Gooseflesh pricked her arms as she thought of it.

Joseph stirred, pulling both of their attentions to his face. His eyes pinched in a grimace, and his head rolled from side to side. A tiny moan slipped from his parched lips.

Emma scooted closer and stroked his hair, then adjusted the wet cloth on his forehead. "Sshh. Here, take another sip of water." She raised a spoonful of the garlic liquid to his lips.

They parted slightly, allowing the moisture to drain into his mouth.

She filled the spoon again. "Simeon, is there any bear fat left? Or something else that would help his lips? They hurt me just looking at how chapped they are."

The rustle of leather sounded behind her as Simeon rose to his feet. "I'll get it."

The rest of the evening passed quietly, Simeon slipping in and out of camp as he cared for the animals and restocked their water and wood supplies for the night. But Emma couldn't bring herself to leave Joseph, even though he never awoke, only occasionally stirred.

His fever burned so hot. Fear had taken hold in her chest, but she knew the Lord heard every one of her frequent litanies. He *had* to protect Joseph. God would make him well again. She only had to believe it and do her part to assist.

At one point, Simeon brought her a plate of Johnnycakes. She tried for a thankful smile, but her weary muscles didn't obey well. After two bites, she set the dish aside. Her stomach didn't submit much better than her face had.

When darkness had shrouded their camp for several hours, Simeon finally settled onto his bedroll, propping himself up against a tree. He gripped his hands around his knees and stared into the fire. This was the same position he'd held so many other times when she would awaken in the night. Now that she knew his story better, she could imagine the pain that lingered over him during his sleepless hours of darkness.

Maybe this night would be different though. *Lord, let him dwell on my words from earlier. Let him feel Your love.*

She was too weary to pray any longer, too tired to think. Good thing the Father knew her heart. With her pallet of blankets and furs stretched beside Joseph, she sank into the softness and allowed her eyes to drift closed.

Simeon's mind whirled as he stared into the fire. *Even*

when we are lost, we're not lost from God. How could Emma have such faith, such unwavering belief in God's love?

Of course, God couldn't help but love her. She always made the best choice for those around her. God had no reason to turn away from her.

But his own past revealed a very different image. God had been perfectly justified in washing His holy hands of Simeon Grant. The Almighty had placed a beautiful family in his charge, and he'd destroyed each perfect piece in less than a week. His recklessness brought the death of his wife, and his grief cost him his children. God had every right to strike him from notice.

Even when we're lost, we're not lost from God.

He pressed his eyes shut to stop the haunting words, but they only rang louder in his mind. He didn't want God to see him. Couldn't bear the scorn. The disappointment.

He surged to his feet and strode into the darkness outside of the camp. Maybe a dunking in the creek could rid him of these thoughts.

Emma woke with a crick in her neck. Her shoulder throbbed where she'd lain all night with nothing to cushion her head, and pain shot through her back as she tried to push herself upright. Her left leg tingled. The angle of her hip pressing into the unforgiving ground must have put the limb to sleep.

A bird twittered in the woods as she blinked and

looked around in the morning mist. Her eyes fell on Joseph, sleeping beside her, and memory flooded in. She scrambled to a sitting position and scooted closer to her brother.

She brushed his forehead. Still fiery. The cloths had slipped from where she'd placed them and were now dry and stiff to the touch. She needed to pack them with snow again to cool him.

"How are you, Joey?" The words sounded so loud in the stillness.

He moaned, his shallow breaths growing loud in her ears. His eyelids flickered but didn't lift.

"Here, have another drink of water." She grabbed the cup from where she'd placed it near the fire and spooned swallows into his mouth as he drank. Still, his eyes never opened.

She scanned his body. They needed to check the wound, maybe wash it and apply a new dose of the garlic salve. Where had Simeon put the extra?

Glancing around the camp, she searched for the man. His bed still lay as it had last night. The brown bearskin stretched neatly over the blankets underneath. Normally, he packed his bedroll when he first rose each morning. Although, maybe he'd left it out today since he knew they wouldn't be leaving. It was like Simeon to straighten the covers when he rose.

Pushing up from the ground, she eased herself to her feet. The muscles in her back complained, but she pressed her hands to them and stretched upward until their grumbling lessened. A new ache made itself felt then, and she headed toward the trees in the direction of the boulder she'd been using as a privy.

After settling that need, she circled through the woods to where Simeon had tied the horses. He was probably feeding them.

But only the four horses stood in the rope corral he'd fastened. Pet and Paint rested with their noses almost touching, eyes closed and each of their left rear hooves cocked. Those two probably breathed at the same time, too. Her mare and Joseph's gelding stood a little distance away, taking advantage of the warm patches of sun starting to peek through the gaps in the pine branches overhead. The ground in the little pen had been churned into a muddy mess, dark where the horses pawed through the snow to find grass underneath.

But where was Simeon?

She followed the trail of hard-packed snow back to their campsite, but the man hadn't returned. Maybe he'd gone out to snare a grouse for breakfast. Or catch some whitefish from the creek further down the mountain. Fried fish was always a nice change from bear meat.

Kneeling beside Joseph again, she refreshed the packs of snow, then drizzled more of the garlic mixture in his mouth. She glanced at his leg. Her queasy stomach preferred for Simeon to manage that part, but he wasn't here, and Joseph's needs shouldn't wait.

She found the salve in a cup by the pot of clean water, then sank to her knees beside Joseph's leg. *Father, let it be better. Please.*

She gripped the blanket with her fingertips, eased it off, and peered underneath. Her stomach churned at the sight. The brown mush of the ointment only served to make the red, swollen leg more revolting. The smell didn't help either.

She tried to peer through the garlic paste to see how the bite marks were healing, but bile rose into her throat, and she had to turn away. She pressed her eyes shut and breathed in deep gulps of clean, mountain air. But the image of the leg was seared in her mind. Her eyes stung with tears, and she squeezed them tighter.

Joseph wasn't getting any better. The leg looked awful. His fever hadn't lessened. Nothing she was doing seemed to help him. Not a thing. Hot tears broke through her barrier, burning and itching as they rolled down her face. She sank back on her haunches and covered her eyes with the heels of her hands.

She was so tired of this. Tired of the fear. Tired of never knowing what was really happening.

Father, where are You? Why aren't You healing my brother? She'd tried so hard to trust. Tried to rest in God's peace, tried to believe He would take care of them. But He wasn't. How could Joseph be lying here burning with fever, his leg so infected he was fighting for his life?

Her chest shook with the sobs as she finally gave in to tears.

It felt like hours passed as she cried, pouring out her heart to the Father. Little by little, peace crept into her soul, soothing her fears like a balm. Amazing how God could use even tears to comfort.

With renewed strength and one of the clean cloths she'd brought to doctor Joseph's leg, she dried her face. She could do this.

While holding her breath, she carefully wiped the old garlic ointment off the angry skin. Her stomach roiled, and she had to turn away again to clear her senses of the smell and the sight. She'd not been ill since early in the pregnancy, but this task was enough to make any person cast up their accounts.

When her head cleared some, she focused on the leg again. Was her memory faulty, or had the swelling grown worse? Especially where the teeth had dug into the flesh, it bubbled in red welts. Was the garlic impotent? Or the infection so strong it required a fiercer treatment?

God, what do I do?

She looked around the clearing again. If only Simeon would reappear. He'd know what should be done. Where was he?

The only thing she could do was apply a fresh coat of the garlic mixture. Mixed with a steady dose of prayer, surely it would help. She swallowed down the bitter taste in her mouth. She couldn't think about what would happen if it didn't.

Chapter Seventeen

Who was it who said, "Lord, I believe. Help my unbelief."
~ Emma's Journal

Emma watched the sun rise high in the blue sky, then crest and begin its descent. Yet still Simeon didn't return.

Joseph had begun to mumble in his feverish state, rolling his head and even jerking his good arm at times. She soothed and sang and soaked him with snow and icy cloths, but nothing seemed to help.

She'd long since stopped caring whether she cried or not. She would do anything—*anything*—to bring Joseph back from this stupor.

"I don't know what to do, Joey." A sob caught in her throat as she stroked his whiskery cheek. "I don't know how to help you. I don't know where Simeon is. I just don't know anything." She bent low to lay her head on his chest, but the bulk of the baby in front of her wouldn't let her lean that far. So she hung there, her head lulling, her shoulders limp. Fear and despair warred inside her.

"I'm here." A hand rested on her back, a deep voice

crooning in her ear.

She jerked upright and stared into the strong features of Simeon Grant. Tears pooled in her eyes again, blurring his image. "Where have you been?"

His arms closed around her, encircling her with his strength and warmth. She clutched the edges of his coat, sobs jerking her body as she pressed into his chest. "He's not getting better." She blubbered the words in between shudders. "I didn't know where you went."

He held her tightly, rocking side to side as his fingers stroked her back. "I'm sorry. I didn't mean to leave you so long."

She tried to stop crying all over him, but her ragged nerves wouldn't let the tears slow. At last, finally, they eased, and she inhaled a shaky breath. His heartbeat pulsed strong under her ear. Everything about this man was strong.

And he'd come back. God knew she would need his strength to make it through this ordeal. But how much more would she need to endure? The thought forced a new leak in her dam, and more tears seeped out. Her Father wouldn't take Joseph. He couldn't. Not her special brother who'd given up his own plans to carry her to safety. Joseph. Always her staunch defender. Her best friend. Selfless to the end.

But it couldn't be the end.

"Shh…" Simeon's fingers stroked the damp hair away from her face. "We're going to work it out."

She shuddered, gulping in air to stop the sobs in her chest. "I'm…sorry."

"It's all right." He pressed a kiss to her forehead.

She straightened, wiping at her eyes and nose. But when she tried to pull away, he kept an arm around her waist. What a sight she must look, a red, swollen face and mussed hair. "So where did you go?"

He thumbed a stray tear from her cheek. "I went looking for grape root. I've seen it grow in the valleys sometimes, and it helps clear the blood. I finally found some, then I saw smoke in the distance."

She met his gaze, her heart picking up speed. "You mean…?"

He nodded. "An old trapper in a tiny cabin. He didn't have much, but gave me some cayenne peppers. That'll do Joseph more good than anything."

A surge of hope swept through her. "Where are they? What do we do?"

Simeon kept an eye on Emma as he took in Joseph's condition. The man was worsening. If the grape root and pepper didn't help, they stood a very real chance of losing him.

The weight squeezing Simeon's chest pressed even harder. He should have prevented this. He wasn't even sure when the man had been bitten, but he'd seen him looking puny those last few days. He should have known better than to assume it was only the elevation and lingering pain from the broken arm. Would he ever make the right decisions?

While Emma steeped the root to make tea, he ground the dried pepper and made a paste of part of it, same as he'd done with the garlic.

He peeled back the blanket covering the leg and scrutinized the swollen limb.

"I applied fresh salve this morning, but I didn't know what else to do."

He met her red-rimmed eyes over her brother's still form. "You did well."

Leaning closer, he studied the teeth marks. Four wide gashes and two smaller ones. They'd sealed over, locking the poison in pockets that protruded higher than the rest of the inflammation. He needed to open them up and let out the infection.

His gaze flicked to Emma, who watched him with wide, blood-shot eyes. This would be painful, for both of them. Joseph might not feel it in his semiconscious state. Or, the pain could be enough to draw him to consciousness in a hurry.

He didn't want Emma here if that were the case. Watching her brother endure that much agony would be more than she should have to handle.

He sat back on his haunches. "Why don't you go down to the creek and get some fresh water. I'll stay with him for a while."

Her gaze grew wary. "I'll stay with him while you get the water."

A memory slipped into his mind. A time when her

face held much the same look it did now. That other time she'd also stubbornly refused to leave while he'd set Joseph's arm.

He locked gazes with her. "Trust me, Emma."

But she shook her head vehemently. "I need you to tell me what you're doing. Don't you see? I need to know." Her voice rose in pitch, and she brushed a lock of hair out of her face. His eyes caught the motion…and something else. Her hand trembled.

But she kept talking, her tone stronger with each word. "You disappear into the woods for hours and hours. I don't know where you've gone or if you're ever coming back. Now you're trying to run me off so you can do something to my brother. I *need* you to tell me what." The stark fear in her gaze, the earnestness begging in her plea—they flayed him.

His throat constricted. He really hadn't meant to be gone so long. Certainly hadn't meant to add to her worries. He opened his mouth to apologize, but she straightened. Her hands fisted at her sides, and she inhaled a breath as if to release another round of emotions. He held his tongue. It would be good for her to get it out.

"All my life, men have been skulking around, planning secrets behind closed doors. I'm done with it." She threw her fists away from her body and her chin jutted high, giving a fierce look to her red-rimmed eyes. They flashed in defiance, but he held her gaze. Waiting.

After a moment, her chin dipped. Those amber eyes lost their fire and narrowed. Now she was ready to hear him.

He swallowed. This was his chance to get it right. "I shouldn't have left this clearing without telling you where I was going and why." His focus slipped to Joseph's prone body. The abscessed gashes. "The poison is building up inside the tooth marks. I need to open the wounds so they can drain." He raised his gaze to meet hers. "If he's awake, it'll be hard on him. Either way it won't be a pretty sight. I thought to spare you that."

Her eyes shimmered like pools of water, clear all the way to their amber depths.

He exhaled a breath. "Stay if you want. I have no secrets from you."

She held his gaze, drawing him in. Piercing through all his barriers, reading his thoughts and intentions. This woman had the power to open him up like no one ever had.

Did she glimpse his sincerity? Did she see how much he cared? The thought caught him short, and he flinched. An automatic motion to shield his soul before she found what he wasn't even sure was there. *Did* he care for this woman? The way he'd sworn to never care again?

Cautiously, he met her gaze once more, guarding himself.

Her look had softened. A sad kind of half-smile touched her lips. "Thank you." The words were little more than a whisper, but she spoke as though they came from a deep place.

Simeon inhaled a breath, his chest shuddering a bit as he looked away. Something strong had passed between them. He wasn't quite sure what, but his mind seemed slow to recover. He blinked, and looked again at Joseph. "I'd best get to it then."

"I'll stay and help."

He didn't look at her, only nodded and stood to put more wood on the fire. This wasn't going to be easy.

While water heated to a boil in the pan, he sharpened the edge of his knife, then dipped it in the boiling water until the blade came away glistening and hot enough to scorch. "Do you have an extra cloth we can wipe away the infection with?"

"Here." Emma sat by her brother's side, holding out a rag. "What should I do?"

"Just be there if I need you." With knife in hand, he made his way around Joseph's feet and settled beside Emma. The mauled leg glared up at him.

It really was in terrible shape, red creeping all the way into the man's thigh. Even if they opened the wounds, the pepper, garlic, and grape root all working together may not be enough to fight this infection.

The leg probably needed to be amputated. But Simeon wasn't a doctor. If he tried to cut off the limb, he'd kill the man for sure. And that just might be the worst possible way to die. No, amputation wasn't an option. He swallowed down a shudder.

"Do you want me to make the incisions?"

He sent a glance toward Emma. Was she serious? Those wide eyes looking up at him sure looked earnest. She had so much more pluck than he'd imagined those first days when the pair showed up at his cabin.

An urge slipped through him to lean over and plant a kiss on her full lips. He almost did it, too, but caught hold of himself just in time. Now wasn't the place for affection. In fact, there wasn't a place for affection. He had to put some space between them.

He focused on the leg again. "I'll do it." But he held his breath as he touched the inflamed skin with the point of his knife.

Everything inside Emma wanted to look away. Squeeze her eyes shut and clamp her hands over her ears. But she forced herself to watch as Simeon's knife sliced through her brother's skin.

Joseph gasped a strangled cry, and she whirled to face him. His eyes had opened wide for the first time in days, and he struggled to sit up.

"Hold him still." Simeon ground out the words as he gripped Joseph's squirming ankle.

She pressed down on her brother's shoulders. He was so weak it took almost no effort to return him to the ground. "Shh. This will help, Joey. Lie still and it'll be over soon." *God, help Simeon hurry.*

Keeping one hand on her brother's shoulder, she used the other to stroke his face, the skin almost too hot to touch. His eyes had drifted closed again, and his swollen, chapped lips moved as if he were praying. He released another strangled sob from deep in his throat.

Please, Lord. Take away his pain. Heal my brother. Her heart sent up a steady stream of prayers as she tried her best to soothe. Every muscle in his face was taut. Pinched.

Then, in a blink, everything went slack. His lips stopped moving except for a slight fanning as air drew in and out. He must have lost consciousness.

She glanced at Simeon. His mouth was pressed tight, his eyes focused on the knife in his hands. She followed his gaze.

Blood and some kind of thick, brown substance oozed from six cuts in Joseph's calf. Simeon had turned the blade over and used the blunt part to scrape more of the pus out of the wounds. She grabbed the extra bandage and held it ready to wipe the stuff away when Simeon was done.

He raised his hands to allow her access, and she stopped breathing as she moved the cloth over the angry skin. Her stomach churned, but she did her best not to think about it. Now was not the time to grow squeamish.

Simeon went back to work on the cuts, ridding Joseph's body of the poison. Finally, he sat back on his heels, and she wiped the leg clean again.

He held his hands and the knife blade in front of him, both covered in blood and other pungent substances. "Clean him off as well as you can, then I'll put the pepper salve on him. Let's sprinkle some in his mouth, too. The sooner it gets in his bloodstream, the faster it will cleanse him."

"What about the other root?"

"We can make a poultice to put on top of the pepper."

She could feel his gaze on her as she wiped Joseph's leg. Simeon had been remarkable through the operation, doing what she wouldn't have been able to.

As he rose to his feet, she turned her focus to Joseph's face. He was so pale, almost as white as the snow she'd packed in the cloths on his head.

And he was so still. Only the shallow rise of his chest and the slight parting of his lips proved he was still alive. Her eyes burned, and she cupped a hand around her brother's scruffy cheek. With her thumb, she stroked the skin under his eyes. "It's going to be all right, Joey." The words were whispered from her heart. "You're going to get better." Her voice broke on a sob as tears slipped from her eyes in steady succession. She couldn't lose him. Her twin. Her other half. An ache throbbed in her chest. Her whole body ached, but nothing compared to the way her brother must hurt.

Strong hands closed over her shoulders. Simeon dropped to his knees beside her and wrapped her in his strength. She sank against his chest, and he pulled her closer, resting his chin on her head so she was covered on all sides. Cradled. Protected.

She sniffed, trying to squelch the tears that flowed freely. But the relief of his arms, the haven they offered, sapped the rest of her waning control. She didn't have the strength to fight.

Giving in to the sobs, she turned to press her face into Simeon's chest.

Chapter Eighteen

My heart is splayed.
~ Simeon

Simeon held Emma close, tucking her shuddering body against his. If only he could take her pain away, make her brother whole again, and clear every tear from her pretty eyes. Everything in him wanted to make things better for her. But he'd done what he could by getting the herbs for her brother. The pepper and grape root poultices were in place. Now they could only wait and see if it would be enough.

He pressed his eyes shut, his chin tucked in Emma's hair. *God, I don't ask it for myself, but for Emma…and Joseph. Make him better. Please.*

If anyone deserved an answered prayer, it was this woman. She'd persevered through so much these last few years, and he had a feeling she didn't break down like this often. Even while he'd worked on Joseph's leg, she'd been remarkable. Soothing her brother, anticipating every need either of them had. She'd lost some color in her cheeks but hadn't swooned or cast up her accounts or even squirmed.

She rested against him quietly now, deep breaths raising her shoulders in a steady rhythm. His thumb stroked her back where his hands rested. She could sit there as long as she liked, taking in what little solace he could offer. It seemed the only thing he could do for her.

After a few moments, he leaned back a tiny bit to get a glimpse of her face. Those beautiful brown eyelashes brushed her cheeks, and her mouth parted in steady breathing. Had she fallen asleep? He leaned sideways to get a better view.

So perfect. Every one of her features. Those long lashes, the even proportions of her forehead and nose, her strong cheekbones, and that chin that jutted every time her stubborn streak flared.

His hand brushed her jaw, still damp from her tears. She didn't stir, though. Poor thing must be exhausted. He reached for an extra blanket lying beside Joseph, and wrapped it around her shoulders.

For the longest time he held her. His weary body ached, every muscle protesting from his long, sleepless night and the tension of working over Joseph. But he couldn't bring himself to move. He didn't want to wake her.

Holding this woman felt too good. Such a feeling of rightness sank deep in his chest, he almost pulled her closer. He'd not been this connected to a woman since Nora. He flinched, waiting for the familiar stab of guilt, the pain that always flowed at Nora's memory. And even more so this time, because he was holding another woman. But the ache barely pressed. Instead of a fierce wave, it drifted in more like a sigh.

He closed his eyes, envisioning Nora in heaven, where she was surely looking down on him. A picture formed in his mind—Nora watching them, her expression so peaceful—and part of the calm settled over him, too. What would she think of Emma? Squeezing his eyes tighter, he pushed the idea away. He couldn't think of that. Not yet.

He forced his eyes open, though a grainy sensation pulled at them. He was exhausted. Every part of him. Glancing around, he spotted a wide pine tree a couple feet behind them. Holding Emma steady in his grasp, he eased them backward to lean against the trunk. It took his weight as he sank against it, and he wrapped the blanket tighter around them both.

There, with Emma cradled against his shoulder, he allowed himself to succumb to sleep.

Emma forced her eyes open against the softness that drew her. Her body begged to stay in the warm peaceful place, but her mind tugged her from it. There was something she needed to do.

She forced her eyelids open and stared into the darkness. Why had she awakened in the middle of the night? And what had it been that called her? She tried to lift herself upright, but something locked her in place. She reached to free herself, her fingers closing over warm flesh.

A hand.

In a rush, memory flooded through her. Joseph. She struggled to sit up again, then realized what held her still. She was wrapped in Simeon's arms. He lay reclined against a tree, and she'd been nestled against the crook of his shoulder. Heat flamed into her face, and she glanced up to see if she'd awakened him. His eyes were shut, and his chest rose in steady breathing. Thank heavens. She wasn't quite ready to face the fact she'd been asleep in this man's arms.

Carefully, she extricated herself from his arms and crawled to Joseph. It was hard to see in the darkness, so she pressed a palm to her brother's forehead. Still warm, but not quite the searing heat like earlier.

A tiny seedling of hope formed in her chest.

She placed her other hand over his chest and focused on the rise and fall of it. Steady, and maybe stronger than before. Was it only wishful thinking? Not enough moon lit the sky to see whether his coloring had darkened any, but he surely needed water. She'd slept so long. Moving quietly, she pushed to her feet and gathered the garlic mixture.

Joseph didn't seem to awaken, but he swallowed some of the liquid she dribbled into his mouth. His breathing was definitely stronger than the faint rasp he'd been making earlier.

What else should she do for him? He needed food to strengthen his body, but he wasn't in any condition to chew. Earlier, Simeon had sprinkled some of the powdered pepper in his mouth to help work it into his blood stream. She could do that again.

When she'd poured a goodly amount through his parted lips, Joseph's eyes still hadn't opened, but his mouth and throat worked in a swallow. Wonderful. She reached for the garlic water, and he downed several spoonfuls.

Thank you, Lord.

She kept at it until Joseph stopped responding, but she'd managed to get much more water in his mouth than she had in previous attempts. Maybe he was turning the corner.

Her gaze wandered to Simeon, who was propped against a tree several feet away, head lolled back, shoulders slumped, and chest rising in steady breaths. He didn't snore, and she wasn't sure if that surprised her or not. Had she ever seen him sleep? She couldn't recall a single time.

Now, as the faint moonlight fell across his face, shadows accented the tired lines around his eyes and jaw. He looked as though he carried the weight of one of these mountains on his shoulders, and now he'd fallen under it. A burden pressed in her chest. The load he carried was much heavier than he was ever meant to bear. If only he could see that.

She eased to her feet and grabbed Simeon's blankets and a fur from his pallet, then crept toward the man. Making as little noise as possible, she spread the pelt on the ground beside him. Any moment, he would awaken. This mountaineer slept with one eye open. It was a wonder he hadn't stirred.

But his steady breathing continued. Finally, she gripped his upper arms and eased him sideways onto the pallet she'd set. He moved where she placed him, toppling a bit like a falling stump. His breathing stopped, but his eyelids didn't flicker open. He just lay in the position she'd planted him.

Without breathing herself, she spread both of his worn quilts over him, then stepped back to watch. Gradually, his chest rose and fell again. Could he have possibly slept through the maneuver? He must be beyond tired.

The urge to lean down and plant a kiss on his temple rose strong in her chest. The only thing that stopped her was the effort it would take to bend so low with her expanded midsection. Especially the getting back up part.

Bless him, Lord.

With the prayer in her heart, she turned to ready her own pallet beside Joseph. She would be close if he needed anything. Anything at all.

Simeon opened his eyes, blinking away the haze from his vision. The effort did little to clear his mind. He pushed upright under his blankets and scanned the area around him.

There lay Joseph, stretched out on the ground and breathing deeply. His coloring looked a little stronger in the early dawn light. On the other side of the man, Emma lay curled on her side, eyes resting in peaceful slumber. It stirred something in his chest, but he looked away before his body had time to react.

The dream he'd had still lingered too strongly in his mind. It had been…so real. He couldn't quite shake its effect. Pushing to his feet, he scrubbed a hand down his face and looked around the campsite again. He needed to get out of here. Stretch his legs and clear his mind.

Turning toward the woods, he settled into a long stride. There was a spot a few minutes out where the trees opened up and he could look out at the mountains and the valley below. That kind of view always re-centered him.

After a quick stop along the way, he found the place he remembered. He settled down on one of the low, wide rocks and looked out over the snowy mountainsides. With the early breeze ruffling his hair, he let his mind wander back to the scenes that had played through his dreams all night.

Nora.

He'd not dreamed of her in months now, and seeing her image again had resurrected a powerful ache in his chest. In the first scene of the dream, it had been Christmastime at church, and the congregation had all gathered outside with candles. They stood in a circle and sang Christmas hymns, one of the few truly happy times he could remember from his childhood. Yet, in the dream, Nora had stood in the circle opposite him, younger than she'd ever been when he knew her. Her face shimmered in the light of her candle. Even while he and all the others lifted their voices in song, she spoke words that echoed in his mind louder than the rest. "I want you to be happy, Simeon, as I am." Then she'd joined the song, voice mingling with the others as pure joy lit her face.

He pressed his eyes shut until he could see the image again. She'd been so beautiful, even in that younger version. Then the picture morphed into another scene from the dream. He'd been with her by the lake at her parents' farm, under the oak that sprawled wide. One of their favorite spots. He'd stolen more than one kiss behind the shelter of that trunk. In the dream, he sat with the tree at his back, guitar in hand, strumming and singing. He couldn't tell what song he sang, but she watched him with her wide blue eyes. She spoke, her words clear despite the fact that his music never ceased. "I want you to be happy, Simeon, as I am." Then she joined her alto voice with his in the song.

The dream had changed a final time, and he'd stood in front of his tiny little cabin. Alone. As he'd stared out into the woods, a voice had sounded. Nora's voice, even though he couldn't see her. She spoke those same haunting words. "I want you to be happy, Simeon, as I am."

Even now as he sat in the frigid morning air, her presence lingered. Hovered. Both in his chest and in the space around him. It had been so long since he felt her this close.

He dropped his forehead to his knees. "Nora." Maybe if he whispered her name enough, she wouldn't leave him. He gripped his upper arms, holding tight to her.

But this wasn't Nora. This sensation was only a feeling. Nora had left him long ago.

Loneliness, sharper than an arrow, pierced through his chest. He slumped forward. "I'm not happy, Nora." A sob caught in his throat, and he dropped his face between his knees, pain clawing at his insides. "I'm not happy." The words spilled out as a strangled whisper.

The agony of his loss split him wide, like a knife severing a fresh carcass. His chest hammered, throat constricting. No sobs could escape, no tears would come. Only raw torment.

A cold wind swept across the back of his neck, howling as it blew through the ravine. He and the wind were utterly alone in this desolate place. His bones ached.

Even when we're lost, we're not lost from God.

Emma's words crept back to him like a voice in his mind. For a moment, he raised his head and looked around. Nothing stared back at him except the snowy landscape. A brown bird skittered on a tree branch down the hill, then fluttered into the air again, disappearing into a tiny speck. As he watched the scene, it was as though all the color had been erased from it. Like the view was blurry, distant.

His mind turned over the words again. What else had Emma said? *God loves you. He'll never stop trying to show you.*

He looked up into the sky above, gray in the morning light. "If she's right, I don't see it." His voice sounded hollow, dull and lifeless, even in his own ears.

For a long moment he sat there, staring at a sky that didn't respond. Waiting for...what? A voice from heaven? His spirit craved something he couldn't define, yet his body was too exhausted to carry on any farther. He'd felt this same overwhelming exhaustion the night before when he'd held Emma in his arms.

Yet then, the exhaustion had mixed with such a strong contentment. A peace. A renewal, of sorts. Holding Emma had resurrected emotions he'd not felt in so long, his weary heart had forgotten they existed. At least he'd tried to make it forget.

Even when we're lost, we're not lost from God.

This time the words whispered to him, lacing around his heart in a peaceful blanket. Was it possible God wanted a connection with him? That He did care about a reclusive man who'd done his best to hide away? But if God cared...

The burn started in his chest and he raised his face again to that great gray expanse. "If You love so much, why would You take my family from me?"

A bird called in the distance, but Simeon's focus never wavered from above. He waited, but still…there was nothing.

He bowed his head, dropping it down to rest on his knees. What was he doing out here? Why was he dragging his heart through this pain again? When would he ever be free?

Guilt pressed hard on his shoulders. He would never be free. He shouldn't be. His question to God had been a mockery. The Almighty hadn't taken his family away. Simeon had lost them all on his own. If he'd been a better protector, a better husband and father, they would all three be with him now.

The burn of tears rose to his eyes, and he squeezed

them shut. But big, salty drops came anyway.

Deep, soul-cleansing tears. And with no one around to see or care, Simeon let them fall. It didn't matter anymore. Nothing mattered.

Chapter Nineteen

Has God brought me on this journey for such a time as this?
~ Emma's Journal

"Simeon?"

He jerked at the voice. Had it been in his mind? Between the dream and the turmoil of emotions in his chest, it was getting hard to tell what was reality.

A rustle sounded behind him. He spun toward the tree line.

Emma stood between the trunks like a mountain fairy in her fluttering blue cloak, tendrils of her brown hair flying in the wind. With the reflection of the morning sun glimmering off the snow, she almost looked like part of his dream. Radiant. Or maybe she *was* from the dream. Maybe, even now, she was a vision come to show him the way.

She stepped forward, drawing closer. Then she reached down and gripped his right hand. The contact made him blink. Definitely real. Firm, yet soft. And cold. Her skin felt like ice in this frosty morning. She should have donned gloves before walking so far from camp.

He pushed to his feet and stood before her, meeting her gaze. Her amber eyes searched his. For what, he didn't have the energy to decipher. He didn't even have the strength to shield himself this time, just let her see everything in him.

She studied him, then stepped forward and slipped herself under his arms, wrapping her arms tightly around him. Even though she turned at an angle, the baby still pressed between them. He closed his grip around them both, breathing deeply of her scent. Her touch. Her strength. And even...whether she meant it or not, the love in her embrace.

Her love? Or maybe it was even more than that. Could it be she was God's way of showing His own love?

Emma's love. God's love. The combination took root in his soul, and he clung to it. Just as he clung to her.

Even while Emma relished the feel of Simeon's arms so tight around her, the strength of his grasp almost took her breath. Literally.

At last, he eased his grip, and she drew in a breath to calm her burning lungs. Then she leaned back and searched his face. What had brought on the intensity of the hug? He'd looked so forlorn, so desolate sitting on this rock at the edge of the world. She'd almost stood quietly and watched, but something had prodded her to speak up. To come forward and wrap her arms around him.

Now, the look of peace that eased his features was different from any expression she'd ever seen on him. The pain lines at the corners of his eyes were gone. His face almost seemed to glow, accentuating the rugged strength of each feature.

Her chest ached with an intense longing. A love forbidden, because he'd be leaving them as soon as they reached Alberta. She couldn't let this man have her heart. She should step out of his arms, but she couldn't quite bring herself to.

"I'm glad you're here." The rich timbre of his voice flowed through her.

She couldn't help a tiny smile. "I came to tell you Joseph's much improved." Elation washed over her anew as she thought of Joey's expression when he'd awakened. "He's alert and eating. I stewed meat for him, and he's talking. I even propped him up for a few minutes." The little one inside her gave a flutter, as if the babe, too, celebrated Joey's recovery.

A grin broke over his features, lighting his blue eyes like the sun shining through colored glass. "That's good." For a moment, she thought he might pick her up at the waist and whirl her around, but instead, he ran his hands up and down her back. "What say we go check on him?" Smile lines crinkled at the corners of his eyes, setting her pulse into a faster thump.

Her own smile responded, and he loosened his hold on her waist. As they both turned to follow their tracks back to the campsite, Simeon's hand found hers, encasing her fingers like a soft leather glove. The perfect fit. Just as if he were made for her.

The peace that settled over their camp kept a persistent smile tugging at Emma's cheeks. Joseph was healing—awake and joking like the brother she loved. Simeon was practically a new man without the weight of sorrow and self-inflicted misery that usually draped him. She'd even glimpsed three—yes, three—full-fledged smiles from him just since they'd arrived back at the campsite a few hours before.

Her heart just might burst from the joy of it all.

After they'd eaten breakfast and she set the camp to rights, they tended Joey's wounds and saw to his other needs. Then she finally eased herself down against a tree with the Bible in her lap.

"It's about time you sat for a minute." Joseph's voice was still weak, but at least he was awake and talking. He gave her a weary smile.

"Simeon's gone to find new fodder for the horses, so I thought you might like me to read to you."

He nodded, but his drooping eyes most likely meant she'd be reading to herself soon. "Can you start in Romans?"

Her fingers had already found her familiar spot in Psalms, but she flipped farther through the pages to the New Testament. Starting with chapter one, she read Paul's instructions of faith to the Roman church. Joseph didn't fall asleep as quickly as she'd expected but lay with his eyes closed and brow furrowed. Every time she stopped to see if he'd finally drifted off, he cracked an eyelid and she went back to reading.

Halfway through chapter seven, Simeon stepped back into camp and strode to his pack. She kept reading but stole occasional glances to see what he was doing. He fumbled with his things for several minutes, looking over at them a couple times as he did so. His brow furrowed, similar to Joseph's. Was he…listening to the Scripture?

Her heart picked up speed, and she continued reading with new fervor. "For I am persuaded, that neither death, nor life, nor angels, nor principalities, nor powers, nor things present, nor things to come…" Her focus was drawn upward as Simeon came to sit on the other side of Joseph. She pulled her gaze back to the page. "…nor height, nor depth, nor any other creature, shall be able to separate us from the love of God, which is in Christ Jesus our Lord."

She inhaled a long breath, soaking in the words. She'd always loved the image of God's love like a wave of water, weaving around and over obstacles in its unstoppable pursuit to reach her.

Her gaze wandered up to Simeon. His head was cocked, and his face held something like perplexed wonder. She nibbled her lip against a smile. Gone was the mask that concealed his emotions. She liked the easy way she could read him now.

A soft snore broke the thought, and she glanced down at Joseph. His chest rose and fell in rhythm with the breath parting his lips. Finally.

She looked back to Simeon. "Shall I keep reading?"

He shrugged, but the way he leaned forward on his elbows gave proof of his interest. "Sure."

As she found her place at the start of chapter nine, she smiled, joy cloaking her like a hug.

Emma gripped the thin, rough trunk of the cedar beside her bedroll and used it to pull herself to her feet the next morning. Standing and sitting were so much effort these days, she'd moved her pallet of blankets closer to this sapling for assistance.

She crept over to Joseph, whose gentle snores proved he still slept. Color finally tinged his face again. A blessed miracle. Simeon's bedroll was empty, the blankets folded in a neat pile. No surprise there.

After grabbing the empty kettle, she headed down the trail toward her privy rock. She could fill the pitcher with clean snow for tea while she was out, then hopefully have a warm breakfast for Simeon when he returned from his morning wanderings. Johnnycakes would be nice, although they were getting low on cornmeal. How much farther until they reached Canada? She should ask Simeon so she would better know how to ration the remaining supplies.

After attending to morning ministrations, Emma perched on the boulder to repair her appearance. She'd not taken time to remove her hair pins and rebraid her hair last night, so she removed the pins now and held them in her teeth. The wooden tools hadn't fared so well on the journey, and she was down to only three. Maybe she should only do a braid today.

As her fingers combed through her thick, brown waves, the back of her neck tingled, almost as if someone were watching. She paused and glanced around, pivoting her bulky girth to see behind her. But there was no one.

The tingle must be due to the frigid morning air. She pulled her coat tighter around her neck, and finger-combed the other side of her hair, then gathered the tendrils on her left side and started a braid. This was the longest her hair had ever grown, almost down to her hips, and it was thick enough to make a ropy plait.

What would Simeon think of it? He'd probably never seen it hanging free, although he'd surely seen the long braid she usually wore when she slept. She reached into her coat pocket for the ribbon usually tucked there.

A hand closed over her mouth.

The shock of the contact caught her so off guard, she didn't move for a single heartbeat. Then terror sluiced through her as her mind caught up with the bitter flavor of the grubby paw cutting off her breath.

Another arm clamped around her waist, locking onto her wrist. She screamed, but the sound was blocked by the flesh in her mouth. A foul taste filled her senses and she fought back a gag.

The arm pressed tight over her belly, and she leaned

backward against the force. But a solid form behind her locked her in place.

Who had her? Not Simeon. Not Joseph. They'd never manhandle her.

Fear leapt through her chest as the rough hands jerked her backward, twisting her around so she landed in a heap, face down in the snow. Her nose and mouth were pressed into the icy powder, hard enough that she could barely draw breath.

Her arms were twisted behind her, and pain shot through both of her shoulders. Without her hands to bear part of her weight, her belly bore the brunt of it, and she drew her knees underneath to protect the baby.

Something rough was being wrapped around her wrists, and she jerked at her arms, trying to shift her head to scream. She wasn't more than a couple hundred feet from the camp. Surely Joseph or Simeon would hear her and come.

She turned her face enough to gasp a quick inhale, but before she could make a sound, a hard knee jabbed into her back, knocking the air from her lungs with a whoosh. A rough hand jerked her braid, pushing her face back into the snow. The knee didn't leave her back, and the fear pounding through her chest intensified.

No matter what, she had to protect the baby. She rounded her back as much as possible, gritting her teeth against the weight pressing on her spine.

The beast jerked her wrists first one way, then another, pulling the cord even tighter with a final yank.

Should she keep trying to fight? Or go along with his mandates and watch for a way to get free? So far, she was no match for the iron strength in his grip. And he had her at a strong disadvantage with her position face-down in the snow. On top of that, if she angered him, there was no telling how he would retaliate. And she had to protect the baby.

What could he want? Had she finally been found by a mercenary out to collect her reward?

He grabbed her braid again and yanked hard, pulling her face from the snow and stretching her neck unnaturally. She squealed, but a cloth settled in her mouth just as he released her hair. Actually, it was more like a pliable buckskin, thick with the taste of leather and grease. He yanked hard on it, tilting her head back so it was almost impossible to keep weight off her abdomen. *Lord, keep my baby safe.*

At last, he tugged a knot in the gag, stretching the side of her mouth but releasing the pull on her neck so her face dropped back into the snow. She struggled to inhale through her nose. Between the knee in her back and her face in the snow, not to mention the thin air and the effort from her struggles, her lungs burned. She focused on drawing in deep breaths.

With a jerk, she was suddenly hauled up out of the snow and pulled upright. Her feet scrambled to find purchase, finally planting themselves as a strong hand on her forearm steadied her. She blinked away the snow clotted in her lashes and strained to see her attacker.

The man stepped around to her front, and she caught her first glimpse. Heavy white furs encased him, and a long, black braid hung from inside his hood. Black eyes pierced from the shadows above his sharp cheekbones.

An Indian.

Chapter Twenty

It's a greater strength I carry now, yet I feel so helpless.
~ Simeon

Simeon stepped into the campsite and glanced at Emma's bed. Empty. The covers were pulled up with no wrinkles marring them. The tea kettle was missing from the spot where it had sat beside the fire that morning, so she must have gone to fill it with snow.

He used a piece of firewood to push the burned chunks of wood closer together, then laid two fresh logs on top. There was a nice bed of coals to cook breakfast over.

His gaze wandered around the place. Everything seemed to be set to rights. He could get started on breakfast, but he needed the snow Emma would bring back. His focus landed on Joseph, sleeping soundly. His color looked better than it had even the night before. The man's recovery was nothing short of a miracle.

The Bible lay next to Joseph, and Simeon's mind drifted back to the verses Emma had read the day before. About how nothing could ever separate us from God's love.

Each word had pierced the shell around his heart, working their way inside him. His fingers itched to thumb the pages and reread that passage. He stepped toward the book. Emma wouldn't mind if he read, surely.

Joseph's light snores paused when Simeon's fingers closed on the Bible, but he retreated to his own pallet, and the sounds from Joseph picked up again.

Settled on his furs, Simeon flipped through the book. Where had Emma been reading? It'd been so long since he'd picked up a Bible, but the passage had sounded like it came from the New Testament. Not the Gospels or Acts. He stopped in Romans and skimmed the pages.

He was deep in a passage about Abraham's faith, when Joseph stirred and pushed himself upright. Simeon raised his gaze from the book to take in the man. "You look a sight better this morning."

He scrubbed a hand over his face. "I feel a sight better. Tired of layin' on these rocks."

Simeon's mouth twitched at the tousled look Joseph presented, his hair spiking in all directions. He probably smelled rank, too, between his feverish sweat and the foul odor of both the infection and the garlic. "We're not so close to a creek, but I imagine we could heat water if you wanna get cleaned up after breakfast."

"That works." Joseph dipped his chin toward his body and wrinkled his nose.

Simeon bit back a chuckle at the expression.

Joseph pushed aside the rest of his blankets as if he planned to get up. "Reckon I'll go find a tree." He eased his sore leg from under the covers, his face scrunching in pain.

He didn't say anything, though, and Simeon let him make the effort on his own. It was probably time Joseph regain some of his strength, and his dignity, too.

Joseph worked to put on his shoes for a while, then pushed to his feet with only a soft groan. Quite a feat, all things considered. When Simeon had checked the leg the night before, it was still pretty red, although the swelling had lessened substantially. It would pain him for a few days, at least.

Joseph limped a couple dozen feet into the woods, then returned a minute or so later. "Where's Emma?"

Simeon looked up from the Bible. "I think she went to get water and do whatever else she does in the mornings." His gaze wandered the direction of the trail she usually took. "I would have thought she'd be back by now." A needle of concern threaded its way through his chest. "Maybe I should go check on her."

But as he thought about what that would entail, heat flamed into his face. The last thing he wanted to do was come upon Emma while she was attending to *personal* business.

Yet she'd been gone for a while now. And maybe longer than he knew. He'd been tending the horses, so he couldn't be sure when she'd first left the clearing. What if she was having trouble with the baby? The muscles through his back and shoulders clutched. Or she could have surprised an animal the way Joseph had with the wolverine.

He lurched to his feet. "I'm going to find her."

Emma's path was easy enough to follow. From the multitude of prints back and forth, it seemed she'd taken the same trail many times. The tracks ended at a boulder, and that was where her route became murky.

The trail seemed to travel behind the rock, but in front of the stone, footprints churned in a large patch of snow. He leaned over them, trying to make sense of the pattern. The snow was flattened in one area, like something had burrowed into it.

As his eyes picked out details, he honed in on one with sharp clarity. Moccasin prints.

A man's prints.

His gut clenched. Who had been here with her? Why? Other than the band of Apsaalooke, they'd not seen anyone else on the entire trip.

Except for the old trapper in the cabin he'd gotten the peppers from.

He'd worn moccasins, although most men seasoned in living out here probably did. Could he have kidnapped Emma? The man hadn't seemed dangerous, although maybe a little eccentric from living out in the wilds by himself for too long. Would that be enough to make him a threat?

He reined in his racing mind and scanned the landscape around him. He didn't know for sure she'd been kidnapped. Maybe she'd wandered farther for some reason.

There. A trail of prints leading away from the area.

He strode toward them, but his heart climbed into his throat at the story they told. One set of moccasin tracks leading toward the boulder. Two sets walking away from it.

The same moccasin prints traipsing behind Emma's smaller boot prints. Her feet seemed to drag in the knee-deep snow as if she were worn out. Or being pushed against her will.

Simeon's hand went to the knife at his waist. He didn't have a gun with him. Should he turn back for it? Or keep following the tracks? He couldn't bring himself to leave their trail.

Emma was in danger. She needed him. And if she hadn't gotten far, maybe he could catch them quickly.

He followed the tracks for a couple hundred feet until they ended in a patch of snow churned by hoof prints. Only one horse. And the animal left from the same direction it came.

He'd never catch up to them on foot. He had to turn back and arm himself properly. And tell Joseph.

"Let's go."

Simeon ignored Joseph's comment as he checked the supply of powder and bullets in his pouch, then opened the rifle's breach to make sure he had a shot loaded.

Joseph was struggling to stand as Simeon strode toward the horses. "I'm going. You're not up to it yet. I'll have her back in a couple hours." He hoped and prayed it would be that easy. *God, keep her safe*.

"I'm going with you." Joseph made it to his feet and limped toward the pack where his rifle was stowed.

Simeon halted. "You're not strong enough. Stay here and wait in case she comes back." The last thing he needed was this man slowing him down. Besides, Joseph was barely a day recovered from the brink of death.

Joseph gripped his rifle, raised it up, swung the barrel around, and pointed the business end at Simeon. "I'm going to get my sister." He ground out the words, his voice made rougher by the raspy remnants of the fever. Even though the gun wasn't cocked—and it quivered in Joseph's shaky hold—he'd made his point. His coloring had blanched a little from the ruddy hue that morning. But the determination in his eyes would carry him aways before his body gave out.

Simeon gave him a flat stare. "Pack some grub while I saddle the horses. I'll swing back to get you." Then he spun on his heel and jogged toward the rope corral.

He wasted no time saddling Pet and Joseph's gelding. Emma had started calling the horse Copper for its chestnut coloring. Maybe not original but easy enough to remember. His chest pulled tighter as urgency for the woman drove his movements.

When he arrived back at the campsite with the two horses in tow, Joseph stood ready with his saddle pack in one hand and the rifle in the other.

Getting the man on the horse was harder than Simeon had expected, though. At first, he held the gelding's head while Joseph tried to mount. Except it was his left leg that still ached from the infection, and the limb wasn't strong enough to bear his weight in the stirrup while Joseph tried to pull himself up. No matter how hard he gritted his teeth.

"Think you can mount on the off side?"

"I guess I'll have to." The frustration evident in Joseph's tone and the set of his shoulders was nothing compared to the fear clawing in Simeon's chest. They had to move out. Emma needed them.

It took quite a bit of effort, but Joseph finally hauled himself into the saddle on the gelding's right side. Simeon handed him the reins and vaulted onto his own mare. "Let's ride."

He kept the horses in a trot as they wove through the trees, following the path of churned snow back to where Emma had mounted the horse with her attacker. There was nothing unusual about the horse tracks they followed after that. Just an unshod mountain pony of medium build and steady gate. The prints could belong to the wooly bay mare he'd seen at the trapper's cabin, or could be one of the Indian ponies.

Or it could be a horse and man they'd never met before. Maybe a reward hunter had tracked Emma all the way up here. His blood pumped faster. There were men in this territory who specialized in such. Any one of them could have seen the wanted poster and come after the price on her head. Maybe they'd seen her in Fort Benton and followed her here. Or been hired by someone who'd known her in Texas. Would they try to take her 'dead or alive'? Had the stranger already killed her?

Oh, God. Protect her.

A muffled sound from Joseph grabbed his attention,

and he reined Pet down to a walk, then turned to better hear the man. "What's wrong?"

"Can we walk a while?" His face had paled considerably since they'd left camp, and he clutched the saddle horn with both hands. This trip was more than his weak body could handle.

Simeon's gaze wandered up to the darkening sky. Another storm was coming, but how much longer would it hold off? Joseph needed a rest or he wouldn't make it much farther. The horses would benefit from slowing, too. They were both breathing hard from the steep terrain combined with the thin air.

While the animals walked, Simeon's mind ran through possible scenarios. They were following pretty much the same trail they'd traveled a few days ago. Which meant the man who had Emma was likely someone who'd tracked them from farther south—a reward seeker or the Indians.

Neither scenario made him feel better. And the more he thought about it, the more he believed the kidnapper had to be someone after her for the bounty. The Indians had no cause to chase them and steal her away. If they'd planned harm, they would have done it when he'd first come upon the band in the cave. Or later, when he'd sought help for Emma's condition.

And if the kidnapper was a lone man accustomed to traveling in these mountains, he'd be able to move quickly. With this slow pace, he and Joseph would never catch up.

He chanced another glance back at Joseph. The man

looked like he'd cast up his accounts any moment. They had to find a spot where he could safely stay. Should Simeon send him back to their camp? Honestly, it didn't look like Joseph would maintain consciousness much farther. Simeon couldn't risk it, especially on horseback.

What other choices did they have? Soon, they'd reach the ledge they'd camped under a few nights back. There was still firewood there that Joseph could use to keep himself warm, assuming it hadn't been covered with snow. And he could keep some of the dried meat for food. Lord willing, Simeon would only be gone a few hours, maybe overnight.

Within a half hour, the rock overhang came into view. Simeon glanced back at his companion. Joseph hunkered low over his saddle, his head lolling with the rhythm of the horse, as though he didn't have the strength to hold it steady.

Simeon reined Pet in at the ledge, and Joseph's gelding stopped alongside them.

Joseph's head raised in a cursory glance. "What?" The word was fuzzy, as though cotton lined his tongue.

Simeon slid off his horse and moved to help Joseph dismount. "You'll stay here."

Joseph blinked and stared at their former camping spot. Almost as though he were struggling to place it.

Simeon stopped beside Joseph's leg. "Climb down."

Obediently, Joseph leaned forward and eased his right leg behind him to dismount. Simeon gripped under his arms and helped him land slowly on his good leg. Joseph kept a white-knuckled grip on the saddle as he tried to shift his weight onto the infected leg. He sucked in a loud breath.

"Let me take your weight." Simeon slipped himself under Joseph's left arm and helped the man hobble to the cave. Joseph must be bad indeed not to fight to continue the journey.

Once he had him settled on the ground, he set to work on the fire. A spark from his flint finally caught hold in the tender, flaming to life, then spreading toward the other kindling.

"My pack." Joseph's voice was breathy.

"I'll get it, and I'll divide up the food in my supplies. You have the peppers and herbs with you?"

Joseph nodded, but his eyes drifted closed as he leaned against the rock wall. "In the bag."

When Simeon had Copper settled and Joseph as comfortable as he could make him, Simeon mounted Pet again and surveyed the scene. "You have your rifle if you need to hunt."

"I'm fine. Go get Emma."

Simeon nodded, but conflict warred in his chest. Was he leaving Joseph here to die? The man was so weak and only had enough food to last a couple days. If Simeon didn't make it back, could Joseph survive on his own? Copper would need a new grazing spot, too, in the next day or so.

But Emma's straits were probably just as dire, if not more so. He didn't want to imagine what horrific actions she'd already endured. And he had to find her before snow came and covered her trail completely. Just when he was finally free to love her, he faced a real chance he might lose her.

His pulse picked up speed. Losing Emma wasn't an option. It was time to move on. Joseph would have to fend for himself.

Simeon reined his horse toward the trail, but as Mustang took up his place beside Pet, he stalled again. Should he leave the dog with Joseph? There wasn't much the animal could do besides alert him to danger. And that would be a more useful quality where Simeon headed. No, best for Mustang to go with him.

Simeon sent one last glance to Joseph. *Be with him, Lord.*

God was the only One who could care for all three of them at once.

Chapter Twenty-One

My heart has but one cry, Lord. Can You hear it?
~ Emma's Journal

Emma held herself stiff against the Indian riding behind her. They'd been on this homely, black pony for hours and hours, and the bony ridge of its back had long ago numbed her lower region.

Every muscle throbbed. More than she'd ever thought possible. And the ache in her stomach gnawed at the last few threads of her patience. The only thing that kept her from fighting against her captor was fear for the child within her.

What did the Indian have planned for her? Surely if he'd wanted to add her scalp to his coup, he would have killed her already. Did that mean he planned to make her his slave? What would he require of her? As her mind wandered through the possibilities, fear clawed in her chest like a wild animal. *God, don't let those things happen to me. Please!*

She forced herself to draw breath. She had to shift her mind to a better topic. *The Lord is my shepherd, I shall not want.* As she mentally recited the twenty-third Psalm, the scenery around them grew familiar.

There, just ahead, sat the cave opening where the Indian band had been camped during the storm. They must still be quartered there. Simeon had said this group acted less friendly than other Indians he'd met from their tribe. Why hadn't she put more weight behind that observation? And what did this group have against white people? Or maybe it wasn't the whites they disliked. Maybe it was something about her specifically that had drawn her kidnapper.

She pressed her eyes shut. She had to stop her thoughts from wandering there.

The Indian dismounted and pulled her off the horse. She barely caught her footing before he pushed her inside the cave.

Darkness and a smoky odor enclosed them, and another burst of panic pressed on her chest. She stumbled, but in the blackness, she couldn't find her balance.

The Indian gripped her wrist tighter and steered her forward, and finally a dim glow grew up ahead. They turned a corner, and the rush of hazy light almost blinded her. Smoke stung her eyes as she blinked to focus.

A cavern as large as Simeon's cabin had been opened before her. Two campfires split the middle, and at least a dozen Indians milled about the space. Some sat by the fires. Some stood. Some lay on blankets around the edge of the room.

She was steered past both fires all the way to the far end of the cavern. The brave spoke a slew of words as he stopped her in front of a thick-waisted squaw sitting cross-legged on a fur. He spun Emma and pressed down on her shoulder.

She scrambled to catch herself, but with her hands bound behind her, she barely had time to lean forward, trying to take some of the weight off her rump. She bit down hard on her gag as spears of pain shot up her back and down her legs.

Tears burned at her eyes, but she pressed them back. *Lord, please keep my baby safe.* It didn't matter what they did to her, as long as they didn't hurt the child within her. That was the truth of it, no matter how many times she had to remind herself.

The brave turned and walked away, and Emma forced herself to focus on her surroundings. The people sitting nearest the campfires seemed to be women. They wore long buckskin dresses decorated with beadwork or boning. The men around the perimeter of the room also wore buckskin with decorations, but their tunics seemed to be shorter, draped over leather pants of a sort. Every person in the room wore their hair in long braids. Most of the men appeared to have longer hair than the women. Their braids to the waist, and the hair at their foreheads was styled in a high wave.

She and Joseph had talked of traveling through Indian country to reach Canada, and she'd known there was danger. It had seemed minimal compared to the threat back in Texas. And in her wildest imaginings, she'd never pictured herself like this, sitting in a cave, bound and gagged, surrounded by a whole band of Indians.

Now that she'd adjusted to the smoky odor, a gamut of other smells permeated her senses. Body odor, grease, food. It all melded together until her nose fought to keep out the air. She breathed through her mouth, trying to filter the mess through the gag. This couldn't be healthy.

A voice sounded beside her, and Emma turned to look at the squaw beside her on the mat. Recognition slammed against her. This was the old woman who'd helped her with the bleeding.

Emotion warred in her chest. The old squaw had aided her once before. Maybe she could find a way to help Emma escape. But she'd just sat there while the brave brought her in and practically tossed her pregnant body on the pallet. Even now, the woman didn't seem concerned in the least about Emma's condition or well-being. Had the woman really helped before? Maybe she'd been only pretending to assist, but really scouting for the brave who would return to take her captive. Maybe even now, the woman was acting as a guard over her. Best to bide her time and see if the old squaw proved friend or foe.

The woman spoke again, and this time her head turned slightly so she could peer at Emma from the corner of her eye. The sounds coming from her mouth were certainly not English, and disappointment pressed in Emma's chest.

She shrugged her shoulders to show she didn't understand.

The woman's brows knit, and she turned toward a younger woman kneeling by the nearest fire. The old squaw spoke to the younger, who rose and walked to a stack of supplies.

She returned a moment later with a leather flask. Her fingers were cool against Emma's cheeks as she worked the gag out of her mouth. The muscles in Emma's jaw cheered at the release of the tight restriction, and she flexed her lips to bring feeling back into them.

The young squaw held the flask up to her. "Drink."

Emma met her dark gaze as the leather opening slipped into her mouth, and she tilted her head back. The blessed coolness of the water slid through her like honey soothing a sore throat. Her eyes sank shut, but too soon, the bliss ended.

She straightened as the woman pulled the flask away. Again their eyes met, and kindness glimmered in the plain face of the Indian. This one she might be able to trust.

And speak with. Sudden realization slammed over her. The woman had spoken an English word. "Do you understand me?" Emma searched her face for an answer.

A softening of the eyes. "I understand."

Emma flicked a glance to the dark cavern entrance where her captor had disappeared. "Do you know what will happen to me?"

If she hadn't been watching the younger woman's expression so closely, she would have missed her quick darted look at the old squaw. In fact, it was so quick, Emma wasn't sure it had happened at all.

But when her kind water-bearer pinched her lips shut, it made the way of things clear. The squaw beside her stood guard as surely as a palace sentry.

Then a grunt issued from the old squaw, and the young woman reached for the gag around Emma's neck and fit it back in place over her mouth. Then she turned and slipped away, fading into the smoky haze.

Within seconds, the tall brave who'd taken her captive strode forward.

Emma's chest seized at his imperious presence. The babe inside her gave a fierce kick under her rib cage, and she clamped her jaw against a flinch. She couldn't let this man see weakness, even if he hadn't been the one wholly responsible for causing the pain.

As the man neared, something glimmered in his right hand. A knife with a blade at least ten inches long. Did he plan to slice her through right there on the cave floor? Bound up the way she was and so heavy with child, she could hardly put up much of a fight if he wanted to take liberties with her.

But then a sliver of hope ran through her. Maybe he was coming to cut her bindings off.

He crouched beside her, one knee resting on the fur mat. His hands reached behind her head, and the hope spread wider through her. He was removing the gag.

His fingers tugged her braid, pulling harder than was necessary to separate it from the leather strip. This Indian was heavy-handed. Especially compared to the gentle fingers of the young woman who'd brought her water.

But something didn't feel right about the steady pull on her braid. As if the man ran his hand down the length of it. The crevice of hope in her chest began to close up again. Dread took its place.

Did he have an affinity for long hair on a woman? Hanging down the way she'd tied it just before he attacked, it reached to her waist.

She craned her eyes, trying to catch a glimpse of what he was doing back there. She caught a quick glitter of metal at the same time the tug on her hair pulled tight, then loosened with a quick release. Her head bobbed forward before she could catch herself.

The Indian sat back on his heels and held something up to the light.

She stared at it, but her mind wouldn't connect with what she saw. There, in the man's hands, hung a long braid of brown hair. At least fifteen inches, maybe closer to twenty.

Tears pricked her eyes, their burn almost more than she could forestall. She bit her lower lip hard to hold them back. He'd cut off her hair? Loose locks curled around her ears, brushing her jaw.

It was gone. All of it.

The long, beautiful strands she brushed diligently, morning and night. Sliced through by a savage's blade. She wanted to strike out. To snarl and kick and rage at this man who'd stolen her crowning glory.

A smile glimmered in his eyes as though he expected her to do all of those things.

The sight calmed her like fingers snuffing out a flame, and cold steel closed over her heart. She wouldn't give him the satisfaction.

A snowflake touched Simeon's nose, light and fluffy. The kind he'd loved to catch on his tongue as a child while he pulled his brothers to the sledding hill and his sisters made snow angels.

He'd loved snow as a child because it meant a small break from chores and a few happy moments with his siblings. He'd always made the youngest children ride with him on the sled. If he was to be held responsible for their protection, he wanted to be the one steering away from rocks and making sure toddlers landed in the softer piles of snow at the bottom of the hill.

But even then, he'd not been so good at protecting. Someone had always ended up with bruises or scrapes from briars hiding under the snow. One time he'd steered too near a tree and Noel, his sister sixth in line and the youngest girl, had pinched her arm between the trunk and the side of the sled. She'd cried all the way home, and Mama had given him extra chores for a week as punishment for not being more responsible.

If only that could have fixed him.

Now, he was on a desperate search to make up for his lack of foresight in protecting Emma. If the few flakes turned into heavy snowfall, it would cover her trail—his best chance to find her.

He pushed Pet faster, and Mustang dropped behind the horse as he struggled to keep up through the snow. The pace and the snow and the rocky trails were a challenge for both animals, but he couldn't let up. Emma needed him.

The snow grew heavier and started to fill the tracks. Simeon's gut tightened, but he couldn't push Pet any faster on the terrain. If she lost her footing and rolled down the mountainside, it would likely be the death of them both.

And if he were gone, who would rescue Emma? And Joseph, too, for that matter. In one fell swoop, all three of them could be wiped off the face of the earth. And no one would even know what happened, no one except the fiend who'd kidnapped Emma. Would there be anyone at all to miss them? An empty despair threatened to settle over him, but he pushed it away. God knew what was happening here. He had Emma and Joseph tucked tightly in His hands, Simeon and the horse and the dog, too.

So while Pet's pace felt impossibly slow, he sent up a steady litany of prayers. He even tried to recall that feeling he'd had when he'd sat on the rock, looking out over the valley, coming to terms with God's love. And what were those verses Emma had read about nothing separating him from God?

The mental exercises almost succeeded in distracting him from the disappearing tracks he followed. He was still an hour or so away from the cave where the Indians had camped, and the trail left by Emma's kidnapper was now almost undiscernible. It certainly seemed to follow the route they'd taken on their journey north, which would pass right by the cave.

But that didn't give him any insight into whether the kidnapper was a mercenary or an Indian. If a white man had been tracking them to secure Emma for the bounty, it made sense that he would go back the same way he'd come.

The only way Simeon could know for sure was to find the Indians and determine whether they had Emma. If they didn't, he'd press on and try to catch up with the real kidnapper. Although, he might have lost precious time by then. And with snow falling, the man could veer off the trail at any time. Simeon might spend the rest of his life hunting these mountains and never find them. This was the perfect country to hide in.

That's why he'd stayed out here these past few years. It had been his best place to lose himself.

But no more. He was on a search now to find a lot more than a bitter, reclusive mountain man. He had to find Emma.

Chapter Twenty-Two

Be Thou my guide.
~ Simeon

Simeon reined Pet to a stop as he recognized the landmarks close to the cave. The mare needed to blow anyway, her sides heaving from her struggle to take in air. Mustang looked up at him with a whine, head cocked. The dog had definitely picked up on Simeon's edginess, but he seemed uncertain of what to do about it.

Simeon wasn't completely sure himself. Should he ride forward slowly until he was within sight of the cave opening, in case he needed to make a quick retreat? Or leave the animals here and move forward on foot so he could sneak in without notice? If the Indians had kidnapped Emma, they likely had a guard posted. Without knowing where that man was, it would be hard to get close enough and not be seen.

Still, moving forward on foot was probably his best option to see what was happening around the cave without disturbing things.

He dismounted and tied Pet to a tree, then gathered

his rifle, pistol, and the pouch containing extra ammunition. He eyed Mustang. "Stay here." The dog didn't particularly like orders, but he knew those two words. He growled but seated himself next to the tree.

Simeon moved quietly through the snow, keeping every sense alert. It was impossible for him not to leave prints in the snow, but the large flakes still falling would cover them soon. He didn't see any motion through the trees, didn't hear any animal sounds that might be an Indian signal. Nothing.

Had the Indians not posted a sentry? Maybe a man stood guard inside the mouth of the cave. It would be too much to hope they'd have Emma outside.

No one stood outside the cave.

Simeon positioned himself behind a scruffy cedar and watched through the tiny gaps in the needles.

No movement except the faint grayish smoke that drifted up from the cave opening. The Indians must still be camped inside. Or someone else.

He held his position for a quarter hour. A half hour. There might have been a flicker of movement in the darkness of the interior, but that could have been smoke. He squinted and tried to relieve the ache in his temples from straining to see.

After a full hour had passed, Simeon's toes had finally stopped their steady wiggle inside his moccasins. Unfortunately, he couldn't feel them at all now. And his muscles throbbed from the constant tension. He had to do something else. He might be sitting out here waiting while the savages tormented her inside. His jaw locked tighter, and he pushed that thought away. *What do I do, Lord*?

Somehow, he had to get a look inside that cave. But if they did have Emma, and if there was a man guarding the cave front, Simeon would probably be shot down the minute he started across the clearing.

Was there another way in? His mind wandered back to the one time he'd been inside, a year or so ago. The cave started off as a dark tunnel that curved to the right. Then it opened into a big cavern. As best he could remember, there weren't any other entrances. He scanned the rock face of the mountain that rose up behind the dark opening. Should he do some scouting and make sure of that?

Assuming his memory was correct and the only entry point was that dark, yawning hole, what were his options? Perhaps he could draw out the guard somehow. No light flickered inside the entrance, so maybe once he got in, he'd be able to snug up next to the tunnel wall and stay out of sight.

But if he were discovered… Even if the Indians hadn't taken Emma captive, if they found a white man in their midst—uninvited—they were sure to think the worst of him and respond accordingly.

But if he were bundled up in his fur coat and hood, would they know he was white? If they shone a light in his face, yes, his coloring would give him away.

And then the seed of an idea planted itself in his mind, and its roots spread through his thoughts until the notion took over like a pesky vine.

He could make himself look like an Indian. Surely he could find something to stain his face and hands a darker color. He could even use some of the bear grease in his pack to make the puffy curl most of the Apsaalooke braves wore. He could find some feathers to tie in his hair with leather strips. It was too bad he'd not let it grow out any this winter. Apsaalooke braves took pride in their long braids.

Ducking low from tree to tree, he retreated from the hiding spot. He had to get back to Pet and his supplies. As soon as he was out of sight from the cave opening, he broke into a sprint, following his earlier tracks through the snow.

What could he use to stain his skin a darker brown? There wouldn't be any berries in the dead of winter. But he'd seen the Indians use tree bark for staining. What kind of tree did they use? Cedar? No, to the best of his memory, it had been a broad-leafed tree. Which meant the branches would be barren now.

Without slowing his pace, he glanced overhead at the towering limbs that steepled like a cathedral. Some held evergreen needles, some spread with leafless fingers. How would he ever know which was good for staining? He had to find another method.

When he made it back to Pet, Mustang trotted forward to greet him. He slipped a hand over the dog's back and slowed to catch his breath. His chest burned from sucking in the icy air, but he couldn't stop to let himself recover. He jerked off his gloves, and his cold fingers fumbled with the ties on his saddle pack. Finally he loosened them, then rummaged inside until his hand closed on the jar of bear grease he kept to salve his chapped lips. Thank God he'd not taken it out of the pack to save room.

Simeon's gaze flickered over the rest of his supplies. In the pack, there was food, the leather wrapped bundle of letters from the Scotts, flint and steel for fire-starting, and a few personal supplies. Tied behind his saddle were two of his warmest furs—a worn grizzly hide and a wolf skin.

His eyes stalled on the wolf fur. The Indian braves he'd seen from this group all wore lighter colored furs. So light they almost blended in with the snow. His own red fox fur coat would stand out in stark contrast to the others. Maybe he should drape the wolf hide over himself in the Indian style.

Once he pulled the lighter fur out of the bundle, he scanned the forest around him. Now he just needed feathers and something to darken his skin.

The feathers were easy enough when he discovered the remains of a recent grouse kill. Though the quills were small, he could use a strip of leather to tie them into his short hair. If only his hair were longer.

He piled the feathers with the bear grease and the wolf skin beside Pet. The mare stood quietly, but the flick of her ear followed his movements as she watched him work.

"Good girl." He straightened and gave her hindquarters a pat as his mind turned over the choices for a stain. She flicked him with her tail, the long black hairs catching on the lacing of his knee-high moccasins. His eyes locked on the sight.

Long, black hair. Or rather…a braid.

It just might work. His gaze wandered up to Pet's head, which came around to look at him as if she could read his thoughts. "You wouldn't mind, girl, would you? For Emma."

She snorted and shook her head, then dropped her nose as if agreeing. For the first time since he'd discovered the man's tracks beside Emma's, a smile played at the corners of his mouth.

By the time he was suited up in his costume, it felt like a whole pool of trout darted and flipped inside his belly. If only he had a mirror to check his reflection. He'd ended up mixing dirt with bear grease to spread over his face and hands, but it tended to wipe off when he brushed against something. Hopefully the cave would be dark enough for the disguise to work.

Now, to get inside.

With the wolf skin draped over his shoulders, he touched the knife at his belt to make sure it was secure. Then he fingered the handle of his pistol, which was tucked in the front of his trousers. He'd carry his rifle as far as the cedar where he'd hidden in front of the cave, but he'd need both hands free when he went inside.

Simeon paused before leaving the horse and scanned his supplies one last time. What was he forgetting? What detail hadn't he covered?

Prayer.

He raised his face heavenward and lifted up his mission to the Lord. *Please keep Emma safe. Let me be in time. Bring us both out whole and healthy.*

Emma's features flashed in his thoughts. Every beautiful detail. The clear amber of her eyes and the way her brows arched perfectly over them. The smooth line of her jaw. The way her stubborn chin jutted.

Purpose washed through him, flooding his veins with strength. Now was the time.

Emma forced herself to sit quietly, not even tapping her boots on the fur beneath her, though the child inside pushed and prodded. The less attention these Indians paid her the better.

It felt like she'd been sitting there for hours, but the time had afforded her the opportunity to study the people rambling about in this cavern. She'd counted eight men, including her kidnapper, who hadn't reappeared since he'd walked out with her hair. Other braves lounged around the perimeter. One had left just before one of the others came in. Guard duty?

Five of the women including the youngest, who looked barely more than a girl, busied themselves cooking around the fires. A sixth squaw snuggled a baby, who was almost covered under the fur skin wrapped around her. The woman was likely nursing the infant. The old squaw beside Emma made eight women in the group.

So sixteen total Indians, not counting the infant. And every one of them blocked her escape through the dark tunnel on the other side of the room. She scanned the edges of the cavern one more time, trying to study the walls without turning her head. As far as she could tell, no shadows deepened to signify a crack in the rock. No openings at all.

One of the women pulled a stick out of the fire. It had some kind of meat that dripped juices on the stone floor. She laid the hunk on a slab of bark, then used another stick to pull smaller pieces of meat from the larger and place them on more bark.

Emma's stomach gurgled as she watched the process. She'd not had anything to eat since her midnight snack of leftover johnnycake the night before. The babe inside her gave a sharp kick against her lower belly, voicing its own complaint.

She forced her eyes away from the meat and onto the face of the woman working with it. At least the baby still seemed alive and well. And while Emma was counting blessings, no matter what the Indian brave had planned for her, the fact that he'd not killed her right away meant she had more time to find a way of escape.

What were Simeon and Joseph doing right now? How long had it taken them to discover she was missing? Would Simeon decipher what had happened from their tracks? Would he come after her? Of course, he would.

But then a niggle of fear wiggled its way through her chest. Eight Indian braves against one white man were not good odds. And if these Indians had a guard posted, they were surely ready for him. There was no way Simeon could get close enough to save her without being murdered himself.

Did the Indians have guns? She'd not seen one yet, only bows and quivers of arrows propped beside the men in this cavern. And of course, the giant knife her captor had used to chop off her hair. But just because she hadn't seen guns didn't mean they didn't have them.

A woman rose to her feet by the fire, snagging Emma's attention. It was the young squaw who'd given her a drink. The one who spoke English.

Emma's pulse picked up speed as the woman walked her direction, her gait elegant, her bearing poised. But then she stopped in front of the squaw who had portioned out meat on the plates of bark. She bent low and picked up the plates, loading six of them on her arms with practiced ease, then carried them around the room, placing one in front of each of the men.

The braves seemed to come to life as the food was set before them. Beside one of the men, what Emma had assumed was a stack of furs in the hazy cavern now came to life. A dog rose to sit and watch its master eat. Across the room, a second dog did the same. How had she missed the fact that there were dogs here with them? What else had she missed?

When the Indian woman finished feeding the men, she returned to the squaw by the fire, who'd pulled out a second spit of meat and dished more portions on slips of bark. The English-speaking woman picked up only one plate this time, then straightened and looked at Emma.

Emma stiffened. Could this be for her? She should try not to get her hopes up, but the sight and smell of the sizzling meat was more than her starving belly could withstand. A fierce rumbling growl emanated from her midsection, probably loud enough for the old squaw beside her to hear.

The younger woman approached and knelt before Emma, laying the food on the fur in front of her. Then she reached for Emma's gag and wiggled the tight leather down to hang around her neck. The corners of her lips burned where they'd been rubbed raw by the binding.

As the woman tore off a bite of meat, Emma's eyes tracked it, its savory aroma wafting up to tantalize her. It looked like beef, but was probably deer or some other mountain creature plentiful in the winter. She could taste the succulent goodness even before its juices touched her tongue. On contact, flavor sprang through her mouth, and her eyes slid closed from the richness of it. As much as she wanted to savor each drop, her teeth worked ravenously, obeying the cry of her stomach to send food.

As the Indian woman fed her bite after bite, she watched Emma, dark eyes shadowed in the dim, smoky light of the cave. At last, the meat was gone, although the ache in Emma's stomach had only started to ease. The squaw picked up the bark as if she would leave.

"Wait." It took effort for Emma to keep her voice low as urgency seized her. This was her chance to get some answers.

The woman paused.

"What will happen to me?"

Those dark eyes took in Emma's face but didn't give away the squaw's thoughts. Did she understand the question?

At last she spoke, the words so quiet Emma almost missed them. "You belong to Daxpitcheehìsshish."

She must have read the confusion on Emma's face. "Red Bear. The brave who found you."

Indignation rose up in Emma's chest. "He didn't find me. He kidnapped me. Took me against my will." She held her hands to the side to show her bindings. "I am not his." She jutted her chin. "I belong to another man." That wasn't exactly true. Her heart belonged to Simeon and likely always would. But the rest of her hadn't been spoken for. These Indians didn't need to know that.

The Indian woman shrugged. "You belong to Red Bear now."

A smothering feeling began in her chest and rose up to her throat. "But why? What does that mean?" She could still feel the volatile fierceness of his rough hands as the brave tossed her about without a care for the babe inside her. "I can't."

The woman's gaze darkened, if that were possible. "Red Bear wishes it."

Emma fought to keep from shivering against the finality in her tone. The blunt edges of her hair feathered her cheek, tickling. "Is that why he cut my hair?"

"It is a mourning ritual. Because your past is dead to you."

This time she couldn't hold back the shiver. She clamped her jaw against any further show of emotion. "He won't touch me while I'm…with child." She glanced down at the swell of her dress not hidden beneath her coat.

Again, a shrug. "Red Bear does what he pleases."

Then the woman rose and walked away, leaving Emma with a dread that spread through her belly like poisoned water. She had to get out of here. Where was Simeon? Watching from outside the cave? He'd never get in here without being shot down a dozen times.

No, it was up to her to find an escape.

Chapter Twenty-Three

Hope is a cruel disappointer, stripping away parts of me until I can clearly see the only things that truly matter.
~ Emma's Journal

Simeon peered through the branches of the same cedar that had hid him earlier. The entrance to the cave stood dark and silent, as it had before. But he wasn't naïve enough to believe no one was watching. Even if the Indians hadn't taken Emma, they wouldn't leave the entrance to their home unguarded.

Now he needed to create a distraction, something that would draw their attention in the opposite direction while he slipped inside the cave. The tunnel appeared black, although surely there was enough light for the braves to maneuver inside. But it should be dim enough for his disguise to conceal his identity.

Something furry touched the back of his hand, and Simeon jerked his arm away as he looked down. Mustang. The dog dropped its tongue down the side of its mouth and panted, looking up at him with soulful eyes. The obstinate creature was supposed to have stayed back with Pet. Of all the times for his willfulness to take over.

Simeon raised his gaze back to the cave, scanning for any motion. Only a faint trail of smoke from the opening.

Maybe the dog could be the distraction. If Simeon could get around to the far side of the cave while Mustang stayed here by the cedar, he could whistle for the animal. Would seeing a dog trot across the open snow be enough to distract the Indians while Simeon slipped inside the dark entrance?

The only problem was, the side he'd be entering was the spot where the Indians had stood when he'd approached them before. He had a feeling that was where at least one of the guards was stationed. Should he risk that possibility? He might not have another choice, but at least he would have the advantage of surprise if he ran into a brave as he entered the darkness. Literally—ran into a brave. He'd have to ready his wits and his knife.

Simeon shifted his gaze to the trees that lined the clearing, searching out a path where he could move around the edge without being seen by the Indians watching. Perhaps he should backtrack to find more cover.

Mustang growled under his hand, rising up to all four feet as his tail stood alert. Simeon glanced at the dog, then followed his focus out into the snowy clearing.

A moose. Wandering out from the trees on the far side of the clearing.

Noise sounded from inside the cave. A scuffling sound.

The moose turned, trying to catch the source of the

noise, or maybe the smell of it. This was the distraction he needed.

Cover me, Lord. With the prayer in his heart, Simeon darted from behind the cedar to the side of the rock mountain. He flattened himself against it, only a dozen feet or so from the cave opening.

The moose saw him then, her nostrils flaring as if she weren't sure whether to charge or retreat. He inched sideways, praying the Indians had her in their sights. Surely they wouldn't pass up such an easy meal. She was only twenty or so feet from the cave. Easy range for an arrow, assuming they didn't have rifles.

The air whistled a split second before an arrow thwacked into the animal's side just behind her front leg.

A mighty bellow filled the air as the animal fell to one knee, and the Indians let out a fierce cry. They surged toward the animal, more arrows flying, and Simeon leaped into motion. With two strides he closed the distance to the cave opening and slipped sideways inside.

Blackness closed around him, and smoky tentacles pressed on his lungs. He paused to make sense of the noises around him. The clatter of stones, male voices, the crunch of moccasins in snow. Something blew by him, just inches away. A person running. He turned to see who had so narrowly missed him and watched for a second as two Indian braves strode through the snow toward the downed moose.

Now was his chance. Turning back toward the darkness, he kept one hand on the rock wall, walking it forward as he crept. Both hands stayed ready to reach for his weapons at the first provocation. Every muscle in his body tensed for action, every sense strained to foresee danger.

A low murmur sounded from ahead. The crackle of fire. He kept inching forward, one step at a time, as the smoke grew thicker. The wall curved to the right, and a sliver of light appeared ahead. He was close to the cavern.

He flattened himself to the wall again, straining to dissect the sounds that wafted through the smoke. A male voice. Then a higher female voice. The man's response. The sounds weren't loud enough for him to pick out words.

He inched farther along the wall, and the opening of light widened. Now he could see a bit of the room. His eyes strained to make sense of the images shifting in the hazy light. An Indian sat on a pallet by the entrance. Another gray-haired man to his left, somewhat facing the tunnel. Both were braves as far as he could tell, but it didn't look like either had seen him. Another Indian walked in front of them, her long dress that of a squaw.

The woman approached the older brave in the corner and leaned down. It looked like she whispered in his ear, though he couldn't be sure.

He took the opportunity to ease out toward the middle of the tunnel so he could glimpse more of the room. Little by little, his view of the cavern opened until he could see all the way to the far end. Two more Indians sat on pallets. No three. One was another brave. Then a young squaw with a babe tucked under part of her robe. Then at the far end, a grey-haired Indian. Was that the squaw who'd come to care for Emma?

He narrowed his eyes. He had trouble summoning any gratitude toward the woman now.

But he still didn't know whether these Indians actually had Emma. How could he see the other side of the room? Maybe if he retreated back to a darker section of the tunnel and moved to the other side.

Then a sound from behind pricked his ears. The padding of feet. The skitter of a pebble. He pressed closer to the wall, not daring to breathe. Then movement caught his eye. Down low, near his feet.

Mustang.

Simeon reached to grab the dog as it trotted by, but his hand came up empty.

A knot tightened in his stomach as the animal stepped from the smoky tunnel into the brightly lit cavern.

Emma watched the commotion at the far end of the cavern near the entrance. There'd been a shout, then one of the men had come to life on his pallet as though called. He sprang to his feet and left the room. Now one of the older women spoke to a brave sitting in the corner near the tunnel entrance. He responded with a command loud enough for the entire room to hear, and a flurry of activity ensued.

What was happening? Her stomach churned as the possibilities flittered through her. Had Simeon come for her?

Had the Indians spotted him and now were preparing for an attack?

The gray-haired squaw in charge groaned as she pushed to her feet. A tiny bit of relief eased through Emma. If the woman assigned to guard her was leaving, maybe she could use this commotion to escape.

Another motion caught her eye near the dark tunnel opening. A dog padded into the room.

She squinted. Even through the smoky haze, something about the animal struck a chord in her mind. A familiarity.

She sucked in a breath as recognition settled over her. Mustang. What in the world was he doing here? She blinked, then focused again. That was definitely Simeon's dog.

Did that mean Simeon was nearby? Her pulse thumped harder. Was he outside even now? This sudden activity had to be due to him.

Or…maybe Mustang spent time with these Indians, too, coming and going the way he did with Simeon. But no, this place was too far from Simeon's cabin. The dog wouldn't roam between two homes so distant.

Simeon had to be nearby.

Excitement built in her chest, and she leaned forward as the dog ambled up to her. She kept her voice quiet as she greeted him. "Hey there. How are you, boy?" Her hands were still tied behind her back, but at least the squaw hadn't put the gag back over her mouth.

The dog sniffed the floor in front of her, not offering

any kind of greeting. But at least he didn't growl at her like usual. She itched to stroke the animal. To stand up and follow him right out of this cave.

But she needed to bide her time. And make sure she didn't give the animal—or Simeon—away to these Indians.

She refocused her attention on the figures scurrying through the smoke. Two of the men still sat on pallets. Women seemed to be traveling in and out of the room carrying baskets. A tall brave bundled in thick fur approached her.

She shrank back and squinted to make out his identity. This brave seemed taller than Red Bear, but it was hard to tell with the fur shadowing his face. He drew near enough to reach for her arm, and she pulled her legs underneath to prepare for when he jerked her up.

He took hold of both her upper arms, but his touch wasn't the same rough treatment Red Bear had given. This man's grip was strong but oddly gentle. Definitely not Red Bear.

Even though he eased her up, her feet struggled to find balance, and needles of pain shot through her right ankle as the blood recirculated. She'd been sitting way too long.

Her leg wouldn't support her, no matter how hard she tried, and the brave pulled her closer to his chest as she wobbled. But the moment she could stand on her own, she pulled away.

His grip on her arms didn't let her go far, though. She increased her effort, but just enough to let him feel her resistance. There was no way she would win a battle of strength against this man, especially not with her hands bound behind her. But he would know she didn't go willingly.

He finally loosed her right arm and pushed her forward with the left. He guided her around the fires and toward the cave entrance, weaving around the flutterings of the Indian women.

Panic rose in her chest, and she slowed her steps, pushing back against the brave's guiding grip. Where was he taking her? Had Red Bear commanded him to bring her for something? Or maybe Simeon was out there. Had they taken him captive too?

Warm breath touched the nape of her neck, fanning the edge of her now-short hair. "Walk forward, Emma. Out of here."

Simeon? She turned to look at the man, but his grip on her arm tightened, pushing her forward. "Walk, Emma. Please." He gritted the words through what sounded like clenched teeth, but it was definitely Simeon's voice. Her heartbeat fanned faster in her chest

She jerked her head straight. How did he get in here? Why had no one tried to stop him? But, of course. He looked just like an Indian brave. She hadn't even recognized him, although she'd not gotten a look at his face. Her fuzzy mind was slow to catch up, but her feet pushed forward, following Simeon's direction.

She wanted to turn and throw her arms around him, but she worked hard to keep her face stoic as they neared the dark tunnel.

Freedom was just on the other side.

A figure stepped in front of her path, glaring at her with dark eyes in a round, leathery face. The old squaw who'd sat beside her all day. Her guard.

The woman pressed a finger in Emma's chest and spat out a string of Indian words.

Simeon's hands gripped Emma's shoulders, steering her around the woman, but the old squaw stepped closer, blocking their path as the pitch of her voice grew higher.

Within less than a second, they were surrounded by braves.

Rough hands gripped Emma, tearing her away from Simeon. Pain seared her upper arms as she was jerked sideways by her bound wrists. Something struck her side, and she bent away from it, trying in vain to protect the baby. She opened her mouth to scream, but a blow struck her right temple, and the sound gurgled in her throat.

Blackness clouded the edge of her vision, but she forced her eyes open, trying to push the dark away. She had to stay awake. Had to protect the baby.

Where was Simeon?

Voices clattered all around her as she sank to her knees. She couldn't make out words. She was hoisted up, staring at the cave ceiling. Carried, as pain continued to bite into her upper arms. Her wrists.

She couldn't sort through the rapid succession of events, but at last a final shot of pain jolted through her rear and back as she landed hard on the ground. The momentum pushed her flat on her back, crushing her hands underneath her. She rolled on her side, curled her legs up, and tried to shield the precious life inside her. *God, please save my baby.*

Chapter Twenty-Four

Your love is my strength.
~ Simeon

Commotion still flurried around Emma, and she tensed for another blow at any moment. It didn't come, though, and she tried to focus on the sounds and bodies moving about her.

A hollow thud sounded behind her, like fist upon flesh. A man groaned.

Simeon.

She strained to hear, wanted to turn over and see.

A sharp intake of air and another groan.

On and on the thuds and grunts sounded. Her spirit cried to stop the beating. To help the man for whom love had flourished in her heart. But she couldn't open herself to blows that might hurt the baby.

At last the beating must have ceased. Two Indians—a man and a woman—spoke in low tones. Then footsteps padded away.

Silence.

Had they both left? She waited. Maybe someone still

stood there, thinking her unconscious. If she moved, would the man strike her again, would this blow be hard enough to hurt the baby?

She waited longer, the sound of Simeon's shallow breathing finally making its way to her ears. At least he was alive. Could she risk turning to see him?

"Emma." His hoarse whisper was loud enough only for her ear, and set loose a rush of relief and fear.

"I'm here. Are you all right?"

"Fine. But you? The baby?"

"I'm fine." The emotion churning inside rose up into her throat, spilling out from her eyes. Simeon was alive. She was alive. They were beaten and bound in an Indian cave, but they were together. No matter what happened, she wouldn't have to face this nightmare alone.

The urge to see him rose strong in her chest, and she strained to roll onto her back first, then her right side.

"What are you—? No, Emma."

She ignored Simeon's words. Once she shifted her weight to turn, she was hard pressed to stop the momentum of her oversize abdomen. She came to a rest on the solid stone floor, drinking in the sight of him.

She squinted to decipher the image before her. He looked…different. Some kind of shiny brown substance covered his face, partially smeared away in some places. It distorted his face but didn't take away from the clear blue of his eyes.

"Emma." He squirmed, wiggling his shoulders as if he were trying to loosen his wrists bound behind him. After a few seconds, he stopped fighting and lay still, his eyes drinking her in. Absorbing her.

She couldn't help but smile at the wonderful sight of him. "I'm so glad to see you."

Simeon's jaw worked, but the shadow of an approaching figure cut off his response.

They both turned to see, and Emma had to crane her neck to look up into the face of Red Bear. Fear clutched at her, and she brought her knees up in a reflexive movement to cover her vulnerability. If he touched her… Simeon wouldn't let it happen. She knew without wondering that he would give his life for hers. But if he did, it would be for naught. His death wouldn't free her.

God, help us.

The man's hard gaze scanned her, then narrowed on Simeon, who was lying on his side on the rock floor. The brave stepped up behind and delivered a swift, hard blow to Simeon's back.

An intake of breath and a sharp flinch were Simeon's only reactions, but Emma could feel the sting of it all the way through her body. She bit down hard on her lower lip to keep from screaming at the bully.

Red Bear bent down and jerked the collar away from Simeon's neck. He grabbed the long black braid and pulled. The entwined hair came away in the Indian's hand, and he raised it with a sneer. He let loose a string of words in a high pitch that rang almost like a war cry. Then his foot struck Simeon's shoulder, slamming into his side on its way back down. The brave shouted—the cry echoing off the walls. But like a whisper in a crowd, the thud of flesh and Simeon's grunts echoed through Emma's mind.

"Stop!" But her cry was swallowed up in the piercing shriek of the Indian's attacks.

She lurched up to a sitting position, searching the room frantically for anyone who might stop the madman.

The old man still sat by the door, not even looking their way. Five braves stood scattered around the room, watching Red Bear as though he were doing nothing more than eating dinner.

Another thud beside her was accompanied by a sharp cry from Simeon. She wanted to grab the cruel brave, shake him like a cloth doll and scream at him. And if she couldn't do that, she wanted to clap her hands over her ears, squeeze her eyes shut and make this awful scene go away.

"Stop him, please!" She turned to the nearest man, but he didn't even acknowledge her presence, his focus on the bully attacking Simeon. All the women had vacated the room, but one appeared now from the darkened tunnel. The young squaw who'd fed her.

Emma's heart leapt in her chest, and she strained forward. "Help him, please!"

But her cry was swallowed by a mighty shout from Red Bear, followed by a high moan from Simeon.

Fury burned through Emma's veins, and she spun to face the attacker.

The man's back was to her, his foot poised for another kick.

Without stopping to think, she leaned back and struck

out with both her heels, plunging them squarely into the back of the man's knees.

His shout turned into a yelp as he plunged forward, landing on his hands and knees almost on top of Simeon. Emma kicked out again, trying to land more blows while the man was down. Simeon lay without moving, his still body feeding her rage as she kicked with her only available weapons.

The Indian lunged to his feet with a roar and spun to face her. His jaw gaped, teeth flashing like a roaring bear as he lunged for her.

Emma shrank back, bracing her heels in the air to repel his attack or at least shield the baby from a direct blow.

With her boots in the way, he grabbed her feet and held them in an iron grip while he landed a hard kick in her right hip. Pain surged through her back, nearly sucking the air from her lungs. She tried to brace for the next blow, but it came too quickly. In almost the same spot. Pain radiated as his foot struck hard.

Emma squirmed, trying to scoot away or at least direct the next blow to a place that didn't already scream with agony.

A shrill whistle split the air, and she squeezed her eyes shut, holding her breath for the next strike.

But it didn't come.

The room grew deathly silent, and she opened her eyes slowly. Her gaze landed first on Simeon. His eyes were open, but they shimmered in the firelight as though they'd glassed over. Panic churned in her chest. Was he dead? Her focus flew to his chest, but it rose and lowered with a steady—if slight— rhythm.

Red Bear stood near them, motionless. His gaze was fixed across the room where another Indian spoke. Emma shifted so she could see what was happening.

It was the old man who'd been sitting in the corner by the tunnel entrance. He stood now, both arms extended like Moses at the red sea. His words came in short guttural sounds, and the eyes of every Indian in the room were fixed on him.

Emma strained to hear, to see the man's hand motions and somehow determine what he was saying.

A sound beside her brought her gaze back to Simeon. His eyes were a little more focused now, like he was listening to the man, too.

"What's he saying?" Emma whispered, but Simeon gave a slight shake of his head.

Then the old man's voice rose, and he spoke a final word. It sounded like a command.

Red Bear shouted back at him, and the old man barked a word in return, then uttered another sentence in a low growl. The tone left no room for argument.

Red Bear stiffened, fists clenched, anger radiating from every inch of his body. He turned and stalked toward the cave entrance, charging past the other Indians, who stepped out of his way.

Emma barely dared to breathe. Had the old man finally put an end to the brutality? Or had he issued a command that they be put to death in a less violent manner?

"What's happening?" She whispered loud enough for Simeon to hear but didn't take her eyes from the Indians around them.

Every person still stood quietly, watching the old man. Waiting for instructions? The old brave turned then to the young woman who'd fed Emma, the one who spoke English. He rattled off a few words, and she nodded in response.

Then she turned toward Emma and Simeon, walking past the Indian men as if she were walking a gauntlet. No one stopped her. No one touched or spoke to her. But every eye tracked her path.

She stopped in front of Emma, then squatted down so she could speak quietly. "You are to come with me. Can you both walk?"

Emma glanced at Simeon. "I can. I'm not sure about—"

"Yes." Simeon spoke the word with more energy than she would have thought he had left. He struggled to sit up, and the young squaw reached for his arm to help him.

Emma squirmed until she could roll on her side and push herself to her knees. As she struggled to get her feet underneath her, the woman's gentle hand gripped her arm and helped pull her up.

When she turned back around, Simeon was on his feet too, although his face was already swelling, and he sagged as if it took all his strength not to collapse.

"Come." The woman turned and followed the path Red Bear had taken out of the room.

Fear churned in Emma's stomach as she fell into step behind her. She glanced back to make sure Simeon was following, but the sight of him staggering forward was almost more than she could stand. She longed to slip herself under his arm and help with the painful task of walking from this cave. But with her hands bound and so many Indian braves staring them down, she dared not do anything except follow the woman.

They stepped into the dark tunnel, and smoky blackness closed around Emma like a smothering blanket, pushing all the air from her lungs. Her muscles tensed even more, and she had to force herself not to dart back into the safety of the cavern. She could hear Simeon's stumbling steps behind her, and his presence eased her fear a tiny bit.

Then a glimmer of light shone ahead, and hope pulled at her chest as the light widened with each step. The glitter of the snowy ground outside was almost blinding. She slowed as they neared the entrance to the new sparkling world. Squinting, she took in the flurry of tracks stomped into the snow leading to a patch of red about twenty feet out.

The knot in her stomach tightened again. Blood in the snow? It couldn't be Simeon's. Had Joseph come with him? Had he been shot down there in that patch of winter ice? But Simeon would have told her. Or would he? He hadn't really said anything yet.

She had no idea where they were being led. Maybe even to that same execution spot. She wanted to step backward. To turn and hide herself in Simeon's arms. Demand he tell her what was happening. She hated secrets.

Hated not knowing.

But the Indian squaw had already walked into the snow away from the bloody stain. She turned and looked at Emma with a frown. "Come."

One foot at a time, Emma forced herself forward. She stepped into the snow, and it covered her boot. Almost as if she were in a dream, the world around her fogged, and she lifted each foot high to clear the fresh powder, walking one effort-laden step at a time.

When they neared the edge of the clearing where the trail began to wind through trees, the Indian woman stopped and turned to them. Her gaze swept Simeon, then focused on Emma. "Your friend will tell you why you were released. But I will tell you why I helped." She reached to touch the gold cross hanging from Emma's neck, barely visible at the top of her coat. "Pray to the Great God that he will forgive my people's sins today." And then she made the sign of the cross, beginning at her forehead and moving to her chest. "Go with God. May He have mercy on us."

With that, she turned and scurried past them to the cave.

Chapter Twenty-Five

Can this be real?
~ Emma's Journal

Emma struggled to take in what had just happened. Were they free? She looked at Simeon.

His face had already swollen so it was almost unrecognizable. His breaths came out in labored puffs, forming a white haze in the air. "Let's go." He started forward, even before his hoarse words made sense in her fuzzy mind.

She scurried forward to catch up. "What happened, Simeon?"

"When we're...out of sight." It sounded like he had spoken through clenched teeth, and his weaving, unsteady stride held an air of determination.

Out of sight. Yes, they needed to get far away from this place before the Indians sent someone to bring them back. She focused her efforts on moving through the snow.

Soon, they made it into the woods and around the bend in the trail so the cave was no longer visible. Simeon's steps stumbled more now, and he swayed with every movement. Teetering.

At last, his legs gave way, and he crumpled to the ground. She dropped to her knees beside him, her heart aching to help. "What can I do for you? I have to get my hands untied so I can help you."

Both his eyes were swollen, the left one more than the right. He gazed at her through the slit in his right eye. "In my left moccasin, there's a knife."

Hope flared in her chest, and she scooted around so her back faced him, using her hands to feel for his leg.

He raised the limb to meet her fumbling fingers, and she groped at the edge of his moccasin laces until she touched something hard. She reached inside the leather, gripped the solid form of a knife hilt, and pulled upward. Her wrists ached from the strain, her upper arms burning, but she extracted the blade from its sheath and closed her hand around the grip.

"See if you can cut your ties. If not, I will." Simeon's words were so weary, they infused a new rush of determination in her chest.

She leaned forward to focus and shifted the knife in her fingertips so it touched her leather bonds. It took several tries, but she finally had it positioned right. She clenched her jaw as every part of her strained to press the knife into the leather and slide the blade up and down. She couldn't tell if it made any headway or not, but her arms throbbed with the effort.

Finally, something popped in the leather straps. She pulled hard to try to separate her hands, but the binding wouldn't give. She pressed the knife blade harder into the cord, working it up and down.

There. With a rush, it sliced through the tie, and her hands separated. The relief that flooded her arms tore away the last of her strength. She collapsed to her knees in the snow, relishing the burn as she eased her arms in front of her. This pain was one she could endure with pleasure.

Still kneeling in the snow, all her energy spent, she touched her left wrist, carefully rubbing feeling back into the skin. Then her right.

A tiny moan from Simeon brought her back to reality. She had to untie him. They needed to get farther from the Indian camp. That was, if he could travel.

She grabbed the knife and scooted forward to Simeon. "I'm going to turn you on your side so I can cut your tie."

He didn't speak, but the tendons at his throat bulged as he struggled to turn himself.

She grabbed his arm and helped him shift just enough for her to gain access to his wrists. "That's all." The knife blade was sharp and sliced through the leather on her second try. She laid the blade aside and pulled the strap off his wrists. His arms still seemed locked behind his back, so she took his left hand and eased it around to his side. "Let's lie you back now."

He groaned as he sank back into the snow. "Need to get to the horse. Away." His voice was strong enough, but his lips barely parted to let the sound through.

Emma leaned over him, craving to touch his wounds. To bring relief to his pain, even a tiny bit. His face was so damaged. The mixture he'd spread on it to darken his skin had been smeared and wiped off in most places, revealing dark blue skin where bruises had already formed. Only his forehead appeared uninjured. She touched the spot, stroking through his hair. Grease and dirt clung to her hand, but she ignored it. She needed to clean his face, though. And maybe the cold from the snow would help his swelling.

She scooped a handful of clean white powder and cupped it over his face, spreading it over his cheeks and jaw. A long stream of breath leaked from his mouth, but it turned into a groan as he pushed the edge of his fur coat away and clutched his right side.

"What hurts, love?" Other than her chest at sight of him in so much pain.

"My ribs."

Her hand found the spot, covering his fingers with her own. "What can I do?"

His breath came in short clips. "Nothing. I think one's broken."

He had a broken bone? She fumbled with his buckskin tunic, trying to work the bottom up so she could assess the damage. "We need to look at it. Does the bone need to be wrapped?"

His fingers found hers, closing over her hand, stilling her. "Not here. My horse is down the trail. Tend it…there."

She raised her eyes to the snowy trail through the trees. His horse was nearby? Energy filled her veins. *Thank you, Lord.*

Dropping her gaze to Simeon again, she scanned the

length of him. "Is there anything else broken?"

"Don't think." But every breath seemed to be a struggle. Were his lungs damaged, or was the broken rib responsible for his shallow breaths? Either way, they had to be careful.

"I'll go get the horse and bring her here. Then we can doctor you, and you won't have to walk."

"No." He struggled to roll on his side, propping himself up on his elbow. "Need to get out of here."

A snap of frustration surged through her chest. "Then let me help you." She pushed to her feet and stepped around to his other side.

"I can do it. Just have to—" With a groan he rolled onto all fours, then stopped as his breath came in short gasps.

"Simeon, please." She touched his back. "Let me help you."

He raised a hand. "All right."

She clasped his hand, but the moment he strained to stand, she realized her grip wasn't strong enough. Grabbing his forearm with her other hand, she braced her feet to pull him up.

He released another groan as he stood and straightened, every inch of his tall, broad strength standing before her.

She couldn't stop herself from slipping under his arm, pressing herself to his side—his good side—and wrapping her arms around his waist. She kept the touch as light as she could, but when his hands settled on her back, she exhaled a long shaky breath. "You have no idea how glad I was to see you." She leaned back to look up into his face. "To have you here now." But the pain so evident in him pushed her into action. "Let's get you to a better place."

With his arm around her shoulders, they turned and started through the snow.

The sight of Pet just ahead gave Simeon enough energy to keep moving when everything in him wanted to collapse. When they were still a dozen steps away, his knees buckled, and he allowed himself to sink into the snow. First to his knees, then down to his side.

Emma fussed around him, and he let his eyes drift shut as he lay on the icy ground. Having her here, alive and well, was worth every bit of the pain flooding his insides. He could let himself rest now, just for a few moments. Then they'd mount Pet and get far, far, away from these Indians.

The cool snow felt good on his aching face, but it was Emma's soft touch and soothing words that eased the pain more than anything. He relished it. Though he didn't have the strength to respond.

A shiver ran through his body, whether from the trauma or the wet snow, he couldn't have said.

"You're cold. I'll get a blanket."

That sounded wonderful, but he needed to do something about his side first. "Need to wrap my ribs."

She rose and moved away, and the loss of her presence seemed to intensify all his pain. Well, if he had to feel everything, he may as well make it productive. With his eyes pressed shut, he catalogued each part of his body.

His right side had definitely taken the brunt of the blows, since it had been nearest the crazed Indian. Both the thigh and hip were pretty bruised, but there was nothing broken. His ribs shot fire through him with every breath, which made it impossible to tell whether any of his internal organs were damaged. Pain radiated through his back, but again, it could just be bruising. There was no telling how bad his face looked, but from the tiny slit he could see through only one eye, he guessed it was only a grotesque caricature of his normal image.

Emma knelt beside him again. "I've got strips of cloth we can tie around you."

He reached for the bottom edge of his tunic and tried to pull it up. But even his fingers lacked strength to do what he asked of them.

Her hands brushed his, taking over the effort. He tried to arch his back to make the task easier. When she pulled his undershirt up, the blast of frigid air that struck his belly was enough to pry his good eye open. The sting of the snow under his back mixed with the ache in his body, easing the pain a tiny bit.

Emma sucked in a sharp breath, and his focus narrowed to her face.

"Simeon." She spoke his name softly, a hint of tears in her voice.

"What?" Was there more damage than he knew about?

"You're hurt. Everywhere."

Was that all? He could have told her that. But the pain in her voice drew his protective instincts. She didn't need to fuss over him. The bruises would heal. She was safe now, and he'd go through a hundred more beatings to keep her that way.

His fingers itched to stroke the sorrow from her face. But he could only reach her hand, so he curled his fingers around hers.

She met his gaze, what he could see through the little slit in his eyelid anyway. As though she could read his mind, she raised his hand up to her cheek and cupped it there. He stroked the softness. So beautiful, those amber eyes almost haunting in their intensity. Only marred by the pain in their depths. Was it there because of him? He had to say something to remove it.

"Don't worry about me, Emma. I'm fine. Just a few bruises, which'll heal."

"I'm so sorry, Simeon. When I saw you in that cave, I was overwhelmed with relief. I knew you'd get me out. Keep me safe. But this"—she glanced over his body—"I didn't know he would hurt you. Mutilate your body like this." She sniffed. "I almost wish I were back in that cave and you'd gone on without me."

A knife of determination pierced through him, enough to jerk his hand from her hold and push himself up to a sitting position. Fire shot through his side, but he ignored it.

"Simeon, don't—" She reached for his shoulders, but he grabbed her hands and trapped them in his lap.

"Emma, listen." He had to fight for breath, but what he had to say was worth the effort. "I would have done…anything…for you. You're worth more…than my sorry hide." He raised one of her hands to his mouth and kissed the tops of her fingers. "So…much more."

Her eyes glimmered as if she were about to cry, and he longed to lean forward and kiss her 'til any thought of those tears was long gone. To tell her how much he loved her. To ask her if he could stay by her side until his last breath—wherever that needed to be. In Canada, in Texas—in Rome, Italy, if that's where she wanted to live. He wanted this woman as his wife, and making a life with her had become the lone desire of his battered heart.

But maybe now wasn't the time to ask. Bruised and swollen the way he was, he surely didn't look like much of a prize. Soon, though. He would ask her soon.

Chapter Twenty-Six

The foretaste is sweet, if only I can make it to the culmination.
~ Simeon

"Thank you for saving me."

Simeon still sat in the snow, Emma hovering over him, waiting to bandage his injured ribs. Her words brought his focus back to her face. A single tear slipped down her cheek, and he reached out to brush it away with his thumb. "I would a hundred times…if I had to. But…I can't claim…the glory." He was able to breathe a little better now if he didn't move. Swallowing, he finished the thought. "Truth is, God did everything back there."

She inhaled loudly enough for him to hear it. "I know. God has us all in His hand."

He shook his head, then stopped as fire pierced through his skull. "No. I mean, yes, but…" He squeezed his eyes shut, but that pulled at his swollen skin and hurt almost as badly as the pounding in his brain. He froze for a moment and focused on breathing only. Not too deep, or his ribs would start shooting bullets through his side.

"Lie down, Simeon. Rest."

Maybe that was a good idea. "All right. Then I'll tell you…what happened back in the cave." The shaman's words had been in Crow, so Emma still had no idea why they'd been released. If he knew her, the not knowing was probably driving her crazy. She must really be worried about him to have not asked yet.

He didn't breathe as he sank back into the snow, then it took a few seconds to get his intakes regulated again. When he was finally able to focus on Emma, she clutched his hand, stroking the top of it with her thumb.

"Could you understand anything the medicine man said back there?"

She shook her head. "You mean the old man who sat by the tunnel entrance? I couldn't tell what anyone said."

"When he came back into the cave and saw them beating me, he told them he'd had a dream the night before that a Mannegishi would come into their cave in the form of a white man. If they let him take what he came for and leave in peace, he wouldn't harm them. Otherwise his tricks would bring devastation to their people."

Her pretty brow puckered. "Mannegishi?"

"The Crow believe there's another race of tiny people with long, skinny arms and big, bald heads. They go around playing tricks on people."

She pinched her lips, but a glimmer of something touched her eyes. "I had a great-uncle like that once."

The chuckle that rumbled in his chest shot pain through his ribs, and he grabbed his side to stop it. "Don't make me laugh."

She covered his hand and side with her own palm. "I'm sorry."

He let his eye drift shut, giving his body a moment to settle.

"So…they thought you were this short, bald trickster?" Doubt laced her voice.

"Yep." He knew better than to nod this time. "Taking a different form was part of the trick."

She was quiet for a moment, and he almost opened his eye to see what thoughts played across her face. But then she spoke. "You think God sent the dream so they'd let us go?"

"That's what I thought at first. But when Quiet Deer said she helped because of your cross necklace…I don't know. She's the shaman's granddaughter, so he would have listened to her." He stopped himself just before he started to shrug. "Whether he really had the dream or only said it to stop Red Bear, I don't know. Either way, it was God's doing."

She didn't answer, but as the quiet lingered, a shiver coursed through him. "Let's get your ribs wrapped, then warm you up."

He didn't argue, just shifted as she directed while she wrapped a cloth around his abdomen several times. She started to tie it, but the thing was too loose to bind his ribs in place. "Tighter."

The bandage tightened a little, but still not enough.

"Tighter."

This time the cloth pulled strong enough to support

his injured midsection. "Good." He released his spent air with the word.

She bustled over him a while longer, wrapping his extra fur around him and feeding him jerked meat from his pack.

He let her fuss, saving up his strength for the ride that had to come soon. They needed to get farther from these Indians. There was no telling whether Red Bear would ignore the shaman's command in secret and come after them. They were far too vulnerable here. Besides, Joseph needed help.

He felt for the pistol at his waistband, but the spot was empty. *No.* Not only had he lost some of their firepower, he might have put it in the hands of the enemy. Assuming the Indians knew how to use the gun. And it only had five shots.

Still…

"Emma."

"Yes?" Her hand stroked his forehead with the lightest of touches. A tingle raised bumps down his arms.

"Hand me my rifle. From the saddle."

The rustle of her dress sounded as she moved away. A moment later, he could feel her presence beside him again, even though he hadn't heard her approach. "What should I do with it?"

"Here." He reached for the gun, forcing his good eye open as he gripped the solid metal and wood. He looked up at her. "When you're ready, we need to get going. Joseph's waiting for us at that overhang where we spent the night."

"Joseph." She murmured the name. "Is he all right?"

"I think so." He couldn't bring himself to dim the hope in her eyes. "Insisted on coming, but he was pretty weak so I left him there with provisions." *Lord, let him still be all right.*

She nibbled her lip. "I don't think you're ready to travel."

"Just give me another minute. I'll be fine." He reached for her hand as he let his eye drift shut. "Tell me what happened before I got there."

She recounted her story from when the Indian attacked her near their camp until Quiet Deer told her Red Bear planned for her to be his squaw. The tale did exactly what he'd expected—it infused fire in his blood.

He rolled onto his side, then up onto all fours. "Let's get going. I want you away from this place."

It took everything he had not to pass out from the pain as Emma helped him onto Pet's back. He positioned himself behind the saddle, leaving a spot for Emma in the leather seat.

As she prepared to lift her foot into the stirrup, she paused and looked around. "Where's Mustang?"

Simeon scanned the area as he thought back through the last hour. "Last time I saw him he was trotting over to you in that cave. He'll show up again. Always does."

She still lingered on the ground, looking almost uncertain. "Seeing him was my first bit of hope." The corner of her mouth pulled upward. "I think it was also the first time he's come near me without growling."

He tried not to chuckle. "I decided that was his way of showing he liked you."

She turned a glare on him. "Hardly. There was more than once I thought he'd take my fingers off."

He reached a hand to her. "Come up. Let's find your brother."

She settled in front of him, and he turned Pet toward the trail. This feeling, this intense rightness in his chest at having her so near, was worth every second of pain.

Emma strained to see through the murky light of the setting sun. Snow had covered Simeon's tracks from earlier that day, so she was relying on her memory and the pattern of the trees to keep them on the trail. Of course, she could ask Simeon, but he'd been quiet for a while, and she could feel the weight of his head heavy on top of hers. He had so many injuries, his body needed to rest.

Her own limbs sagged from exhaustion, and her hip ached where she'd been kicked, but she still pressed on. Joseph was somewhere ahead. He needed them.

Darkness fell in earnest, and she could feel Simeon's steady breathing through her back. She could see almost nothing save a few feet around them. Should she stop? Wake Simeon and let him guide them?

"Simeon?"

Her pulse jumped at the voice coming from the

darkness ahead. She tried to peer through the haze. "Joseph?"

Simeon shifted behind her, his breaths changing as he straightened with a groan.

She reined Pet toward the voice. "Joseph, are you there?"

"Emma!"

Her heart sang as the sound of her twin's voice wove through her. "We're here, Joseph. We're coming."

The light from his campfire appeared through the trees, although it was more like a faint glow from the coals. Joseph's figure took shape beside it, a shadow sitting on the ground, propped against the rock wall. "Is Simeon with you?"

"We're both here." She urged Pet the last few feet, then reined in at the camp. She touched Simeon's arm, which rested around her protruding abdomen. "We're here, Simeon. Do you think you can get down?"

"Yeah." The word sounded thick, but he shifted behind her and slid slowly to the ground. A gasp slipped from his mouth as he descended, but he landed on his feet.

She raised her leg over the mare's neck, as she'd started having to do with her belly so big, and slid sideways until she landed on her feet on the ground.

Simeon still stood beside the horse, clutching the saddle as if it alone held him upright. She slipped her hand in his. "Come lay down beside the fire." She tried to find his eyes, but the shadows were so deep, it took a moment for her to realize his eyelids were closed.

But when she pulled on his hand, he followed like an obedient child. She'd never seen him so passive. Normally, Simeon would be the one guiding her. Was his complacency due to pain only? Or had the beating injured something more? Maybe the blows to his head had done more damage than just bruises on his face.

A new panic crept into her chest. She'd read in *The Westhaven Daily* about a man who died after a blow to the head because his brain swelled inside his skull. Could something like that have happened to Simeon? Once she had him settled and saw to Joseph, she'd check for symptoms.

Her eyes roamed over her brother as she led Simeon to the fireside and helped him lie down. "How are you, Joey?"

He looked decent, although it was hard to tell much in the semi-darkness. His face was so pale it shone in the moonlight.

He gave her a tired half-smile. "Fine and dandy now that you're here. What happened to you? Looks like you gave Simeon a good beating anyway."

With Simeon settled on the ground, she stroked his hair one last time, then rose and made her way around the fire to her brother. "That was Red Bear's doing. How're you feeling? Is the fever gone?"

She knelt beside him and brushed her fingers across his forehead. A little bit of heat there, but nothing like the way he'd burned while he'd been unconscious. Sitting back on her heels, she scanned his form, all the way down to his leg, covered by his trousers. "The leg still getting better?"

Her gaze came back to his face.

"Yes, ma'am. Healing just fine."

She studied his eyes. The exhaustion there told another story. Once she got them all fed, she'd check his leg over better. The thought of how much work lay ahead of her settled a blanket of weariness over her shoulders, but her men needed tending.

She turned back to Simeon. His breathing barely raised his coat, and in the dim light washing his features, she saw that the swelling in his eye looked worse than earlier. Between the two of them, he likely needed attention the most.

After stoking the fire, she added more wood until the blaze leapt high enough to cut the edge from the frigid night. Pet still stood patiently in the snow, and Emma removed Simeon's rifle, packs and blankets, then dished out provisions for the men. Joseph took it with a thankful smile, but Simeon had begun a soft snoring. As she inspected his face, she saw the swelling around his eyes and nose had definitely increased, maybe even to the point of hindering his breathing. She hadn't thought about whether his nose might be broken, but maybe she should do something to keep his airway open.

She ran her hand over his head, brushing her thumb across his forehead near the hairline—the only spot on his face free from damage. Seeing him like this made her chest ache with an intensity that pierced through her bones. He'd endured all this because of her. Certainly she hadn't intended it, but watching his pain was almost too much to bear.

His eye opened in a thin sliver, just enough for her to see the darkness of his pupil.

She summoned a smile for him. "How are you feeling, love?"

"You're…so…beautiful." His voice graveled as if he'd dragged it over a dry creek bed, but the intensity of the words soaked through her like a warm tea on a snowy day.

She raised his hand to her lips as his image blurred. "You are, too."

His chuckle turned into a cough, then a groan as he gripped his side with his free hand. "Don't…make me…laugh."

"I'm sorry." She stroked his hairline again. "Do we have anything I can give you for pain?"

He shook his head in a slow deliberate movement, his eyelid coming to rest on his lower lashes again. "No, just need…sleep."

"Can you eat something first? All I could find was jerky, and I've melted snow to drink."

"All right."

He chewed the meat methodically, letting her raise his head to drink between bites. Every movement seemed to pain him, and her weariness paled against the effort he had to put forth for each breath.

When Simeon finished eating and his hoarse, steady breathing took over, she glanced around the campsite. Was there anything else that couldn't wait until after she'd slept a few hours?

A flash of movement outside the light grabbed her attention. She'd already reached for the rifle before she realized it was Pet, waiting patiently in her saddle and bridle.

Emma pushed to her feet and trudged out to the horse. "I'm sorry, girl. I need to get you settled too." She was pretty sure she remembered where Simeon had tied the horses the last time they'd camped here. But would there be anything there for the mare?

"Just leave her with us, Em. My gelding's in a pen about a hundred yards out, but she's fine where she is."

They had no grain tucked away in Simeon's pack, and the snow was too deep here to provide fodder. Tomorrow, if both men were well enough to travel, they had to get back to their main camp. There was so much they needed. Food, medicines, feed for the animals. Not to mention the other two horses still camped there. Tomorrow would be soon enough, though.

For now, she was ready to collapse.

After stripping Pet's tack and hobbling her the way she'd seen Simeon do, Emma added another couple logs to the fire, then sank onto a blanket beside Joseph.

What a day.

"You all right, Em?" Joseph's words sounded drowsy, like the sleep-tousled boy who'd climbed into her bed when they were kids and one of them had had a bad dream. They'd shared a bedroom at the house in Baltimore, and she couldn't ever remember running to their parents' room for solace. There was no need as long as Joseph was there to defend her.

"Fine, Joey. How 'bout you?"

His blanket rustled as his hand slid out, fumbling across the ground between them. She slipped her fingers into his the same way she'd always done in those nighttime moments.

"I'm glad you're back."

Warmth flooded her chest, seeping out through her veins to every part of her body. It overshadowed even the profound exhaustion and ache in her muscles. "Me, too."

Thank you, Lord, for Joey. And Simeon. A sharp kick pressed into her lower belly. *And this sweet life inside me.*

And for sleep.

Chapter Twenty-Seven

God has proved so faithful. Why do I still cling to this worry?
~ Emma's Journal

Pain was the first thought that niggled in Simeon's brain, like a worm eating through an apple, leaving a putrid waste everywhere it touched.

A moan slipped from his lips, then something icy touched them. A cloth. Damp and cold. He sucked the fabric, taking the liquid in his parched mouth. But the effort pounded through his skull.

He froze, not daring to breathe as his head pulsed, feeling like it expanded with every beat. Was it possible for a head to explode? That might be the best course at this point. At least then the agony would come to an end.

"Take away his pain, Father. Lessen the swelling."

The soft murmur of the angel voice sounded so far away, but the words gradually permeated the pain to reach his awareness. Emma?

He fought to open his eyes, but only his right eyelid would respond, and then only a crack. Why did the skin pull so tight on his face? It felt like he'd been left to bake out in the sun for days.

He focused on the light coming through that sliver, forcing himself not to blink as he struggled to clear the fog in his mind. "Emma?"

"I'm here, Simeon."

Something cool and wet brushed across his forehead, easing the burn of his skin. "What's happened?"

"You were beaten. Badly." Was that a hitch in her voice, or was his mind just slow to process her words?

He tried to focus on her face, but it was hard to make out details when his eyelid wouldn't open any further. "Where am I?"

"We're still camped under this ledge. You've been asleep for two days now. We were afraid to move you."

Ledge… He struggled to place where they were, but nothing seemed familiar. He remembered a cave. Remembered lying on a stone floor being kicked by an Indian. Emma beside him. Was she hurt? His pulse picked up speed, and he struggled to push up.

Shots exploded inside his head, almost knocking him sideways as everything went black. Sounds still echoed in his mind, but he couldn't tell what was inside and what came from around him. "Emma." He reached out, grasping for anything that could pull him up. If the Indians were still there, Emma wasn't safe. He had to get up. Had to push through this pain to get her to safety.

"Simeon."

His fingers gripped skin. Smooth, cool flesh. It was Emma. He knew by the touch of her. He clutched what must be an arm, not willing to let her be pulled away from him.

"Shh. It's all right, Simeon." Another cold hand touched his fingers where he held her.

"We have to get out of here." Had that been his voice? It sounded hoarse, like a man he'd never heard before.

"It's all right, Simeon. We're safe." Her angel voice again. How could she be so calm? Didn't she understand?

"The Indians." He had to make her see. Using his grip on her arm for leverage, he tried to pull himself up. But he was so weak.

"They're gone, Simeon. The Indians let us go free. We're far away now."

Far away? He sank back to the ground, letting his eyelid drift closed. He didn't have the strength to sort through the fog in his mind anymore. But he still didn't release her arm. He had to know for sure. "You're safe?"

Her hand brushed his brow again. "I'm safe. Rest now. Let your body heal."

Fine. He would have to believe her. He couldn't hold back the darkness any longer.

Emma stroked Simeon's hair as she replayed his confused words. She'd been so relieved to see him awaken, but was the confusion because he'd slept for two days, or had the swelling done permanent damage?

Joseph stepped into the camp and sank to his

haunches across from her. "Found a good spot for the horses. The snow'd melted so you could actually see the grass poking through."

She glanced up at him, but her mind had trouble shifting to the new topic. "That's good."

His brow pinched, and his gaze dropped to Simeon. "Any change?"

"He woke up."

"Great." Her brother seemed to be waiting for her response. Reading her too closely. "Right?"

"Yes." She tried to find the elation she'd felt when she saw his eyelid flutter. "It is good."

"But?"

"He was pretty confused. He remembered the Indians but thought we were still there. In danger. If he hadn't been so weak he would have jumped up and started fighting."

Joseph's lips pursed. "That's probably normal, what with all the swelling on his face and the jarring to his brain. I think it's just good he woke up."

She inhaled a breath. "Yes. Good." She had to focus on their blessings. Simeon had awakened. Joseph was up and moving and looked so much better now. He was her old Joey again, although he still tired quickly. But at least he'd found the strength to travel to their main camp and bring back supplies and the other horses. He'd even regained some use of his broken arm. They could stay in this spot until Simeon was better and Joseph healed even more.

Simeon. She scanned his face, cataloging the changes from the day before. The bruising seemed like it might be turning a yellowish black. That made it look worse, but the sooner it ran its course, the sooner it'd be gone. The swelling appeared to have lessened a tiny bit. Maybe. Or that might be her mind grasping for what she hoped would be. The stubble on his jaw almost hid the skin there, and she brushed her fingertips across the thick hairs. He always kept himself so clean-shaven, she itched to find his razor and do at least that small task for him. But she didn't dare attempt it with the way his left side bulged larger than the right.

She had to be patient, no matter how much the helpless waiting drove her mad. *Father, heal him. Take away the pain. Please, Lord.* Her strongest solace came in knowing that God loved this man as much as she did. *Thank you, Lord.* She brushed a kiss on her fingertips and touched it to the swollen, scabbed skin of Simeon's lips. He was God's now, and God would return him to her. She had to trust that.

Simeon parted his eyes a tiny bit as they adjusted to the brightness of the light. A dull throb pulsed through his temples, but he pushed through it to focus on the sounds around him. Steady breathing, like someone lay sleeping. And a rustle.

The ache in his skull was strong enough to keep him from moving his head, but he shifted his eyes, opening the lids a little wider. The skin around his left eye felt tight, and he had to work harder to make the muscles move.

Emma sat up on the other side of the bed of coals that had once been their campfire. Her hair was mussed and puffed out in a short, sleep-rumpled bob.

Short? He studied her, a snippet of memory tugging at him.

The Indians. The beating. The miracle of walking out alive. The memories unfolded more the farther he pushed. He remembered mounting Pet with Emma climbing aboard in front of him. But beyond that…nothing.

He scanned the rock overhang above and the bit of sky he could see without moving his head. It was barely past dawn, if the color creeping near the tree line were any indication. The rock seemed familiar, but all this studying had increased the pain in his head. It hurt too much to think.

A movement to the side pulled his focus back to Emma. She was watching him, her amber eyes glistening even in the morning shadows.

"You're awake." A soft smile curved her mouth.

"I think." His throat ached when he spoke, and his voice graveled so that he barely recognized it.

"Hungry?"

He tried to clear his throat, but a knife of pain shot through his ribs when he tensed his midsection. "Yeah."

Her smile brightened, and she struggled to pull herself to a standing position with the swell of the baby making movement hard. A pang hit his chest that had nothing to do with the sore ribs. Her time would be on them soon. There was so much he'd wanted to do before then. So much he *had* to do, with the most critical item being to deliver them safely to their family in Alberta. How much longer did Emma have before the baby came?

They'd traveled for five weeks before Joseph took sick, but he wasn't sure how much time had passed since then.

He swallowed, trying to clear the cotton from his throat without angering his ribs. "How much time do we have left, Emma?"

She paused, a log in hand ready to lay on the coals in the fire ring. Raising her gaze to his face, her expression grew guarded. "You mean how much farther to Canada? I was going to ask you that."

He shook his head, but stopped as a bullet shot through his temples. He gripped his forehead, willing the ringing to stop. "No. I mean how much time before the baby comes."

He wished he could see her face, but the pulsing in his skull wouldn't allow him to even open his eyes.

"I don't know exactly. Maybe three or four weeks."

Dropping his hand, he did open his eyes then. "Three or four weeks?" The emotions that coursed through him were too much for his mind to decipher. How far were they from Alberta? Could he get them there and talk Emma into marrying him in that much time? What if she said no? What if she didn't want the babe to carry his name? What if she didn't want to marry him at all?

"What is it, Simeon? What's wrong?" Emma was by his side, though he hadn't heard her come. "You're pale as snow. Are you chilled?"

Chilled? No, fire raced through his veins. He had to get up from this sickbed. Push through the pain and get them packed and on the trail. It wasn't safe for Emma to travel so close to her time. He'd already risked too much.

Propping his elbows on the ground, he squeezed his eyes shut and pushed upward. He clenched his jaw to hold in a groan, then barely allowed himself to breathe as his side screamed. At last, it lessened enough for him to unclench his jaw. "Wake your…brother. We're…leaving." He measured his breaths, preparing himself to push all the way up to standing.

"No."

A hand touched his shoulder, but he shook it off.

"Simeon, lie down."

The command came so sharp, he stopped midway through his movements. His lungs burned to breathe in deep gulps, but he knew better. Instead, he forced in shallow intakes of air.

Emma's hands pressed his shoulders again, and he opened his eyes. Her face was inches from his, her amber eyes searching him. "Please, lie down."

This time the words were so achingly soft, his body obeyed without him telling it to. He held her gaze, though, as he sank to the ground. Indeed, he would have been hard pressed to look away. It was as though his spirit latched onto her and clung for dear life.

She brushed a hand across his forehead, and as soothing as the gesture was, it made him feel too much like an invalid. He wanted to rise up and be strong for her. To slay a thousand dragons and bring her to their destination in safety.

He slipped his hand over hers and brought her fingers to his lips, his eyes still lost in the strength of her gaze. He pressed a kiss to the tips of her fingers, considered reaching for her face so he could capture her mouth.

Instead, he reached up to cradle her cheek. She was so soft. So smooth against his rough, work-hardened hand. And wasn't that symbolic of the two of them? She was elegance and beauty, an angel in a wild country. He was hardened, brought low by a past he couldn't let go. Yet God had released him from the pain. Forgiven him. Poured a love into him that pressed through every boundary he'd set.

He could still feel the freedom in that love, even now as his body ached. It made him want to try with Emma. He wasn't much of a prize. She may not want him. But he had to try.

"Emma."

She leaned into his hand on her cheek, and he stroked her with his thumb. "Just one more day, Simeon."

He had to focus on the words to make sense of what she was saying. She must still be talking about when they'd begin traveling again. But he had other things to say.

He locked her in his gaze. "I don't want just one more day. I want all the days."

She drew in a sharp breath, but he pressed on.

"I love you, Emma. I never thought I'd be capable of love again. Never thought I'd want to. But between you and God…" His throat clogged, but he pushed forward. "I want to spend all my days with you, if you'll have me." He suddenly felt so vulnerable, as though he were lying exposed while a bear charged.

He tried to study her face. To read her thoughts in her eyes. But they shimmered so much he couldn't see through the moisture. Were tears a good thing? Probably not.

His heart tried to shutter itself, but he inhaled and forced himself to wait.

Chapter Twenty-Eight

I wait with bated breath.
~ Simeon

Simeon didn't breathe again as he awaited Emma's response. But when a tear slipped through her lower lashes, the realization swept over him. She was trying to find a way to say no. Despite the passion he'd felt in their kiss, the way his heart connected with hers. The times he'd read in her eyes what he'd foolishly thought was love.

His gaze dropped to her chin. "If you don't feel the same…"

"I do."

Her words spilled out so quickly, he wasn't sure he'd heard them right. He raised his focus back to her eyes, daring to hope.

She sniffed. "I do." A smile touched the corners of her mouth. "I didn't think you'd ever… I mean, I was guarding myself because I knew you'd be leaving." An unsteady breath hiccupped from her chest as another tear slipped from her eyes. She sniffed hard and wiped the drop with her fingers, a wobbly smile peeking through. "I'm so happy."

His chest burned with the joy that surged through him. But the tears? He had to make those right.

Releasing Emma's hand, he rolled to the side so he could push himself to a sitting position. Fire exploded in his midsection as he sat up, but he clamped his jaw tight to hold the groan inside.

At last he was upright, facing Emma's worried expression. He focused all his attention on her, pushing the pain to the back of his mind. Taking her face in both his hands, his gaze dropped to her lips, but he raised it back to her eyes. There would be time for that after he got things straight. "Does that mean you'll marry me?"

A bubble of laughter slipped through her lips. "Yes. I'll marry you."

He could stand it no more. Joy overflowed in his chest as he pulled her to him.

She snuggled in, and the wonder of it was worth every bit of pain from the extra pressure on his ribs. The scent of roses slipped over him, melding with her softness as she rested her head on his shoulder. Their breathing slipped into unison, and his mind wandered to all the times to come when he would to hold her this close. He reined his thoughts in. There was still one more thing to set straight.

Leaning back a little, he tried to see her face. She straightened, putting distance between them so he could look in her eyes. He'd be happy staring at her beautiful face forever, but his body missed the contact.

"There's one other thing." He reached up to stroke the short hair that feathered over her face.

She pushed the strand behind her ear, a hint of irritation at the hair evident in her motion.

"Have I told you how much I like your hair short?"

Her amber eyes widened. "You do? It was so long before. My best feature." The longing and sadness in her gaze tugged at his chest.

He fingered the ends that curled around her ear, brushing her chin. "Your best feature? Your hair is beautiful, but I love these eyes that show your heart." He moved his touch to her temples. "Your strength that never questions whether you'll do what's right. Your faith that never wavers, even when your world is turning upside down. Your devotion. Your love. I think your best feature is all of you."

Her eyes shimmered again. Hopefully those were still happy tears.

"That's beautiful." She sniffed, an unsteady smile touching her face. "What was it you were going to say?"

Yes. A knot of nerves tightened in his gut. He studied her face as he tried to decide how to best word the question. His eyes dropped to the swell of her midsection, the baby inside. He longed to reach out and stroke the child, but he wasn't sure how she'd feel about that. Then he raised his gaze back to her face. He should just say what he wanted.

"Emma, I want to be a papa to this little one. I know I don't really have the right, but… I want to love him or her like my very own."

Her smile softened. "No child could be luckier."

He searched her eyes. "Would you want the babe to…have my name, too?" He could barely breathe as he tried to decipher her thoughts.

"I would."

"You would?"

A shadow crossed her eyes. "Lance's name was Carter, but I changed my surname back to Malcom after he died. It seemed better for both of us." Her smile was sad. "I might not be tracked as easily, and this sweet babe wouldn't have so much to overcome." She rested a hand on her midsection as she met Simeon's gaze. "We would both be honored to take your name."

As satisfaction pulsed through him, he leaned forward to capture her mouth with his. The taste of her was sweeter than he remembered.

Intoxicating. Drawing him in with aching gentleness. He savored every second, craving the rest of his life spent with this woman.

"You two gonna stop that long enough to make breakfast?"

Emma jumped at the sound of her brother's voice and jerked back from Simeon's kiss. She glanced at her brother, who'd awakened and now sat on his pallet eyeing them with raised eyebrows.

Her gaze lowered to her hands where they rested on Simeon's chest. She dropped them to her lap. "I…" Her mind was so befuddled she couldn't think of a proper answer. "Yes, um…" She darted a look at Simeon, but the cheeky grin on his face didn't relieve her fluster.

She pushed up to her feet and grabbed the coffee pot. "Yes, I'll gather water while you make the fire."

"Wait." Simeon's sharp command paused her mid-stride. She pivoted back to eye him.

Gone was the impish grin. It was hard to tell his expression from the swelling that distorted his features, but the pinch of his lips made the change in his mood clear. "You're not going off on your own again. That Indian could be waiting to get you alone. I'll go collect the water." He leaned forward and placed his hands on the ground like he was trying to rise, but slowed as his breathing grew quick and shallow. He teetered on his hands and knees and looked like he might fall sideways.

She lunged forward. "Stop, Simeon. Lie down. You're not ready to get up yet." His memory was just now coming back to him, the last thing they needed was for him to jar his brain by falling.

"Aw, both of you sit. I'll get the water." Joseph pushed to his feet and grabbed the pitcher from her hand, then stomped off toward the trees.

Emma watched him go, then turned back to Simeon.

Even the way the swelling distorted his face, she could tell he was trying to raise a brow at her, and the way his mouth twitched made a giggle rise up in her chest. She let it spill out, probably sounding like a school girl, but she didn't care. Simeon had asked her to become his wife.

She started for the pile of logs they'd been using for the fire and tried to contain her grin as she set about bringing the ashes to life.

Simeon sank back onto his pallet and watched, his eyes dipping to half-mast. Their little tete-a-tete had probably been more than he was ready for, but she didn't regret it for a moment. Simeon loved her. And wanted to marry her. Even wanted to love and care for this sweet bundle inside her. She pressed a hand to the underside of her belly, and the babe responded with a sharp jab. This sweet, feisty bundle.

Her gaze wandered to Simeon again and found him watching her. She couldn't have wiped away her smile if she'd wanted to, and his own mouth pulled into a grin.

"You know, I need to ask Joseph for his blessing." Even in his tired state, Simeon's voice poured over her like honey.

Her gaze flicked to the woods where Joseph had disappeared. "Oh, he'll give it."

That raised brow again. "You sound so certain."

She cocked her chin. "He likes you. Besides, I'm older. He knows better than to resist me."

A soft chuckle turned into a wince as he grabbed his side. "What am I getting myself into?"

Simeon waited to talk with Joseph until after breakfast when Emma was scrubbing the frying pan in the snow at the edge of their camp. She'd helped him prop up on a roll of furs, but he still hated to be in this reclined position for such an important conversation. But the activity this morning had used up much of his strength, and it was a struggle just to keep his eyes open.

Joseph sat on the other side of the fire, taking in the scenery as he sipped a mug of tea. "Ya know, I think I'm actually getting used to these teas you drink. Thought you were crazy not to drink coffee like the rest of the civilized world, but this isn't half bad if you brew it strong enough."

Simeon gripped his side as a chuckle forced its way out. "A lot easier to obtain out here. I thought about trying to grow my own coffee beans at first but finally decided I'd be better off if I kicked the habit." And at the time, he'd been so deep in his grief, any deprivation to punish himself had seemed like a good idea.

Silence settled over them for a moment, but the seconds ticked in Simeon's mind with an urgency that tightened his nerves. He needed to ask the question soon, before he lost his opportunity. And his nerve.

"Joseph, I've a question for you."

The man turned to eye him. "Oh?"

"I'd like your blessing to marry your sister."

His brow crinkled and his lips pursed. "I wondered when you'd ask." But then he was silent. Was that his agreement? By the unsettled look on his face, probably not.

Simeon held his tongue, something that seemed much harder to do now than before he'd met Emma and Joseph.

At last, "Where would you live?"

Simeon raised his brows. "I'm assuming Alberta

somewhere. Figured I'd build us a home near your aunt's ranch. I'll work to get Emma's name cleared down in Texas, but I imagine she'll still want to be close to family. That is, unless you're planning to go back to Texas or Baltimore?"

That thought hadn't occurred to him, but if Emma wanted to move back to one of the eastern states, so be it. Her happiness meant more to him than the state where he resided. Or the country, for that matter.

Joseph took a sip of tea. "These mountains have kinda grown on me. Thought I might hang around and see what kind of trouble I can find up here."

A slow breath slipped from Simeon, easing the tension in his shoulders. He'd move back east for Emma, but the idea of staying in the Rockies appealed to him so much more.

Joseph narrowed a look at him. "So you're not planning to move her away from me?"

Simeon met his gaze. "Wouldn't dream of it."

A small nod. "Well, I won't ask how you'll provide for her. I imagine she'll be a sight better off in this country with you than with me. I expect you to do right by her, though. And if you don't, you can be assured you'll have both me an' God to answer to."

A grin pulled at Simeon's mouth, but he tried to keep a straight face. "No concerns there."

"And the baby? You'll raise the child as yours?"

Simeon swallowed, the image of his own twins flitting through his mind. "It would be my honor." *God, make me worthy.*

"Then you have my blessing and my thanks. And I'm pretty sure you have Emma's love, too, or my answer would have been different."

Simeon nodded. "I'll do my best by her." And if God helped with His best, maybe things would go better this time around.

Joseph was silent, his gaze lingering over Emma's form as she knelt in the snow about twenty yards out. "She's special. My best friend."

Was that the kind of bond that would have existed between his own children? That old familiar longing tightened Simeon's chest. "I don't take that lightly. And I don't plan to take her from you, Joseph."

The man only nodded.

By the next evening, they'd only made it as far as the main camp, where the whole mess with the Indians had begun. Simeon's spirit chaffed the slow travel, though his body told him even the three or four hours in the saddle had pushed him to the edge of his physical limits. He'd had the chance to examine his wounds that morning— aside from the ribs, mostly bruising. The vision in his left eye was still limited due to the lingering swelling, and he could just imagine how bad his face looked with the bruises mottling yellow and green. It was a wonder Emma had said yes to him in this condition.

Nay, it was a miracle. Something only God could have orchestrated. *Thanks again, Lord.*

The short day of travel seemed to have exhausted Emma, too. She'd stretched out on her pallet after the meal and said she was going to rest a while before cleaning up.

"Lie still. It's about time I earn my keep." Joseph pushed to his feet and grabbed their used plates and spoons.

Simeon sank back against his own furs as Joseph puttered around the place. He'd just close his eyes for a moment, then go check the horses a final time before dark.

But when he opened his lids again, darkness had fully taken over, and Joseph was sitting on his bedroll, strumming the guitar. The soft strains lingered in the clear mountain air as he strummed a series of single chords.

Simeon let the sounds soothe him, his eyelids drifting shut as the chords progressed in a rhythmic pattern.

When a soft soprano rose above the notes, his eyes popped open. Without moving his head, he focused on Emma's pallet across the campfire. She sat upright, leaning against a tree. But in the darkness, he couldn't see her expression.

Her voice was so clear, almost haunting as it rose in a descant over the minor chording. He let his eyes drift shut, absorbing the music within him, feeling his soul respond in a way that only music could draw from him. This woman had abilities beyond what he could ever imagine. And soon she would be his. His soulmate. The thought was almost too wonderful to fathom.

A single tear of gratitude slipped from the corner of

his eye.

Chapter Twenty-Nine

How can it be so close? All that I've longed for, yet part of me fears the changes.
~ Emma's Journal

The next day they moved on, and what a relief to finally leave the campsite that held so many aching memories for Emma. Joseph's infection. Her own kidnapping. Yet they'd pushed through every traumatic event and maybe they'd become stronger for it. Mostly.

Simeon no longer carried the weight of guilt from his past. And he loved her. And wanted to marry her. She should pinch herself to make sure she wasn't dreaming. She would if she weren't so bone-weary and aching everywhere.

By the middle of the third day, they maneuvered downward on the mountain trail, which finally leveled out into a wide valley, surrounded by mountains on all sides. A small lake stretched before them, its water as green as the moss that grew on the trees around Baltimore.

"Do those look like buildings up there?" From his spot at the front of their caravan, Joseph pointed past the lake. Emma squinted to distinguish the images, and Simeon pushed his horse into a jog around hers, riding up beside Joseph.

"I think so. I've been wondering if we'd crossed into Canada. I reckon these folks will know." Simeon's deep voice drifted back to her.

They let the horses stop for a drink at the lake's edge, then kept moving toward what looked like it might be a small town. Even the horses seemed to know something good was coming as their strides lengthened on the even terrain.

People. It seemed almost a dream to suddenly be faced with human interaction. Would there be women in the group? Was this Canada? How close were they to Aunt Mary's ranch?

A few minutes passed in silence as the buildings grew closer. There weren't as many as she'd first thought. Maybe four or five wooden structures, some as small as storage sheds.

Simeon still rode beside Joseph, his pack horse trailing him. The trail was much wider now, and she maneuvered her mare up to Simeon's other side. She was just in time to see him pull his rifle from its scabbard and lay it across his lap.

"Do you think they're dangerous?" She scanned his face, but it had settled into an emotionless expression. The swelling had mostly disappeared, but the bruising had turned a yellowish color that still made her heart ache for the pain he endured. Just now, it made his expression look especially fierce.

"Hope not. But we may as well be prepared."

Out of the corner of her eye, she saw Joseph reach for his rifle and place it the same way Simeon had.

Honestly. These men were awfully untrusting. Even so, a knot tightened in her stomach. The baby inside her responded to the tension with a sharp kick low in her midsection. It seemed the pokes had been focusing in that lower region the past few days. She rarely felt them as high as her ribs anymore. Did the change mean she was nearing her time? If only she had a mother or physician to answer these questions.

When they were within a hundred yards of the buildings, a figure appeared from the nearest structure. His broad form was clothed in brown furs, but she couldn't make out much more than that.

As they neared, the man's features became clearer. A dark, bushy beard covered much of his face, and atop his head sat an animal peering out with dark beady eyes—almost like those of the man. A raccoon skin hat?

The stranger wore the same buckskin clothing as Simeon. And like Simeon, he gripped a rifle at the ready.

He stood with his feet spread as they approached, but no other signs of life moved around the buildings. Did he live alone in this place?

Simeon reined his horse to a stop when they were about twenty feet from the man, and the rest of the horses halted with his. Even the beasts followed his lead without question.

"Howdy." Simeon's voice rang deep across the

distance.

The man only nodded, his gaze a mix of curiosity and wariness as it crawled over them, stalling on Emma for a long moment before dragging back to Simeon.

"We're wondering if we've reached Canada yet."

"*Oui.*" He spat a stream of dark liquid to the side. French? At least he seemed to understand Simeon's English.

"Is this a settlement then?" Simeon nodded toward the buildings behind the man.

Their unusual greeter twisted to look where Simeon pointed, as if he weren't aware of the cluster of ragged structures behind him. He turned back and spat another stream. "Wouldn't call it that. Just a few trappers found ourselves a place to tan hides." Each word rolled in a heavy French accent, but they were decipherable.

Simeon leaned forward to rest an arm on his saddle horn, affecting a casual stance. Although he still gripped the barrel of his rifle. "You know of any ranches in these parts? Owned by a Lockman?"

The stranger studied him, taking more notice than he had so far in the conversation. Then his gaze wandered back to Emma before focusing on Simeon again. "You lookin' to hire on?"

Simeon glanced at Joseph. "We're family. Come to visit."

Joseph nodded, affirming the vague comment.

The man and his coonskin hat scrutinized Simeon a moment longer, then glanced to his left. "About a day's ride through that pass."

Emma followed his gaze, focusing on the V where two mountain slopes met in a gentle hill. Aunt Mary was only a day's ride away? Relief almost sapped the last of the strength from her aching muscles. So close. Then she would finally be done with the constant jarring of long hours in the saddle. Her back ached more with each mile.

Simeon straightened in his saddle, turned Pet toward the pass, and saluted the man. "Much obliged." All the horses set off at a walk, following Pet's lead.

That was it? The first white man they'd seen in weeks and they were leaving after only a handful of questions? The least they could do was stop and eat lunch here. Pick the man's brain about the area and Aunt Mary's ranch.

She pushed her mare into a longer stride to ride up beside Simeon, although his horse had picked up speed too. "Simeon." She tried to keep her voice low enough that the trapper wouldn't hear.

"Yep?" He didn't look at her, just kept his head pointed toward the mountain pass.

"Why don't we stop here for a while? He could tell us about the area."

"I didn't like his look." A muscle flexed in his jaw.

His look? Sure, the man had been scraggly and greasy, but he was a mountain trapper. She wouldn't expect many of them to keep themselves as well as Simeon did. "He didn't look any different than what I'd expect from living in such a remote place."

His jaw worked again. "I mean the way he looked at you."

She couldn't stop the chuckle that burst out, nor the flood of warmth through her chest. Simeon *was* the protective sort. But after everything she'd been through in the last year—especially the last two weeks—she'd take protective. In truth, she craved protective.

Settling back in the saddle, she let her mare fall into stride beside Simeon as they rode three abreast.

One day. Just one more day, and they'd finally get to rest.

They rode a few more hours, then set up camp for the night. Once she had a stew simmering on the cook fire, Emma collapsed onto her pallet for a few minutes of rest while the men tended the horses. Honestly, she had almost no strength left to keep going.

Simeon seemed to be feeling much better, and Joseph was practically running circles around them both. It was good to see him healthy again, smiling and telling his silly jokes. He even pulled out his guitar after darkness settled in.

But Emma only heard the first part of his opening jig before sleep claimed her.

She slept soundly that night for the first time in days and awoke after dawn had already lightened the sky. She sat up to stretch the soreness from her back and breathed deeply of the cold morning air.

Anticipation tightened her chest. Today would be the

day. This time tomorrow, she'd probably be rising from a real bed. Or at least a bedroll on a wooden floor, under a real roof.

The men were already up, and she hurried through her personal tasks, then readied breakfast. Her stomach roiled at the bear meat sizzling in the pan, and she nibbled on a stale johnnycake, but it crunched like powder in her mouth. She forced down a few bites, then prepared plates for Simeon and Joseph. They were likely more than ready for the variety of food Aunt Mary would serve. At least it'd be better than fried bear and johnnycake for every meal.

When the men came for breakfast, they seemed as ready to get on the trail as she was, scarfing down their food and following it with tea.

"Everything's packed, just need to add your things." Joseph pushed to his feet. "I'll load the dishes while you pack your bedroll."

Emma obeyed orders, rolling her blankets in a neat bundle.

A sound from the patch of woods a dozen feet away made her pause. A growl? She peered toward the barren trunks. Something moved beside one of the trees. A wolf? Or maybe a wolverine like the one that bit Joseph.

She glanced around for a weapon but had nothing. Simeon had already taken her pack to load on the horses. A scraping noise sounded behind her, and she whirled to see Joseph scouring the pan behind her. "Joey." She turned back toward the trees, focusing her eyes to catch any movement.

"What? What's wrong?" Her brother was by her side

in a moment, his hand touching her shoulder.

"There's something there. In the trees. I heard a growl."

"Do you think it's an Indian?"

Her breathing froze. The thought hadn't even crossed her mind. Gooseflesh crawled up the back of her neck, and she wrapped her arms around her, stepping back behind Joseph's shadow. "I…I don't…"

Then the flash of fur moved again, separating from the tree and taking the shape of…a dog. Mustang?

He trotted toward them, the familiar sight feeling like a dream after her fear just moments before. Another growl drifted from his throat, in direct contrast to the friendly swish of his tail as he pattered their direction in the thin snow.

Mustang.

She dropped to her knees as the dog reached them, relief stealing the strength from her muscles. She took his face in her hands. "What are you doing here, boy? You scared me silly."

The dog looked up at her with pleasure in his eyes, his tongue lolling to the side and a strange little half growl rumbling from his throat. She laughed as she stroked his ears flat against his neck. The poor dog had lived such a secluded life, he might never learn social niceties like not growling at people while they performed a kindness for you. But he had his own unique way of showing affection. And she could live with that, now that she understood the language.

"I'm going to check those trees."

Emma glanced up as Joseph strode forward, the butt of his rifle pressed into his shoulder. The sight didn't worry her, though. Mustang wouldn't act so carefree if danger were near.

The animal licked her hand, and she resumed her stroking, happiness bubbling inside her chest as she lavished her joy on the dog.

Emma's eyes kept drifting shut as Simeon signaled a halt that evening.

"Let's camp here. The horses need a rest."

She summoned the energy to straighten and look around. They'd stopped in a snowy patch of uneven ground sprinkled with a handful of pines and rocks jutting through the white blanket.

Not Aunt Mary's ranch. Urgency mixed with annoyance in her chest. "We need to keep going. The ranch can't be much farther."

Simeon had already slid from his horse and strode back to stand beside her. He gripped his hands under her arms and pulled her down. "We're going to stop here for the night."

She didn't have the strength to do anything but obey, sliding to the ground and into his arms. She clung to his shirt, resting her head against his chest. Breathing in his scent…his strength. She was so weary.

He held her for a long moment, then ran his hand up and down her back. "Let's get you to a spot where you can rest."

"I need to start dinner." The words were mumbled into his shirt, so they may not have been discernable.

He turned her, keeping his right arm locked around her back and his left gripping her elbow. "Joseph said he wants to do the cooking tonight."

Emma let him lead her and settled on a fur that magically appeared on the ground. If she could just keep her eyes open… She had to snap out of this and get started on her evening chores.

She ate the food Simeon brought her, washing it down with big gulps of bitter tea. At last she raised her head and looked around.

Simeon sat beside her, and Joseph knelt a few feet past him near the fire. Both men watched her, wary concern in their eyes. She offered them a smile. "I didn't realize how famished I was."

Simeon's gaze flicked to the darkening sky. "I should have stopped us hours ago. Shouldn't have pushed so hard."

She reached forward to slide her fingers into his. "I'm fine, Simeon. And I wouldn't have let you stop hours ago. Every mile we covered today means we'll get to Aunt Mary's earlier tomorrow."

He met her gaze, and she saw it then. Fear. She didn't want to be the cause of that look.

She squeezed his hand. "Have you eaten?" It was a

shame she didn't know the answer to that question, even though she'd sat right beside him. She'd been in such a fog, but her head had cleared some now. She'd have to be more careful not to let herself get so hungry.

While the others ate, Emma scanned their surroundings. If she weren't mistaken, the sound of running water gurgled from somewhere off to the right. The trail grime seemed to cloak her in layers, and although it was too cold for a full bath, she could at least wash her hands and face.

She pressed up from the ground, going to all fours to make it easier to rise to her feet.

Strong hands gripped her upper arms. "Let me help."

She accepted Simeon's assistance with relief. Every movement seemed to take all her strength, and her back ached enough to bring tears to her eyes. She should probably sit down and get some rest, but the sound of that water called to her. She finally made it to her feet and stopped to let her breathing even.

"Emma, sit and rest. Whatever you need, I'll get it." Simeon's gaze entreated, but she tried to offer a reassuring smile.

"I thought I'd take a walk. I think I hear water somewhere."

"Emma…" Simeon scrubbed a hand through his hair, worry lines etching the corners of his eyes.

"I'm fine, Simeon. Honest."

His gaze searched her face, and she willed him to believe her. At last he sighed, dropping his hand to his side.

"I'll walk with you."

Her chest surged. Time alone with Simeon would be a treat, even if it meant she wouldn't get a private moment at the water. "If you insist."

Chapter Thirty

I never thought I could feel so whole.
~ Simeon

Simeon kept a wary eye on Emma as they wove around clusters of fir and pine, but she seemed to be recovered from the exhaustion that had overwhelmed her before. Maybe food really was all she'd needed.

He could shoot himself for pushing so far today, but he kept thinking they'd see the ranch around each curve of the trail. It wasn't until he'd looked back to find Emma practically asleep in the saddle that he'd called an end to the madness.

He inhaled a deep breath, then released it, letting the strain slide from his muscles with the spent air.

"It feels like we've found a secret trail out here, doesn't it?"

He glanced around and nodded. The way the trees clustered did give the space an intimate feel. The sound of water gurgling had grown louder. "I think that might be a spring up ahead. It sounds too fast for a creek."

They wound around another group of trees, the low, bushy cedars blocking their view of what lay ahead. Then a pool appeared before them, water gurgling into it like a spigot from the rock at one end.

"Oh." Emma gasped, then released his arm and stepped to the edge. She dropped to her knees, shucking her gloves before she plunged her hands into the liquid. "It's warm." She turned to him with eyes rounded, delight lighting her face in a way that tightened his chest. What he wouldn't do to keep that look on her face forever.

She splashed the water over her face, then lowered her hands back into the pool, letting the liquid flow through her open fingers. "Come feel it."

He sank to the ground beside her, pulling off his own gloves so he could do as she asked. It was hard to deny her anything.

The heat from the water seared his skin, especially the spots chapped from cold and snow. But it was a good kind of burn, slowly eating away at his tension and soaking through him like a warm tea on a cold morning.

"I'd heard there were hot springs up here."

Emma settled into a sitting position on the ground, keeping her hands in the water. She looked like she wanted to stay a while, so Simeon eased onto his haunches, too.

She flashed him a shy smile, then her gaze fell to the river flowing through her fingers. "Think we'll be able to find a minister out here? I hadn't expected it to be so unsettled."

He'd been wondering that himself, but he hadn't

wanted to voice it. He was beginning to get the feeling the little cluster of buildings they'd passed might be the only town around. "I'm sure your aunt will know where to find someone." He couldn't help but reach out and rub the backs of his fingers down her cheek. Would he be able to find a preacher before the baby came? He had to believe God would make a way. Like the ravens bringing bread and meat to Elijah, surely God could provide someone to marry them before Emma gave birth. *Please, Lord.*

Emma sucked in a hard breath, jerking Simeon's focus to her. "What's wrong?"

She pulled a hand out of the water to rub her rounded side. "Just this little one kicking. When the babe wants to be heard, she gets forceful."

His fingers itched to reach out and touch the spot she rubbed, but he didn't dare. Not yet. Instead, he focused on her face. "You think it's a girl?"

She raised her brows, though her weariness was plain in the way her eyes drooped. "Maybe not, but I've been thinking of her as a girl for a while now." She shrugged. "A boy would be nice, too."

He stroked a piece of hair off her cheek, tucking it behind her ear. "Either way, I hope he or she has your eyes."

She turned that amber gaze on him, plunging its intensity through his defenses. He swallowed, trying to keep himself from getting lost completely. He brushed her chin with his fingers. "And this stubborn chin, too."

A dimple pressed into her cheek. "I wish she could look like you." Was that longing in her tone? He couldn't let himself follow that trail.

Instead, he ran his hand down the length of her arm, weaving his fingers through hers. "Have you thought of names?"

She turned and stared into the bubbling water. "I thought about Hannah, but I'm not sure."

Was that a family name? There was so much he didn't know about her, but he was ready to learn it all. "Do you know any Hannahs?"

Shaking her head, she gripped her fingers tighter around his. "No. I just like the name."

He nodded. "I do, too."

She searched his eyes as if she were looking for something there. "Are you sure?" She took in a breath. "I mean, are you sure you want to do this? Take me and…another man's child." Her last words faded to a whisper, and her expression took on such a fragile edge, he wanted to swoop her into his arms and shore her up.

Instead, he rested their joined hands on her rounded middle, feeling the firm swell of the babe inside. "I'm sure. I know I don't have real claim to the baby. This child's father would have loved him or her, I'm sure. But since he's not here, I want to love her. I want to give the babe…" He wasn't prepared for the crash of emotions that swept over him as he thought about the twins he could no longer love and protect. His voice broke, and he struggled to push back the moisture that clogged this throat. He blinked, forcing his rogue thoughts into control.

"I want to love and give this baby what I couldn't

give my own little ones." He risked a lot as he looked at her, but he needed to know she understood what he meant.

Emma's eyes shimmered, and her lips curved in a soft smile. She pulled her hand from the water and reached up to cup his cheek, the damp warmth of her soft hand infusing him with strength. "You're a good man, Simeon Grant. The very best."

He was tempted to pull her into a kiss, but the connection in the moment seemed too strong to break. He was content enough to stay just like that.

But then she winced and pulled her hand from his face to rub her lower back.

Fear stabbed his chest. "What's wrong? Do we need to go back?"

She shook her head. "No, just the baby kicking." Her smile didn't quite reach her eyes. "This is an active one."

"That's good, right?"

Emma nodded. "Yes, very good. I think."

He eased out a breath. "Just tell the little one it's not time to come yet. I need to take care of a few things first." He took her hand again. "As soon as we get to your aunt's."

Sitting like that, they watched the water for a few more moments. She breathed out a long breath. "I don't know for sure, but I think we could probably be ready to leave a month or so after the baby comes. Two months at the most, I think." She turned those piercing eyes on him. "Will that be all right?"

His mind stuttered to make sense of her words. "Leave?" Where was she going? Surely not back to Texas.

Not until he had her name cleared, and who knew how long that would take communicating from this remote place.

A line formed on her brow. "Back to your cabin." She said it like she was reminding a forgetful grandparent.

He struggled to keep his jaw from dropping open. "You want to go back there? But…" His mind scurried to make sense of what she was thinking. "To visit or to live?"

A second line joined the first on her pretty forehead. "I thought that's where you'd want to live. Isn't it?"

He let out a breath, then tilted his head back with a chuckle. If she thought he'd planned for her and the baby to live in that dirty shack, it was a wonder she'd said yes to his proposal.

He met her curious gaze, raising her knuckles to plant a kiss on them. "Emma, there's not a way in the world I'd make you live in that uncivilized cabin. I can't believe you'd consider it."

The corners of her lips danced. "I was going to ask you if we could put in a wood floor."

Another chuckle built in his chest. "Anything for you." He paused a moment to regain his wits. "Seriously, though. I'm happy to go back to the territory, but I thought you'd want to stay here, near your aunt and Joseph. Your family."

A sweet smile took over her face. "You'll be my family."

When she looked at him like that, it was all he could do not to take her up on that idea. Soon, but not yet. And not too soon, considering her condition. He could handle the wait, though. He hoped.

Luckily, she kept talking, and he forced his mind to focus on her words.

"I would miss Joseph, of course. But there are always letters. He's been my protector for so long—my champion. It's time he got to live his own life." She looked a little sad as she said the words, like she'd resigned herself.

He squeezed her hand. "We have a while to figure everything out. I was thinking this looks like a nice country, though. Besides, I kind of like the idea of being around family again."

She raised her brows. "One cantankerous brother is better than four?"

He nodded, although his family back in South Carolina no longer seemed like the burden they once had. In fact, nothing in his life seemed like a hardship these days. It was amazing what finding love could do for a man—both from God and now from this woman.

Emma pressed a hand to the underside of her belly, willing the muscles there to relax as she strained to make out the words scrawled on the paper. These letters should be more than enough to distract her from her aches. What a precious gift Simeon had offered by letting her read them.

When they'd returned from their walk last night, he'd pressed the bundle into her hand with a mumbled explanation, then slipped out of camp. It wasn't until she'd sat on her pallet by the campfire that she realized exactly how much of himself he was revealing with the gesture.

She'd cried when she read of the Scotts' gratitude in the first letter as they'd thanked him for trusting them to raise his children. Even now, her eyes burned as she thought about how hard it would be to give away her own babe. No wonder Simeon had carried the pain for so long.

Then the second letter came, and Mr. Scott told of baby Nora's passing. It had taken a while to stop blubbering enough to finish it. And from the dried water stains spotting the paper, she wasn't the only one who'd cried through the reading.

But the next letters had been happier, detailing the growth of little Reuben. They said his eyes had turned a deep crystal blue, like Simeon's, no doubt. Her heart craved to see the boy. To wrap him in her arms and love him like she now loved his father. How did Simeon bear this deep ache? Moisture clouded her vision as she reread a section that described how much he'd grown as a two-year-old.

Simeon stirred on his pallet across the fire, and Emma wiped the tears from her face with a sniff. He sat up, finding her with his gaze, and she gave him a wobbly smile. "Good morning."

"Is it?" His brow furrowed. He must have realized she was crying.

She let out a shaky laugh. "Yes. Don't mind me. I'm just over here blubbering."

He rose with his usual grace and came to sit beside

her, leaning close to see the letter. "That's a good one. Did you read the part where he learned to feed the chickens?"

She smiled, skimming for the section. "He sounds so cute. I imagine him with pudgy legs and your blue eyes, waddling out to give them what he was supposed to have eaten for lunch."

Simeon's rich chuckle filled her ear, gravely from sleep. "She said it took two days to catch all the hens after he left the door open and fell asleep in their laying nests."

He slipped a hand around her waist, and she sank against him, resting her head on his shoulder. She could hear the longing just under the surface of his tone. The same longing that filled her chest. It would always be there, no doubt. But together, they could share the pain. The loss. And maybe someday they could find little Reuben and reconnect with him. Not to take the place of the Scotts, but to shower even more love on the precious boy.

A pain wrapped through her lower back, and she stiffened against the fierceness of it.

"What's wrong?"

This one was much stronger than the others, and she focused on taking steady breaths. She shifted, pushing away from his side in case her position was what had brought on the pain. But she had an inkling nothing would ease this pressure until it was ready to pass. They'd been coming too consistently.

She turned to Simeon, biting her lip to keep the burn in her eyes at bay. "I think…it's time."

Chapter Thirty-One

Finally.
~ Emma's Journal

Simeon pushed his horse harder, too many memories pressing through his mind to hold them back. The other time he'd had to get help for someone he loved about to give birth.

The memory of that day kept pressing into his mind, blurring his vision. The way Nora had braved through the pain, had held on until they'd reached the Scotts' doorstep. They'd landed there at God's leading, no doubt. Yet that had been one of the worst weeks of his life. Losing Nora…giving up the twins.

He couldn't let himself be sucked into that dark place again. Emma needed him to find help. They couldn't be far from the Lockman ranch, and surely her aunt would know what to do. He just had to find the woman and get her back to Emma before it was too late.

At last, he rounded the bend in the rock, and the land spread before him into a wide valley. In the distance, a house sat on one side of the open land.

He pushed Pet into a canter, opening up her stride as the ground leveled out. He'd made it. *Lord, let this be the right place.*

As he neared the cluster of ranch buildings, figures began to take shape. Horses and a couple cows moved inside corral fences. A man rode a bay in one of the pens, and he reined Pet that direction, slowing to a jog as they entered the yard.

The cowboy met him at the fence, and Simeon struggled to catch his breath enough to speak.

"*Bonjour*." The other man touched the brim of his hat.

It took a moment for his brain to process the French word, and his heart plummeted. He knew only a few words of the language. Surely someone here would speak English, though. Emma's aunt and uncle for sure. Right?

"Bonjour. I'm looking for Mary Lockman. Is this her place?"

The man tilted his head, the wide brim of his hat cocking. "You know my wife?"

A rush of relief coursed through Simeon, loosening the knot clenched in his gut, his tongue with it. "Yes. I mean, I know your niece and nephew. Where is she? Emma needs her. I think the labor's started, and she has to come quick. Can she come? Emma needs her. *Now*."

The man just stood there looking at him until the final commanding *now*. That seemed to clear the dust from his leathers, and he turned the horse toward an opening in the fence, then plodded the animal in a steady walk toward the house.

Simeon turned Pet to fall into stride beside the bay. But he had to tighten his reins as the mare danced under him. She must feel his urgency through the tension in his legs.

"Your name, *monsieur*?" The man cut him a sideways glance as he spoke in a heavy French accent. He'd not realized Emma's aunt was married to a Frenchman, but it made sense, living up here in Canada.

"Simeon, Simeon Grant." He forced himself to give the surname. There was no need to hide from people any more. And soon, Lord willing, these folks would be family.

Family. The word still held a hint of taboo in his mind. Something he no longer deserved. But God was giving it to him anyway. He thought of Emma, of the pain he'd seen in her eyes right before he ridden out, the fear in Joseph's. *Please, God.*

A woman with graying hair met them on the porch of the ranch house, and the first detail he noticed about her were her eyes. A striking blue.

She raised a hand to shade her eyes, and the next thing he noticed were the trousers she wore. Yes, *trousers*. Why had he not seen that at first?

The couple conversed in French, then Mary turned to him. "You know my niece? How is she? Are she and Joseph coming soon?" The man must not have understood the gush of information Simeon had spewed at him. No wonder he'd dawdled so.

"Emma's time is here. The pains have started. She needs you, ma'am. *Now*."

It didn't take Aunt Mary long to catch on. "Emma's with child? Where is she?"

But before he could drag in a breath to answer, she spun to her husband and spit out a string of French. The man dismounted and draped his horse's rein over a hitching post, then jogged toward the barn.

She focused on Simeon again. "You said the labor's started? Where is she?"

He motioned the way he'd come. "About an hour back, I think. If you're moving fast. A little ways down the trail through the mountain pass."

"Let me gather some things, then we'll ride out. Adrien will come with the wagon." She spun and started for the door.

"There's one other thing, ma'am."

She halted and turned to look at him.

"Is there a parson around? Or a priest, maybe?" Weren't the French mostly Catholic? He couldn't remember for sure, but he'd take any man of God at this point.

Her face paled visibly. "I'm sure Emma will be fine. She's tough."

He didn't doubt her toughness, but the direction the woman's thoughts had taken speared him. He cleared his throat. "It's not that, ma'am. We need a wedding performed."

She cocked her head in the same way her husband had, scanning him up and down as if seeing him for the first time. "Is the baby yours?"

He'd expected her to ask this, and a big part of him

wanted to say yes. The child would carry his name and he would love it with all his strength. Yet the last thing he wanted was for this woman to think ill of Emma…or him. He met her gaze. "Emma is with child by her deceased husband. But I'm honored she's agreed to take my name for both her and the babe."

Aunt Mary nodded, her eyes gentling a touch. "I'll have Adrien send a man for Father Bergeron."

Then she disappeared inside, leaving Simeon to fidget. Was there anything he could do to hurry these people on? Even now, Emma could be bleeding to death on the snowy ground. His mind formed images far too vivid, and he pressed fingers into his eye sockets to purge the pictures.

"Let's go, young man."

He jerked up at the commanding voice. Aunt Mary stepped from the house and pulled the door closed behind her. It'd been a number of years since he'd been called by that moniker.

She stepped to Simeon's horse and handed up a bundle of blankets. "Tie these on your saddle while I tell Adrien where to find us."

Within minutes, they were riding out of the ranch yard. He pushed Pet into a canter, and Aunt Mary's horse matched the stride. Then his eyes widened as the animal stretched out into a gallop, passing them as if they were out for a Sunday jog.

His mare picked up her pace, but she'd been going hard all morning and didn't have much more speed to give. He settled back into an easy canter. This savvy ranch woman would be able to follow his tracks. He had no doubt she'd be what Emma needed. *God, give her wisdom to keep Emma and the baby safe.*

If only he'd pushed farther last night, they might have made it to the ranch before Emma's pains started. But she'd been so weary, there was no way she could have ridden much more. Her body preparing for the efforts of today, no doubt.

He'd expected to catch up with Aunt Mary when the pass narrowed to a winding trail between the mountains. Pet had to slow to a jog to make it over the rough terrain, and surely Aunt Mary's horse had to do the same, but the woman must have had a strong lead on him.

By the time he arrived back at camp, their horses were in a line tied to trees, saddled and loaded with all their supplies.

He slid to the ground and jogged to where Joseph and Aunt Mary clustered around Emma.

"Let's get you up, darlin'. You wanna ride your own horse or with your brother?" Aunt Mary was giving orders, something that seemed to come naturally to her.

Simeon pushed through and knelt beside Emma. She sat on a fur, legs stretched in front of her and hands braced behind to prop herself up. Her weary gaze landed on him.

He soaked in the beautiful sight of her. "How are you, love?" He stroked a strand of damp hair from her cheek.

"Fine. I'm good."

"We're taking her to the trailhead where she can ride back to the house in the wagon. Help her to the horses."

Aunt Mary barked the order as though it would be obeyed, but everything about him fought against the idea.

He turned to face her. "Should she be moved?"

"She has hours still. Better to get her to the house now while we have a chance."

Hours? He turned back to Emma and ran his gaze over her.

She gave him a brave smile, a look that was probably meant to be reassuring, but only tightened his protective instincts. Could her aunt be right? The woman had to know more about birthing babies than he did.

They could follow the woman's advice for now, but if it seemed too much for Emma, he'd put his foot down. "Joseph, bring Emma's mare over here. I'll ride with her for now and give Pet a break."

A scuffling noise told him the man was obeying. Simeon slid one arm under the crook of Emma's legs and wrapped the other around her back. Every bit of him strained as he stood with her in his arms.

"I can walk, Simeon. I'm fine."

But she didn't struggle. Instead, she tucked herself into his chest, resting her head on his shoulder. With her cradled in his arms like this, he'd walk the rest of the way if he had to.

The pains were steady, hitting at least every five minutes.

Simeon fought his helplessness as he cradled Emma across his lap and pushed the mare harder. When a new pain would start, Emma would grip his shirt in both her hands, pulling tighter and tighter until there were times the collar almost cut off his breathing. But then the contractions would lessen, and she'd sink against him. In those moments, he could feel the hard intakes of breath and the pounding of her heart. The intensity of it all had just about worn his nerves to their marrow. If only he could take this agony on himself so she didn't have to endure it.

At long last, they reached the spot where the trail opened into the valley, and there sat a wagon, Adrian Lockman standing by the horses. The man started toward the rear of the vehicle the moment he saw them.

But as Simeon reined his mare next to him, Emma gripped his shirt again, her eyes pressing tight as her mouth pulled in a pinched line. Adrian reached up to take her, but Simeon raised a staying hand. "Wait till this pain passes."

Emma whimpered as she burrowed into him, and Simeon stroked her back, then rubbed small circles at her waist. If only there were something—anything—he could do to take this from her. The helplessness was driving him mad.

At last, Emma relaxed and barely stirred as he passed her down to her uncle. Possibly an uncle she hadn't even met. They settled her on blankets in the wagon bed, Aunt Mary kneeling beside her. Simeon fit the board in place to close up the back, then reached for the mare's reins.

But Aunt Mary motioned him. "Ya might as well climb up. It seems you're special to her."

Simeon met the woman's gaze, emotion churning in him. His body ached to *do* something. Something that would actually make a difference for Emma. Ease her pain. But maybe staying near was the only thing that might help. Although he wasn't sure it really made a difference.

Still, if Aunt Mary thought it might…

He tossed his reins in a loop around the wood tailgate, then leapt up into the wagon. He settled on Emma's other side and took her delicate hand in his. So fragile, this woman. But not really. She'd already proved tougher than he'd ever have imagined. *Lord, let her have enough strength left to pull through this, too.*

And if it's not too much to ask, send the priest. Please. Urgency to make her his wife surged in his chest, maybe more than it should. Words spoken before God couldn't possibly fill him with any more love than what already coursed through him. But his spirit drove the desire, which was almost as strong as his desire to keep her alive.

Chapter Thirty-Two

Terrifying bliss.
~ Simeon

Everything had faded to a blur for Emma, making only the steady labor pains seem real. One gripped her now as she clawed at the hand that held hers. The burning squeezed so tight, she couldn't breathe. Couldn't think. Couldn't do anything except try to escape the agony wrapping around her middle.

"Shh… We're here."

Something warm stroked her face, and she struggled for breath. There, she sucked in tiny gasps as she finally found air. Slowly, too slowly, her muscles eased. The pain relaxed.

"We've got to get you inside now, Emma. I'll carry you in."

She squinted to focus, finally finding Simeon's face as he hovered over her. "I can walk."

"Let's get you to the end of the wagon, then I'll carry you."

She slid and shifted where he motioned for her to

move until she was sitting with her legs draped over the back of the wagon. He slipped a hand under her legs as if he would pick her up, but she touched his shoulder. "I can walk, Simeon. I'm fine until another one comes."

She pushed off the wagon, landing on her feet with more force than she'd expected. But she had a grip on the wood, and the hands that grabbed each of her elbows helped her balance. She focused on the ground ahead, forcing her feet to move her forward. Up three wooden steps, across a porch, into the darkness of a room. She was blinded for a moment, and reached out to find support.

"Keep going straight, dearie. I've a bed ready down the hall on the right." A woman's voice? She couldn't place it at first, then realized it must have been Aunt Mary.

Then the band around her middle tightened again, shooting hot coals through her belly and up her back. She gasped, grabbing for something to cling to. She found a hand and clutched it with both of hers as the pain nearly lifted her off her feet.

Then she really was airborne, wrapped in strong arms. Then something soft. A blanket. A bed. She clawed the covers, trying to find escape from the agony in her belly. Trying to find a breath. A cry gurgled in her throat, surging out as her chest burned for air.

As quickly as it tightened, the band around her middle released. She sank back against the covers, dragging in breaths. They were shallow, but any kind of air would do.

Simeon's voice settled over her, and she struggled to focus on his words.

"What do you think? Would you rather wait?"

She forced open her eyes and found his worried face hovering beside her bed. "Wait for what?"

"Till after the baby comes. To get married. The priest is here, but you need to focus on the birthing. We can wait." He looked as though he'd made a decision and started to turn away.

She grabbed at him, catching part of his shirt and dragging him back to her. "No. Now."

He searched her face. "Are you sure?"

"Hurry." Another pain would hit any moment, and she wanted to be this man's wife before the baby was born if there was any way possible.

A throat cleared behind her. A man's throat. Emma turned to see an older man in a black cloak and a white collar. His hair was almost as white as the cloth around his neck, and it gave him a kindly smile. Or maybe it was his eyes that brought the kindness.

"My dear, I'm Father Bergeron. Are you sure you're feeling up to this?"

A woman stood beside him, and as Emma focused, she realized it must be Aunt Mary. Her red hair was cut short, much like Emma's own hair, although probably not for the same reason. Her aunt offered a soft smile, similar to that of the priest. "It's up to you, dearie."

She squeezed Simeon's hand, which had once again taken over hers. Then she met his gaze. "Yes. Of course. But we'd better hurry before…"

And there it was again, that pain that wrapped so

tightly it stole her very breath.

Simeon stroked the top of Emma's fingers as she squeezed the blood out of his arm with both her hands. The cry that slipped from her open mouth gripped tighter around his chest.

He couldn't do this. Couldn't be here and see all her pain. But he couldn't leave either. What if she needed him?

But first things first. As soon as this contraction passed, they had to be ready to say the vows. He looked up to the priest. "Are you ready as soon as this one's over?"

The man stepped forward with raised brows. "I'm not the one you should be worried about." But he opened the book in his hands and found the spot he wanted, then kept a finger at the place while he looked up at Emma.

Simeon turned to the man on his right.

Joseph met and held his look, then nodded. He approved. Or at least wasn't going to stand in their way. And that was all Simeon needed for now.

He turned his full attention to his bride, who seemed to be coming out of the pain now. Her face gleamed with sweat, and her short hair was matted to her forehead and cheeks. So beautiful, it created a physical ache in his chest every time he looked at her.

Her long brown lashes rose, and her gaze met his. "I'm ready."

Together, they turned to face the priest.

As the man started into the ceremony, Simeon realized he should have asked the Father to keep it as short as possible. Hopefully he wouldn't need to be told.

After a short Scripture passage, the priest looked up at Simeon. "Simeon Grant, do you take Emma Malcom to be your wife? Do you promise to be true to her in good times and in bad, in sickness and in health, to love her and honor her all the days of your life?"

Inhaling a breath, Simeon nodded. "With every ounce of strength in me."

That seemed to satisfy the priest, and he turned to Emma and asked her the same question. Her soft "I do" pierced all the way through to Simeon's soul.

Father Bergeron glanced at the others in the room. "Let us ask God for His continued blessing on this couple." He bowed his head and spoke in a voice that quivered with fervor. "Holy Father, Creator of the universe, Maker of man and woman in your own likeness, Source of blessing for married life…"

As the prayer continued, Simeon focused on each word, absorbing them into his heart. A smile pulled at his mouth when the man spoke about enriching God's church with their children. They were about to get a head start on that.

When the final words ceased, he joined his "Amen" with the others, then lifted his face to Emma's. She had such a look of peace, it stole his breath. So much like an angel, with the light shining through the window behind her bed.

He couldn't help but lean forward and press a kiss to her forehead.

The priest cleared his throat. "I suppose now you may kiss your bride."

Simeon pulled back a few inches to grin at Emma. "It's about time." He swooped down to seal their promise properly, and Emma's lips were soft and warm against his.

But he'd barely touched her before she stiffened, gripping his shoulder with a strength he wouldn't have guessed she had left.

He pulled back, but couldn't go far because of her clamp on his shoulder. Since he was locked there, just inches from her face, he stroked her forehead, pressing a kiss to her cheek. "Hold on, darling. You can do this. It'll be worth it for our child."

And with every word, he sent up a prayer. For strength. For safety. And he couldn't help but add his abundance of thanks for this double gift he was being given.

Exhaustion dragged at every part of Emma, yet nothing could diminish the giddy feeling bubbling from her chest. "She's perfect. Every inch of her."

"She is." Simeon's breath caressed Emma's cheek as he leaned close to see the baby's face.

Their baby.

She looked up to smile at him and lost herself in the

tenderness of his eyes. So much love this man possessed. What a pity it had been wasted all these years.

Of course, not a pity for her. God and Simeon must have been storing it all up just for her. She gazed down at the perfect features of her daughter's face. For her and this sweet new life.

The baby squinted through long brown lashes as her tiny red lips worked. "Are you hungry, my sweet?" She turned to Simeon again. "What shall we name her?"

He raised his brows, pulling his gaze from the baby to meet hers. "Hannah?"

Once more, she turned to her baby, snuggling the little bundle even closer. "I think so. Hannah Joy." She flicked her gaze up to her husband. "Hannah Joy Grant."

The kiss he bestowed on her said more than his words ever could.

Epilogue

The end is a glorious beginning.
~ Emma's Journal

SIX MONTHS LATER

Simeon peered over the top of the blanket, widening his eyes as he dropped the quilt to the floor. "Peekaboo."

Dimples pressed into both rosy cheeks as Hannah erupted into giggles. She threw her cloth doll to the floor in her glee, rocking so much he reached out to keep her from falling over. She'd been sitting up by herself for a few weeks, but she wasn't always steady.

After she'd settled, he raised the blanket back in front of his face. "Where's Papa?"

He eased the barrier down again as he peered over the top, then dropped it with a jerk. "Peekaboo!"

She collapsed into giggles again, merriment wracking her pudgy little frame. He reached forward and tickled her belly. "Funny bug."

She giggled again, and he couldn't help but join her

laughter. He'd been sitting on the floor but lowered himself to lie down, propping an elbow on the boards as he soaked in the sight of his daughter.

"I think she's getting another tooth on the top."

He glanced at Emma, who sat in the rocking chair he'd just finished for her. She was stitching something, probably the quilt she'd been making for their bed. "You think?"

Turning back to Hannah, he tickled her belly again. "Can I see those teethies? Let me see that new tooth." She giggled again, curling her chin into the rolls at her neck. Too precious for words.

After her bout of merriment calmed, Hannah snatched her doll from the floor, and Simeon's gaze tracked to Emma again. She was focused on her stitches, and he took the moment to watch her. So beautiful with the light from the fire illuminating her face. She'd slimmed quickly after Hannah's birth, and now the soft planes of her face were more angular. If possible, she looked even more like an angel. His angel.

She met his gaze, and the love in her eyes resonated in his chest. Now might be a good time to steal a kiss, while Hannah was occupied with her toy.

But before he could make a move, a horse whinnied outside the cabin's front door. He raised a brow at Emma. "Are we expecting visitors tonight?" Just that morning, she and Hannah had ridden across the valley to see her aunt and uncle.

The distance wasn't too far, but he'd expected Aunt

Mary and Uncle Adrian would enjoy some solitude now that they finally had their house to themselves again. They'd been so hospitable while Simeon built their cabin, but surely they'd be thankful for time alone.

Maybe they'd sent one of the hired men over on an errand.

He sprang to his feet at the knock on the door. Out of habit, he touched the knife strapped at his waist. They may be within view of the big ranch, but this was still the mountain wilderness. And he had a family to protect.

He peered through the tiny slit he'd cut in the door and caught a familiar profile on the other side. After pulling the latch string, he jerked the door wide. "Joseph, come in. Didn't expect you for another day or so. You're family though. You don't need to knock."

Joseph stood in the doorway looking a little sheepish. He shrugged one shoulder. "I figured with your new cabin and you being newlyweds...." He shrugged again and raised his brows. "Better to knock."

Simeon held back a grin. Yes, better to knock. He stepped aside. "How was the ride from town?"

Joseph moved into the room, doffing his hat as he turned toward Emma. "Long, but fine."

Emma laid her sewing aside and rose to greet her brother. He met her halfway, and she slipped her hands around his waist in a hug. "Good to have you back, little brother."

He chuckled and patted her shoulders. "I see my niece is still growing." When Emma released him, he hunkered down to Hannah's level. "How are you, muffin?"

"Ba." She babbled around the doll's hand she'd stuffed in her mouth.

"What's that? Did you say Uncle Joey?" He glanced up at Emma with one side of his mouth quirked. "I think her first words were 'Uncle Joey.'"

Emma rolled her eyes and chuckled.

Joseph's expression changed then, and he looked past Emma to Simeon. He straightened and pulled a paper from his pocket. "Brought your mail from town."

Simeon's gut tightened, and he stepped forward to take it. A reply already? Did that mean they'd received confirmation? Or maybe they'd decided not to help. Surely the latter wouldn't be the case.

He stared at the folded paper in his hand, his fingers turning white as he gripped it. Emma stepped close and touched his arm. Her presence infused a measure of peace, and he inhaled a deep breath and looked into her face.

Her expression was guarded, but he saw hope there. "Open it."

If he'd raised her hopes only to dash them with this letter, he'd never forgive himself. He shouldn't have told Emma what he was doing. Should have kept it between him and Joseph until he knew how things would turn out.

But he wasn't any good at keeping secrets from Emma. One piercing look from those amber eyes, and he bared his soul. Maybe because she'd proved trustworthy. Maybe because she didn't judge him. Either way, she made him want to be the man he saw reflected in her gaze.

"Open it." Her words were soft. Prodding.

He glanced down at the letter again, then fumbled with the seal and unfolded the paper.

Dear Son,

I can't begin to tell you how relieved we were to receive your letter. We thank God for your safety, as we'd long believed he'd taken you on to Glory. Your mother sends her love, and I believe she's cried as much these past days since receiving your letter as she did the past six years we've waited for news of you. She assures me these are tears of joy, however. We grieve the loss of Nora, but we are glad you've found joy again. Please pass along our love to Emma, and we hope to one day be given the chance to tell her so in person.

I sent the wire you requested and have received a speedy reply with news which I think will relieve you. His message stated:

> *Mrs. Emma Carter proven innocent of fraud STOP Reward no longer offered STOP Signed Sheriff Howard Mason STOP Westhaven Texas STOP*

I've responded with another telegram asking him to send us a letter with more details of the case. I'll write again when I receive the correspondence. For now, I hope these details will ease your concerns.

He could feel Emma's presence as she stepped near, and he paused to look at her. There was still another page of script, but he handed the letter to his wife. Her gaze searched his face, but he did his best not to give away the news. It was hard, though, to fight the grin that wanted to split his face apart.

She was free. He'd never had a doubt of Emma's innocence, but he'd figured it would take more than a telegram to clear her name of the charges laid against her. What had transpired in that Texas town after she left? Maybe a thorough investigation had uncovered the truth. It had always perplexed him that anyone who knew Emma could think she'd be involved in unsavory business, but desperate people sometimes lost their sensibilities.

He studied his wife's face as she read the note, her lips moving silently as she drank in each word. Her eyes widened at one point, and her gaze darted up to his. Then her focus returned to the paper.

"Good news, I suppose?" Joseph's words broke through Simeon's focus, and he turned to the man.

Finally, he let his smile slip out. "Yep."

Emma turned to her brother, holding the letter out. "Read it, Joey. I'm cleared. Sheriff Mason said there's no reward anymore." Her voice sounded like a child's on Christmas morning.

Joseph took the letter as his gaze flicked to Simeon, a little triumphant. "It's about time."

Emma scooped up little Hannah and swung her around in a circle. "Your mama's not a wanted woman anymore. Isn't it wonderful?" She snuggled Hannah close to her cheek as she turned back to Simeon.

The warmth in his chest spread up his throat to burn

the backs of his eyes. How had he ever deserved these two? It was too much sometimes, this love that burned in him.

He tried to push through the lump in his throat to smile. "Oh, you're still wanted."

Emma gave him one of those looks that stirred his blood. She stepped closer, and he slipped an arm around her waist, relishing her softness as she leaned into him.

"Pa." Hannah pressed a slobbery hand against his chest.

He raised his brows at her. "Did I hear you say Pa, little bit?" He shot a glance at Emma to gauge her reaction. He knew as well as she did that Hannah hadn't meant the sound as a word, but he still loved the thought of it.

Emma tilted her head at him. "I think that's exactly what she said." Then to Hannah, "That's your papa, isn't it, sweet one?"

The joy that surged in his chest was more than he deserved. Here he stood with his family, in their own home. And outside their front door rose the majestic Rocky Mountains that had taken root in his soul and become a part of him. He'd never felt so loved.

Did you enjoy this book? I hope so!

Would you take a quick minute to leave a review?
http://www.amazon.com/dp/B0783H565P

It doesn't have to be long. Just a sentence or two telling what you liked about the story!

~ ~ ~

Receive a FREE ebook and get updates when new Misty M. Beller books release: http://eepurl.com/bXmHwb

About the Author

Misty M. Beller is a *USA Today* bestselling author of romantic mountain stories, set on the 1800s frontier and woven with the truth of God's love.

She was raised on a farm in South Carolina, so her Southern roots run deep. Growing up, her family was close, and they continue to keep that priority today. Her husband and children now add another dimension to her life, keeping her both grounded and crazy.

God has placed a desire in Misty's heart to combine her love for Christian fiction and the simpler ranch life, writing historical novels that display God's abundant love through the twists and turns in the lives of her characters.

Sign up for e-mail updates when future books are available!

www.MistyMBeller.com

Don't miss the other books by

Misty M. Beller

The Mountain Series
The Lady and the Mountain Man
The Lady and the Mountain Doctor
The Lady and the Mountain Fire
The Lady and the Mountain Promise
The Lady and the Mountain Call
This Treacherous Journey
This Wilderness Journey
This Freedom Journey (novella)
This Courageous Journey
This Homeward Journey
This Daring Journey
This Healing Journey

Texas Rancher Trilogy
The Rancher Takes a Cook
The Ranger Takes a Bride
The Rancher Takes a Cowgirl

Wyoming Mountain Tales
A Pony Express Romance
A Rocky Mountain Romance
A Sweetwater River Romance
A Mountain Christmas Romance

Hearts of Montana
Hope's Highest Mountain
Love's Mountain Quest
Faith's Mountain Home

Call of the Rockies
Freedom in the Mountain Wind
Hope in the Mountain River
Light in the Mountain Sky

CPSIA information can be obtained
at www.ICGtesting.com
Printed in the USA
LVHW050037230520
656338LV00001B/95

9 780999 70122